The Third Breath

DCI Bennett Book 7

By

Malcolm Hollingdrake

First published in 2018 by Bloodhound Books

www.bloodhoundbooks.com

Print ISBN 978-1-912604-65-4

Also By Malcolm Hollingdrake

DCI Bennett Series

Only The Dead (Book 1)
Hell's Gate (Book 2)
Flesh Evidence (Book 3)
Game Point (Book 4)
Dying Art (Book 5)
Crossed Out (Book 6)

Praise For Malcolm Hollingdrake

"This was a complex piece of story-telling with a lot of characters but it all worked for me. A very enjoyable read." **Kath Middleton - Kath Middleton Books**

"Fantastic read ... I absolutely loved it, and can't wait for the next installment." **Liza Murray - Turn The Page**

"The gripping investigation and various layers held my attention throughout and I love how Malcolm Hollingdrake is able to light the mood occasionally to give us a well-earned break from all the crazy." **Eva Merckx - Novel Deelights**

"The various plotlines are well-crafted and draw you right in, one of the reasons this excellently written thriller with its beautiful descriptive sentences is captivating and intriguing." **Caroline Vincent - Bits About Books**

"The action in this book started on page one and didn't let up until the very end – it was a classic detective/police mystery with a creepy plot and villain." **Ashley Gillan - (e)Book Nerd Reviews**

"The story is written well, thrilling and fast paced. You really won't want to put it down." **Gemma Myers - Between The Pages Book Club**

"Another excellent book by the talented Malcolm Hollingdrake I am looking forward to more in this series." **Jill Burkinshaw - Books n All**

"Fans will not be disappointing with Crossed Out it is one hell of an engaging read which I couldn't put down and highly recommend giving..." **Shell Baker - Chelle's Book Reviews**

"Crossed Out is an intense, criminally insane book which encompassed every piece of my soul with literary salivation." **Diane Hogg - Sweet Little Book Blog**

"The writing style as always was superb and I thoroughly enjoyed the whole thing, being gripped by the end of the first chapter." **Donna Maguire - Donnas Book Blog**

Dedicated to Lal and Jim Grice.
Dear family friends.

Man is not what he thinks he is, he is what he hides.

André Malraux
Novelist

Previously

Knowing his father was critically ill had impacted little on Cyril's emotional state, but the news had brought with it a moral dilemma. He knew that he had neither the appetite nor the enthusiasm to reconnect with his past, a past that he thought he had successfully locked away in his memory, deep within a vacuum, hidden, closed off and forgotten.

Why he had gone to see his dying father in his last days, he would never really understand; maybe it was his partner Julie's sensitive guidance, maybe his own copper's curiosity, or was it the last opportunity to eventually tell his father what he truly thought of him? Whatever the answer, after that visit Cyril was assured that the correct decision had been made. He had matured and he could see that life and relationships were not purely black and white. His ice-like emotions towards his family were beginning to thaw and for that reason, he had decided to attend the funeral.

***

You will find, as with all books, that turning over the first page is easily done with a simple flick of the finger. You will, I hope, feel a flutter in your stomach and a keen sense of anticipation of what is to come... Well... I feel those same emotions; I feel that tingle of illicit excitement as I prepare each step, even now, as I lift the white enamelled freezer lid and look inside at my work; every victim is a new chapter.... And I remember that I must do unto others as they have done to me but I must do it with a greater degree of subtlety.

As the results of my labours unfold in the local and national press, I receive the same excitement, the same anticipation you feel as you start this book... so... it could be said that we are not too dissimilar... are we?

Chapter One

The tiny ice crystals had formed what looked like an armoured sheath of semi-translucent particles that seemed to hover above the frost-burned flesh. The hair, almost white, spread halo-like around the head. With the introduction of the relatively warm air, a milky-white mist mingled and hung just above the cadaver, a protective, smothering layer.

"You look at peace. It's good to have you close where I can see you. What do they say, *Keep your friends close and your enemies closer*? Yes, closer."

He lowered the lid on the old chest freezer and his fingers tapped out an indiscriminate tune on the lid.

***

He found it difficult to hold the fine wires and to work as intricately as he had anticipated. It was a struggle on account of the limited sensitivity and feeling in the ends of his fingers, even when wearing the ultra-fine latex gloves. No matter how warm the room or what time of year his fingers seemed semi-paralysed. They had diagnosed Raynaud's disease but then what did they know? Before starting each delicate process he blew on them and rubbed his damaged fingers to generate what he hoped would be greater blood flow, therefore bringing some feeling to the numbed flesh.

As he blew warm breath across his hands he frowned but then let his focus drift to just above the bench to the news cutting pinned to the wall, one edge curled in defiance. He dabbed it with his finger as his gaze shifted to study the technical drawing taped alongside; it was hand drawn but no less detailed for that. Every wire and miniature circuit board was coloured and sequenced. His finger pressed against the paper and followed each wire until stopping at one, a green and white striped line that snaked from its starting position to its conclusion. He repeated this action on the bench but instead of being spread flat over a distance of six inches as in the wiring diagram, the work was constrained into an area no bigger than an egg cup. By using a large, illuminated magnifying glass he ensured that there was no snagging or corruption of the soldered joints.

Every few minutes a wisp of smoke, the result of the hot iron melting and fusing flux and solder to the wire, would drift to one side as each connection was secured. Once finished, the electronics looked like a coloured crochet disc as it was fitted into a stainless steel cap.

After two hours of careful work, the electronics-filled cap was connected to its base. It was then easily attached to a container. A small, disc battery resembling a silver coin was placed in the designated holder. He closed the lid before locking it in position with the safety catch, trapping tightly the neoprene seal ensuring that nothing could enter or escape. It was a perfect fit. There was silence apart from the occasional cooling click from the gas soldering gun.

After a further inspection the engineer flicked off the lid's safety catch before making some minor adjustments. He moved away from the bench to the far side of the room before picking up a remote key fob similar to that found attached to a car key. He was satisfied that things were ready for the first test.

"Three, two, one!" His thumb gently pressed the button as excited eyes focussed on the container. Nothing happened. He sighed out of frustration but soon a string of expletives bombarded the container. Putting down the fob, he moved back to the bench, adjusted the magnifying glass into position and stared at the electronics. It only took a minute for him to detect his error.

He cursed a second time. Fingers fumbled with the battery and he turned it over before checking carefully that it was correctly fitted.

"You go to all this trouble with a fine, detailed design and then you go and put the battery in the wrong way," he admonished himself before moving back across the room and picking up the fob. He was ready and his heart rate accelerated.

"Three… two… one!"

As he pressed the button for the second time, the lid of the container flicked open automatically with a degree of force that momentarily startled him. It remained wide open, held with a spring, one hundred and eighty degrees from its closed position, therefore opening the mouth of the container fully.

"Boom!" he shouted. "Got ya!" A large smile spread across his face.

Moving back to the bench, he unpinned the news cutting and reread through it. He looked at the date he had written in the margin. *No mention of the human cost… There never is, it's all down to money…. Was it so long ago?* It was time to move on and he carefully folded the paper. Striking a match he lit one corner and allowed the flames to lick his fingers. The heat brought a smile before he dropped it onto the asbestos mat he had used when soldering. He then brushed the delicate ashes into the waste bin.

"Ashes to ashes, dust to dust, it shall be," he whispered. "Boom!"

He needed sleep.

***

The morning dawned fine as the engineer split the venetian blinds and peered out. At least the weather would be on his side. A flask sat on the windowsill already wrapped in a quilted jacket. He flicked off the safety catch, picked up the remote and pressed the button. Just as on the previous day, the lid snapped open. He was ready for the difficult part of the operation. He needed to arm it and for that he would work with care. He could make no mistakes at this stage he knew that to his cost. He would then be ready to travel.

***

The late afternoon train journey from York to Harrogate had been pleasant enough. As his carriage approached the station, he breathed on his hands and rubbed them together before carefully collecting his rucksack and moving to the automatic door. He enjoyed the growing feeling of excitement as the adrenalin slowly flushed through his system. Even though the day was warm, he wore thin, breathable running gloves. The light on the side of the door turned from red to green and as he tapped it, the warning beeping sound signalled its intention to open.

There was always something special about a station, the enclosed passageways, the echoes, the order, possibly the anonymity of being in a crowd, a crowd seemingly moving in one direction with a purpose to escape. He stood for a moment to allow those eager, those possibly late, the uncertain, the sightseers or simply the unrushed, to leave before him. The smell of coffee and pastries filled his nostrils and for the first time that day he felt hungry.

When he reached the entrance to Station Parade, the traffic was busy, all heading in one direction. He stood momentarily, allowing the warmth from the sun and light to welcome him. Turning left out of the station, he knew that it would take only ten minutes to walk to the car park. There would be time to sit on a bench near The Stray, to watch the world go by and to remember the good times. He did not want to reach his target too early; he needed the car park to have emptied of shoppers' and tourists' vehicles. He needed it to be quiet.

Patience was the key to success. He had hours to wait but he would walk The Stray. Simply to watch would be reward enough as the time to act would come soon. He had all the time in the world.

The distant trees silhouetted against the blue, a bank of mountain-like clouds had slowly built from the east creating identifiable shapes that became real to his furtive mind.

As the clouds began to dissipate, the light slowly diminished leaving the increasing traffic to flow along the A61. It was time to move, time to check and take stock before crossing the road and walking up Tower Street.

The concrete multi-storey car park was to his right. He knew the vehicle would be in there, it would just require a brief search. He looked away as a car waited by the barrier, the driver eager for the metal arm to lift. As it quickly departed he entered. As yet the lights had not come on, leaving the corners of the building wrapped in partial shadowy dark. Walking up the first ramp, he heard a car engine start on a level above, the echo making it difficult to determine the floor it was on. He found a dark space and waited.

Within minutes, the car's headlights danced along the walls as it made its way to the exit, the engine note amplified within the hollow space. The building was cooler than he had expected but then the sun never penetrated the lower levels.

He inhaled and the familiar aroma, a smell found in many multi-storey car parks, stung his nostrils, a cocktail of exhaust gas and urine. As the car turned onto his level the headlights briefly illuminated his target, the blue Jaguar F-Type, parked on level two.

It was situated away from the dark corners and positioned below a CCTV camera. That brought a smile. Holding a key fob that he had cloned earlier, he approached the car. Obediently, the lights flashed as the alarm was turned off. The locks sprang open. From his rucksack, he withdrew the container he had worked on; it was armed and a very different vessel. Much larger than a family thermos flask, it was much heavier too. It was wrapped in a thick, black quilted jacket. He flicked the safety clasp that helped secure the top, checking that the seal was still intact before opening the passenger door. With great care, he placed it in the footwell of the car before then moving to the driver's side. From the pocket of the rucksack he took a small box. Within was a cocktail glass. He held it up, carefully removed a glove and flicked the rim with his fingernail. It rang, bell-like, the sound faintly echoing within the low-ceilinged space.

"For whom the bell tolls," he whispered as he placed it in the shallow space under the driver's seat before adding one more item. He grinned inwardly as a rhyme played in his head, a rhyme from his childhood. The next step would demand great patience as he would have to wait indefinitely for the owner to return, but then time was the one thing of which he had plenty. For this to succeed, the timing was critical and if his calculations were correct, it should all soon be over with one press of the key… over in a flash!

Chapter Two

Cyril was the last to go to bed. He sat nursing a glass of red wine and stared out into the darkness of the garden. He was trying to put everything into a perspective that he could reconcile and therefore come to terms with the situation in which he found himself. The funeral of his father had affected him more than he had ever thought possible. An owl called somewhere in the distance.

***

It was not unusual for cars to be left in the multi-storey car park overnight. Often it was a result of the owner having one drink too many. It was exactly nine thirty when the shutters came down cocooning the Jaguar in the darkness that only held the echoes of the outside world. It would be another nine hours before the discovery would be made and only then by accident.

***

It took a while for Cyril to realise that it was the silence that woke him. Smiling at this thought, and the sudden awareness of his surroundings, he opened his eyes fully allowing them to focus on the leaching, early morning light that played and danced with the mottled shadows flickering across the strangely familiar ceiling. Hearing Julie's slow, rhythmic breathing, semi-muffled within the bed sheets, was reassuring and he let his body relax before stretching out his hand to feel her familiar warmth. He looked back at the moving patterns and thought of his father, reflecting on the previous day's funeral, on the coffin and the ceremony. Cyril had been emotionally dead, he knew that he would be. There was no love lost between them, but to him, after a great deal of soul-searching, it felt important he should be there, the right thing to do; an only son has responsibilities, irrespective of the bitterness and history. In his mind it was simply an obligation, and now his duty had been fulfilled. He recalled the words of one of his heroes: *When in doubt, do the courageous thing.* It had been far from easy but he knew that he had honoured those emotive words.

He closed his eyes and his mother's face swam into the space he had just created. It suddenly felt as if she were there with him. In his mind he could hear the low melodic tones of her violin, the bow caressing the strings as she smiled at him; the lark was ascending with each careful note and he felt wrapped and enveloped within the security of the fine, misty image; a mother's love. It was in this state of peace that he thought he heard her whisper the words, *Thank you, Cyril, thank you. We are now together.*

Suddenly confused, he quickly opened his eyes as if to grasp a semblance of reality. He felt a warm tear run from his eye before catching it on his cheek with his finger. "Don't be a bloody fool, man!" he admonished himself before slipping from the bed and moving to the window. Julie stirred a little but immediately settled again. Parting the curtains, he allowed the morning brightness to stab his wet eyes. If Julie were to wake, at least he would have an excuse for the tears.

He looked out across the garden. It was as if he had never been away; it seemed the same, so familiar, the place he had spent his formative years. The time rolled back and in his mind's eye he could see himself, a small boy again, throwing the newly made balsa wood model aircraft with great enthusiasm, watching it take flight, lift, twist, soar and turn before slowly coming in to land. Cyril smiled at this memory.

Out of nowhere, a figure moved into his peripheral vision, causing the phantom child to vanish as quickly as it had appeared. It was Wendy, his stepmother. How frail she seemed as she carried a small cutting-board of broken bread for the birds. He watched her scrape it onto the bird-table. Smiling, he noticed the birds begin to mass immediately within the outer hedges of the garden; their calls seemed clearly audible for the first time, a morning ritual.

She had been brave at the funeral. Cyril was amazed that she had chosen to read the eulogy, an emotionally demanding task for any loved one. Standing proudly at the lectern, she had been in control and for her diminutive size, imposing. He was also surprised that she had mentioned sincerely his mother throughout her delivery; the warm words paid homage, celebrating the lives of both her husband and her dear friend and his first wife. She clearly loved them in equal measure. How difficult for her that must have been, how dignified she was.

Cyril's respect for her had grown over the days they had been together but it was that moment in the packed church when he realised what a wonderful human being she truly was. The years of resentment were immediately replaced with a deep respect and in some ways he felt a pang of regret that he had not really given her a chance to be closer to him, to be his surrogate mother in his early years.

Swallowing his distress, he watched her retrace her steps and disappear inside. Lifting his eyes beyond the surrounding hedges, he followed the rise of the land across the fields towards the silhouetted copse of oak that lined the morning-fresh horizon. It brought a degree of comfort. Relieved, he smiled. If he had a pound for every time he had played in its hidden darkness he would be a wealthy man. His eyes then caught the fine straight line of a jet's vapour trail bringing him clearly back to the present.

"Is it fine or wet?" Julie's mumbling emerged from beneath the sheets.

"It's fine, the same as yesterday. I'll bring you some tea."

She released a hand from the covers and waved her approval. Cyril moved back to the bed, leaned over and kissed her forehead before grabbing a dressing gown and going downstairs.

***

The blue Jaguar had been in the Harrogate multi-storey car park for twenty-one hours and would have been there longer had it not been for a driver scraping the rear bumper during a clumsy reversing manoeuvre. She could never reverse into gaps so why she had done so she would never know, but could only berate herself for trying. If her morning had started badly it was only going to get much worse.

She had approached the car to place a note under the wiper-blade giving her contact details and an apology for her carelessness. What confronted her as she looked through the windscreen shocked and startled her more than the accident itself. Her scream pierced the relative silence as it echoed through the stark concrete building before finally rallying two members of the public to her assistance. Within twenty minutes, it had also brought the police.

***

The kitchen was warm and the smell of baking bread was welcoming. Wendy was sitting at the large table, writing. She stopped and lifted her head as Cyril entered. A smile, as welcome as the bread's aroma, flashed across her face. Cyril raised his hand and returned the smile.

"Good morning, Cyril, I trust you slept well?" she asked as she replaced the top on her fountain pen and stood. "I'll make some tea, the bread will be ready soon. Your father loved the smell of boiled eggs and fresh, warm bread soldiers." She sounded quite carefree but her eyes spoke a different language and Cyril was quick to interpret the depth of her sadness.

As she moved away, Cyril glanced at the book. The beautiful, blue handwriting seemed to flow in regimental rows across the page. He immediately spotted his name within the sentences; it seemed to be some kind of diary. Wendy glanced up and could sense his curiosity.

"I write to her every day, it's to your mother and now your father too. When your mother died, I promised myself to have a daily chat with her just as we did when she was alive. It was usually about your father or about the house, the news and the ever-changing world. I'd write about concerts and films and what we'd been doing. When I heard any news of you I'd tell her. There's a book for each year she's been gone."

Cyril, feeling himself blush slightly, immediately looked away from the diary and focussed on Wendy as she busied herself making the tea.

"I've told your mother about the funeral and how your father was so pleased that you'd come to see him before he passed away. You'll never know just how much pleasure I felt telling her about those precious moments, how much it meant to your father. Sadly, Cyril, neither of us will understand what it would have meant to your mother." Wendy moved across the kitchen and put her hand on his shoulder. "What I do know is that God is good and that one day we shall all meet again." She paused and went to close the diary. "When I die, these books, my private conversations with your parents, will be yours to do with as you see fit." She turned and smiled. "But until then, my ramblings must stay with me."

She brought the tray and placed it on the table. "There's one for Julie. You take it to her. I'll put the cosy on the pot so you can pour yours when you come down. I know you like it strong."

Chapter Three

The blue and white police tape fluttered lazily across the entrance to Tower Street car park, a sixties concrete monstrosity that could only be politely referred to as an architectural blot on Harrogate's elegant Edwardian stone buildings. A degree of traffic confusion had been created by the discovery of the body as regular users of the car park were turned away. Most of those already parked would not need their cars for an hour or more but additional police had been drafted in to keep the traffic flowing and sightseers away.

Owen leaned against one of the concrete columns, his fingers dancing on the keypad of his phone. He made a few further notes and then tucked it into his inside pocket as the Crime Scene Manager approached.

"One dead, no suspicious circumstances from first inspection but..." The CSM shrugged. "The car doors were unlocked and left open, can you believe? Not fully, ajar like. Laptop and phone are in the car. According to one of the lads the key might well be in his pocket, does everything for you, the Jag… keyless entry. It's one of the flash sporty type cars. No room in it at all and so if you're not interested in going fast it's bloody useless, if you ask me!"

Owen immediately thought of Cyril when he heard the word *Flash*. It had been Cyril Bennett's nickname ever since he had known him but very few brave souls would say it to his face. Many thought he had been given the sobriquet because of his love of smart clothing but they were wrong. He was originally given the cognomen, *Gordon,* after the nineteenth century publishing magnate, James Gordon Bennett. Someone thinking Gordon was his real name called him Flash Gordon and it had simply stayed with him.

"The lad thinks all those electronics can be a nightmare if they go wrong; he's a bit of a petrol head, see? The guy in the car probably had a heart attack after having to fill the bloody thing with petrol." He chuckled to himself as if realising that he might have made a joke but it was short-lived. Owen's facial expression never altered.

"Who's attending?"

"Caner."

Dr Isaac Caner was one of four Home Office pathologists designated to the north east. There would have been a day when the thought of meeting Caner at a crime scene would have brought a sinking feeling to Owen's stomach, but over the course of time they had warmed to each other; Owen knew that Caner certainly was impressed by his ability to stomach an autopsy.

Owen grunted. "May I?" He pointed in the direction of the car.

The CSM simply smiled again and lifted the tape offering the pad for Owen to sign himself into the sealed area.

As Owen walked up the incline to the next level and approached the second row of police tape, he noticed a white Suzuki Swift parked away from the Jaguar. The repeated flash from the camera accompanied by the echoes from the passing traffic and the chattering of voices created a strange ambience within the close confines of the car park, not enhanced by the slight but distinct whiff of stale urine. There seemed to be a chill, even on this warm morning. The damage to both cars was evident. Caner was clearing items into his case while his assistant continued to take more photographs. The driver's door was still gaping and Owen could see the occupant's legs.

It took a moment for Dr Caner to spot Owen. "Morning, Owen, still lurking in the shadows? Didn't think this would be Cyril's bagatelle even though he just lives round the corner."

"He's away, father's funeral. Died a week ago. Cyril's had to travel to Nantwich. Surprisingly, that's where the family home is and that's where he was born. I always thought he was from this neck of the woods but apparently not." He shook his head emphasising his disbelief. "You work with someone all this time and you still don't know everything about them."

Caner looked at Owen, his facial expression saying everything. "Cheshire? Bloody hell! Thought he was carved from Yorkshire grit stone and his features were weathered by the four winds and the driving rain. Always did play his cards close to his chest. Still, waters certainly run deep within Bennett."

Owen chuckled. "Might be from a different county but he still has all the traits of a Yorkshireman; bloody short arms and deep pockets and as you know, he certainly calls a spade a spade. True there is a real depth to his character."

"Not too good in an autopsy, Owen, whereas you my lad..." He smiled before turning to point at the Jag. "Our man here's been dead for about twelve hours but I'll give you a more accurate time of death once he's back on the slab."

"What do you guess to be the cause of death?"

"No sign of any visible injuries and, Owen, a word to the wise, we never guess." He exaggerated the word elongating the sibilant. "So, in answer to your question, my professional judgement right at this minute would be natural causes. If that checks after examination I'll file my report with the coroner."

"David Stephens is the owner of the Jag according to the DVLA, not had it long either, poor bugger. Fifty-six and lived in Leathley. From what we've managed to ascertain, he owns a couple of bars and a restaurant. Officers are on their way to interview the family. Interestingly, he was reported missing yesterday just before two in the morning. He'd phoned home at 9pm to say he'd be there in about forty minutes but he never arrived."

"Age is about right. Well done. We'll see what the coroner has to say but I feel that there'll be no need for you to attend this one, Owen. Cut and dried. No signs of distress, nothing taken from the car as far as I can see and no damage to... Stephens, did you say?"

Owen nodded.

"So, apart from the scrape to the back of the car, there's nothing to suspect foul play. Is this car park attended at night?"

"No, locked at nine-thirty and opened again at around seven." Owen pointed to the CCTV camera. "That doesn't work either. According to the chap downstairs it was reported a month ago but as yet nothing's been done about it. I bet they'll sort it now."

"Could your boffin chaps not have tracked him by his phone?" Caner asked as he ducked beneath the tape.

"Most people prefer to have that facility switched off for very obvious reasons." Owen looked at Caner and winked. "We've checked his phone records and last call made was from the area where his bar is."

"I see. Forgive my naïvety, Owen. I'm but a simple doctor." He removed his blue protective clothing, dropped it in a yellow clinical waste bag before walking towards the ramp, his assistant in tow. "I'll be in touch. My condolences to Cyril when you next communicate."

***

Cyril left Julie and Wendy chatting as he walked to the garage. Once inside he reread the letter addressed to him by his father. The writing was almost illegible but the content was quite clear, he had requested that Cyril keep the car. *It mustn't be sold. If you will not cherish it, then it must be destroyed, scrapped.* He read it over again and glanced at the car. What was he going to do with this aged behemoth? It was the only request his father had made. Cyril opened the door and sat in the driver's seat running his hands on the wheel. It had a smell of its own, it always did have and that was the problem; it hoarded memories, to him it was a Pandora's box on wheels. To his annoyance his phone rang.

"Bennett."

"Owen, sir. Just wondering how things went yesterday. Wanted you to know we were all thinking about you."

Cyril's annoyance immediately waned. "As well as funerals go, Owen. Thank you for your concern and please pass my thanks on to the team." He paused for a moment. "Anything to report?"

"Body found in a car in the multi-storey just by your place but looks as though it's natural causes, no suspicious circumstances as far as they can see. Forensics have done a check and the body is with Caner so we should hear within twenty-four hours. He seemed fairly confident. Family called to say he was missing. There might not be an inquest. Car was locked in the car park overnight. Shakti's on leave, somewhere near Nice, that's in the South of..." He stopped himself going geographically further and quickly changed the route and subject. "...April's busy with a cold case. She sends her best wishes. You could say that we're sailing along fairly smoothly without the captain at the helm. No choppy seas just yet but when're you back?"

"Do we have a name?"

"Sorry?"

"The deceased, Owen?"

"Yes, sorry. Stephens, David Stephens. Family didn't seem overly traumatised by his sudden death. He'd been diagnosed with a heart condition a while back. Had a bit of a scare a few months ago too, heart attack, but they were assured it wasn't anything too serious. DVLA didn't see fit to cancel his driver's licence but the CAA has put a temporary stop on his pilot's licences."

"Licences? Plural? He held two?"

"Two, yes, fixed wing and rotary, I think the correct terms are. He owned a small helicopter that he kept at home and also flew an aircraft at Yeadon. All that from some bars and a restaurant! I'm in the wrong bloody job, sir. You used to fly, didn't you?"

"I did indeed, learned to fly at Liverpool, Speke, as it was known then but that was many years ago, now it's named after a Beatle. My flying is another story and as for your career? Believe me, Owen, you're where you should be, trust me."

Owen glanced at his watch and remembered the words inscribed on the back of the case, *Keen as mustard.* It had been a Christmas gift from Cyril and it meant a lot. "I know, thank you. When do you feel as though you might be ready to return to Castle Greyskull?"

"Sorry?"

"Beckwith Head Road. The station."

Cyril chuckled. "Greyskull! I'm ready now to be honest but just need to finalise a few things here, a couple of days at most. Keep me informed of anything, Owen, anything. And Owen?"

"Sir."

"What would you do with an old Bentley and I mean old?"

There was a sudden silence. "My gran used to watch a cop show where the detective had one with a black roof, Morse, I think he was called."

"That was a Daimler, Owen. Never mind. I was just thinking out loud. Thanks for the call. Means a lot."

"Never watched it myself."

Cyril smiled as he popped the phone on the bench seat of the car. "What on earth am I going to do with you?" he said out loud, tapping the steering wheel with more affection than he had imagined possible.

***

Julie and Wendy had moved to the garden. Slowly, Cyril's childhood past was being revealed as if Wendy were explaining the Bennett family life story. Although Julie was fascinated, she also felt uneasy; secrets were being disclosed to which only family members should be privy. On more than one occasion she had tried to change the subject but it was clear that Wendy had but one objective in life and that was to ensure at least one person knew the truth. They stopped as the Bentley moved slowly from the garage and down the gravel path to the road. The gravel crunched under its tyres as though in protest.

"I know Cyril, Wendy, he's a torn man. That car holds conflicting memories. May I be honest with you?"

Wendy nodded. "Please. Now is the time for honesty on all sides. We've nothing to hide and therefore nothing to fear."

Julie considered her words carefully, she felt as though she were passing bad news to a bereaved relative but knew it must be done for Cyril's sake and for Wendy herself.

"I know a little of Cyril's past. He's talked of many things but one thing that seemed to affect him more than anything else was his telling of the day he discovered his father's infidelity. Had it not been for spotting that car, the one his father wants him to cherish, on a country lane, he might never have known, he would have remained ignorant of the facts. However, he did know and only recently learned that this affair, your relationship with his father was condoned by his mother, maybe even instigated by her. Imagine the maelstrom of confusion that was generated in his young mind, interpreting the confronting situation as he did. I think he still has to come to terms with the fact that his own mother wanted you to be part of their lives so that when she had gone, Cyril, her little boy would not be without a mother figure, but in the care of someone who truly loved them all."

She watched as Wendy removed a handkerchief from her sleeve before raising it to her nose.

"His mother and I had discussed it over many weeks. As she grew weaker she became convinced it was best for all concerned. Had we known that Cyril had witnessed what he had, we would have done things differently. You must remember that time was not on our side. His mother, bless her, and I for that matter, did it for the right reasons, to protect the ones we loved."

Neither spoke. The birdsong seemed to fill the uneasy gap perfectly as each considered their conversation and what might happen in the future.

Chapter Four

Owen was sitting at his desk trying to fish food crumbs from his computer keyboard using the end of a penknife and a paintbrush. Occasionally he blew at the stubborn objects but with little or no success. His tie had often worked effectively as a food chute to send lost morsels directly to the computer's keys where they had lodged in the crevices and seemed to stay indefinitely. Why he was endeavouring to clear the detritus today of all days was anyone's guess. He then looked at the screen. That too had been the target of a number of coughs and sneezes considering the spatter patterns that, in the artificial light, looked not too dissimilar to a Jackson Pollock painting. He soaked the end of his tie in his mouth and attempted to wipe clean the screen.

DC Stuart Park walked past Owen's desk, dropped a blue file into the tray and whistled the tune, *When I'm Cleaning Windows.* The subtlety went over his sergeant's head.

Owen sat back and admired his handiwork. He could almost hear Cyril's comment, *"Bloody hell, Owen, you've improved it worse!"* He frowned.

Grabbing the file, he removed the autopsy report on David Stephens and flicked through it. He quickly scanned the more technical terminology:

...no evidence of epilepsy and tests show ischemic hypoxia looking at the metabolic dysfunction and cell death. History of heart failure and recent infarction...

It was not as Caner had initially suspected, natural causes. The advice was that the death should be considered as *open* owing to some contradictory factors running parallel with the severe nature of the long-standing heart problems. There was little evidence to contradict his original theory but there was doubt.

Considering the conflicting findings, it would be impossible at that stage to say whether they were or were not contributory or resultant factors. Caner's advice was that they were resultant. Owen flicked back hoping to discover the exact reason for the change in diagnosis.

...tested results for blood oxygen saturation demonstrate that it was less than eighty-six per cent and therefore severe and rapid...

Owen tossed the file back onto the desk. In some ways he was reassured but an open verdict seemed contradictory to the confident first prognosis. However, he could see that there would be no reason to investigate further as the autopsy results and David Stephens's medical history suggested that his death was the result of a sudden heart attack. Some toxicology results were still outstanding, but from those received to date, there was evidence that he had been taking his prescribed medication but, more pertinently, there were positive signs of cocaine use. Further peripheral blood tests had been sent for analysis. Owen was intrigued to read that the findings suggested that Stephens was more poorly than at first thought by his family. Owen read an attached handwritten note from Caner.

Owen,

Drug use may prove to be a contributory factor in the further development of his medical condition but more tests will help. However, normally cardiac troponins are released four to six hours after a heart attack and can stay elevated for up to two weeks. If you compare the figures here you can see that our man was in rather poor health and that he had possibly suffered a number of minor heart attacks recently. We shall await further toxicology results but it seems clear. I feel there will be no inquest, even in light of the Class A drug use.

Regards,

Isaac Caner

Although concerned at the findings, Owen thought that if all the cases were as easy as this he would be able to spend more time rooting around the keys of his computer and less time actually on it. His desk phone rang.

He listened. "Ask them to come in, sooner rather than later. A cocktail glass you said? Under the driver's seat? And a..." He paused as if checking what he was about to say made any sense. "A potato? Ring me as soon as you have an appointment time."

Owen put the phone down, stood and went in search of DC April Richmond.

***

Wendy and Julie had returned to the kitchen when they heard the Bentley crunch its way up the drive. Glancing out of the window, a mug of coffee in her hand, Julie watched the car come to rest. She observed Cyril as he climbed out of the car and she could see from his demeanour that he still had the same dilemma. She grabbed a cup and saucer from the cupboard and prepared a coffee for him. It was going to be a difficult day.

***

Paul Ashton had been shocked to hear of his partner's death. He tried to busy himself in the lounge area of the *Bauhaus Cocktail and Champagne Bar* but he realised he was not achieving very much. He had initially been the sole owner until the venture faced serious financial difficulties. It was then that Stephens had proposed a partnership; he had been part owner for just over nine months and business had flourished. David had brought not only the necessary funding but also years of operational experience. They had become close friends. Although Paul did not like to think about the welfare of the business at this sad time, he was a realist and knew that David's death could not have come at a more difficult moment.

Paul had decided to close at lunchtime out of respect but to open for the evening trade as closing for the whole day would have been the last thing David would have wanted. It was, however, very clear that Paul's heart was not in it. His two staff would be able to handle the bar. Being a weekday it should not be too busy. He would be around in case they need him.

***

Mrs Stephens sat in the informal interview room, accompanied by her son and daughter. No one had chosen to accept the coffee offered and it was clear that they were all still in a state of anxiety. Owen and April entered, Owen introducing them both. It never ceased to amaze him how formalities continued in the most difficult of circumstances. He noted that Mrs Stephens looked a good ten years younger than he had imagined even at such a traumatic period in her life.

"Thank you for coming in at this difficult time, our condolences to you and your family." He paused, giving her time to compose herself. "Can you tell me why you contacted us, Mrs Stephens?"

"It was the glass, the glass my son found under the seat when the car was returned to us."

Owen failed to comprehend the significance. He looked across at April hoping she had picked up on something he had failed to see. She too seemed in the dark.

"Jonathan, my son, had washed and cleaned the car the day before. He'd vacuumed the inside and he knew that the glass wasn't in there the morning my husband left for Harrogate. I know that he didn't take it with him; he only took his phones and laptop. I walked him to his car."

"Was there a potato found too?"

"Goodness me, yes, a small one. How could I possibly forget that? It was sprouting too. I threw it away. I can assure you that he'd never go shopping in his car and certainly not to buy vegetables!"

"So it could have been there a while considering the state of it?" Owen said.

"No, the car's new. It can't have been and it wasn't there the day before." Jonathan's tone left Owen in no doubt that it must have been added on the day his father died.

"So how do you think they found their way under the seat?"

There was a disconcerting pause as Jonathan's mother raised her eyebrows. "Mr Owen, Sergeant, I'm not a policewoman. The potato, goodness knows, but what I do know is that this glass..." She took the glass from her bag and peeled away the bubble wrap as she continued to speak,"...Was not in the car when he left home so either he collected it from somewhere else that day and it fell under the seat at some point on his journey or someone put it there."

"Did you know your husband's timetable for the day?" It was April's turn to speak.

"Yes. He was in Harrogate all day. He has two businesses in the town. The other is in Knaresborough. He rang me as he was leaving the Bauhaus."

"At what time?"

"About nine. He said he'd be forty minutes, that the car was parked in the usual place; Tower Street, I assumed. He always parks there. He liked the security of the CCTV. He never liked parking on the roadside."

Owen simply looked down. "Cameras, right! Could the glass have come from the bar?"

"Mr Owen, forgive me, but I believe David passed away before taking his car from the car park. If he had collected it that day, why hide it beneath the seat? Surely it would be on the passenger seat?"

Owen took a deep breath and glanced at April.

April responded immediately. "So he didn't stop anywhere before he arrived in Harrogate, as far as you know?"

"If he did, then it's a surprise to me. Maybe your roadside cameras could answer that question, the ones that check number plates against road tax and the like. They seem to be everywhere these days."

Owen raised his eyebrows and made a note to check. "We'll need to keep the glass. I'll get our Forensics Team to take a look. We'll need your fingerprints to eliminate you from the procedure." Owen noticed her look of horror as she looked at her beautifully manicured nails.

"There's no ink, we scan them digitally now."

Owen turned to Jonathan. "You cleaned the inside of the car yesterday?"

"Yes, it's new. We have a few cars and I simply enjoy the task. I can assure you that the car was perfect when I'd finished. There was certainly neither a glass nor a potato in the car when he drove away."

Owen tapped his fingers on the table, glancing at the daughter too upset to be questioned. He considered the implications of the find. "Thank you, thank you for coming in at this difficult time."

"Do you know the F-Type?" Jonathan asked looking at both officers in turn. "It has two seats and very little room. The back of the seats cannot come forward other than by adjusting the rake angle to suit the driving position. That glass could not have fallen from a parcel shelf during a drive, it had to have been deliberately placed under the seat. The potato could have fallen from his pocket and rolled but why would he carry a potato? It just doesn't make sense."

"Thank you." A small bell rang in Owen's head. He did not like the way this interview was going. Clearly there were questions and he had to find the answers. So much for it being a simple case.

An officer entered with a digital laser scanner and within minutes the prints had been taken. April escorted them to the front desk where they were signed out before she returned to the interview room. There was a momentary silence as each glanced at their notes. Owen sat back, folded his arms and stared at the cocktail glass.

"Where the bloody hell did that come from and why was it there?"

April jotted down a few notes before she spoke. "She's obviously read the autopsy report but showed no real concern. Neither did she mention the poor state of her husband's health nor the use of drugs." She repeated Owen's internal words. "So much for it being a simple case."

"Drug use I've kept for later. Put someone on to checking journey times using available ANPR cameras. That should give us a clear idea of where he went on that day."

Chapter Five

Cyril threw a cover over the Bentley, releasing a cloud of dust particles that were immediately caught in the sun's beaming light. He marvelled at them momentarily; they had the appearance of minute fireflies. He ensured that the battery was connected to the trickle charger, wondering if that small action was an admission that the car would survive. He had connected it to a life-support system. The drive and the menthol vapour from his electronic cigarette had helped focus his thinking.

The house would eventually be his. All the mystery and secrets that he believed it once held had somehow drifted away over the last few days. It held no ogres but it still retained within its walls some bad memories. He would also admit for the very first time that it held some fond ones too. He neither needed to nor was he about to make a decision about the car but would leave it here in the garage.

As often as work demands permitted he resolved to return knowing that he needed and wanted to see Wendy. She was the custodian of his past and he was aware of his obligations if he wanted to discover the inner truth about his mother and the complexity of the tangled relationships of his parents. Knowing the truth might finally allow him to break down the barriers and escape his own personal demons.

***

On returning to his desk, Owen pulled up a chair for April. "Have you read the autopsy on David Stephens?" He looked up as April nodded. "Although it's an open verdict and Caner clearly feels that it's natural causes why am I not fully convinced? Is it because of that?" Owen pointed to the glass wrapped within the protective bag. "Or is it the discovery of traces of cocaine in his system? We need to discover why that glass was there and more importantly why it might have been put there. We need to get it to Forensics pretty smartish."

She smiled at Owen, knowing what she would be doing for the rest of the day. "For it to be anything else, and I know you're edging towards unlawful killing for whatever reason, you'll need clear and indisputable evidence to back up that claim. What you expect to get from… " She didn't finish but collected the glass. "A thought. With respect, you might also need permission to expend valuable resources on what might be a wild goose chase." She held up the glass.

Owen frowned realising her words were wise. "Thanks, April. What's the state of David Stephens's businesses, I wonder? Before you take the glass to Forensics, please ask Smirthwaite to do some digging. You know the drill. Check for loans, lease agreements, family debt, maybe too many financial commitments. Something's just not right here unless Stephens was a bloody brilliant actor and kept his health issues and his drug use a closely guarded secret. But if so, why? I think I'll pay a visit to the *Bauhaus Cocktail and Champagne Bar*."

April simply smiled and shook her head. Owen would do what he felt to be necessary and he would make the request when he had a little more to go on. "Lovely. Have one for me when you're there."

***

Owen parked on Raglan Street just behind Harrogate's library. He remembered that this was the area from which Stephens had made his final phone call. The traffic was busy for late morning but then the sun was out and that always attracted the shoppers. The Bauhaus was a well designed double-fronted bar positioned in a large, modern stone development. Grey frames were filled with distinctive frosted glass bedecked with lettering spelling the word,

Bauhaus, the ascenders of letters 'b' and 'h' extending to the top of the window. It was elegant, well executed and probably cost a small fortune to build.

The bar was busier than Owen had expected. He glanced at the large room; the paint scheme continued the grey theme giving the room a sophisticated yet dour air. Large coloured block posters were beautifully presented around the room and the settees and chairs, all grey leather, added to the overall appearance. He made his way to the bar.

"What can I get you?" The young lady behind the bar slid across a cocktail menu. Owen in return lifted his ID.

"Mr Paul Ashton, please." Owen smiled wanting to add, 'shaken, not stirred' but resisted the temptation.

Her response was professional, as if it were a normal, daily occurrence. She smiled and moved away towards a door at the rear of the bar. Owen watched as a few metres away a cocktail was poured into a glass. What appeared to be steam drifted downwards from the rim until it settled around the stem making him immediately think of a miniature witch's cauldron; the purple contents only enhanced the image.

"Rather have a pint," he mumbled to himself as he fidgeted uncomfortably. The entry of Paul Ashton came as a relief.

"Paul Ashton. How may I help?" He offered his hand across the bar.

"I'd like to talk about David Stephens if you have somewhere more private?"

***

Julie dropped Cyril on Robert Street.

"Ring me later." She blew a kiss and drove away.

Within an hour, Cyril had unpacked, loaded the washing machine and made a pot of tea. He checked his watch, shook his wrist and looked again, 3.55pm. He settled in a chair, removed the cosy from the pot and poured a cup. Dialling Owen's number, Cyril put his phone on speaker and sipped his tea.

"Owen, just wanted to let you know that I'll be in tomorrow. How's the car park death going?"

Cyril listened to the explanation. "So you've interviewed his partner? What about the other businesses, didn't you say that he had three? What about the CAA medical report… has the coroner also asked for that to be checked by Caner and his GP medical records?" He sipped his tea as he listened to the responses.

"Early start. Brief me tomorrow at 7.30am, and I want Richmond and Smirthwaite there also. You said he was checking finances, yes? Good. See you in the morning. And Owen, have ANPR records been checked for Stephens's car?"

"Yes, sir."

Cyril could tell from Owen's tone that there was some doubt in his mind as to whether the death was from natural causes. However, unless he had proof and hard facts natural causes would be the outcome. Cyril felt an excitement at returning to work. "Castle Greyskull indeed!" he said quietly and smiled. He somehow felt as though a huge weight had been lifted from his shoulders.

Chapter Six

It was with some relief that Cyril turned out of the passageway linking Robert Street with West Park; it was always a conduit for a cold draught of air even in the summer months. Crossing the road, he suddenly felt the early morning warmth. It would be good to get back to work and clear his head of the domestic complexities that had plagued him for the last few weeks. Even after being away a relatively short time, being back in Harrogate felt like the cure-all that he needed, its security and familiarity and Julie.

He turned to look at the spire of Trinity Church, a grey obelisk set within a verdant sea made up of the many trees that surrounded and edged The Stray; all seemed to be competing for his attention. A car horn sounded and a hand waved as the vehicle slowed and the driver smiled. Cyril suddenly felt as though he were home and safe, a feeling that persisted when he reached the station. He received a warm welcome upon signing in, and slipped the security ID lanyard over his head before approaching his office.

Owen knew immediately to whom the shoes belonged to as they appeared and crossed the room while he groped on the floor beneath his desk; it was the shine and the neatly tied laces.

"Morning, Owen. In search of the truth or merely looking for inspiration down there amidst the detritus of your everyday life?"

Owen's head popped up like that of a prairie dog emerging from a hole, a huge smile of success on his face.

"Morning, sir. Dropped my mint ball when I squeezed it from the packet." He grinned before blowing on the retrieved sweet and popping it into his mouth. "Search and thou shall find, my gran always said."

"Some things don't change, Owen, we've to be grateful for that. One day, I'll wager, I'll come to work and find that you've contracted the Black bloody Death. My office in ten and please don't forget to bring Richmond and Smirthwaite with you."

"Meant to tell you on the phone that Caner sends his condolences."

Cyril simply smiled. "And was he amazed that I wasn't born in God's own county, Owen?"

"Funny that. We both were to be honest."

"You can never judge a book by its cover and sometimes neither can you judge it by its contents! My office…" He looked at his watch. "In eight."

"Never did like books," Owen mumbled as he went in search of April.

***

Owen presented his causes for concern about the irregularities in the case but quickly admitted that he was reacting purely on his instincts. He had looked across at April before mentioning the need to commit resources to ensure that David Stephens's death was not through foul play. Cyril had simply nodded.

The evidence suggested there had appeared to be nothing untoward in Stephens's relationship with his business partner and, according to Smirthwaite, all the financial and business dealings appeared to be above board. There was debt, but that was managed through business loans and mortgages. The family home was owned outright. It was difficult to ascertain the amount of savings Stephens and his family held but it could be assumed by his lifestyle that he was a very wealthy man.

Questions were asked about his ability to sustain such a lavish lifestyle. It was evident that although the businesses were performing well, it was questionable as to whether they were healthy enough to support a helicopter and a personal aircraft. There was, at this stage, a belief that a good deal of his wealth was through inheritance.

"His wife?" Cyril rolled the electronic cigarette along his lower lip.

"Originally worked in the business but stopped when the children reached school age. The son is presently on holiday from Nottingham University; he's studying sciences. For some reason he wants to be a teacher." It was the inflection in Owen's voice that made Cyril sit up.

"Does that not seem right to you, Owen? It's a good profession for anyone to take. It's a vocation."

"You'd think he'd follow his father. He's seen what rewards are to be had and… Well, you would wouldn't you… it's there on a plate."

It was April who answered with an astute observation. "He might also have seen the long anti-social hours that could have had a direct impact on family life, seen the effect on his father's health and maybe, just maybe, he's seen a part of life that at this moment is hidden from plain sight. He could be the wise one. The daughter doesn't seem to have an interest in the business either. She's a model and trying to break into acting."

"I believe Caner's convinced that it's natural causes?" Cyril questioned, knowing the answer but wanting to hear Owen say so.

"To quote Caner, sir." Owen shuffled his notes until he found the page. *"I don't work on gut feelings or whether a pinecone is open or closed. As a pathologist I work on facts. I make judgements based on hard facts, indisputable, medical evidence that after years of training and many more years' experience this profession has bestowed on me. What I write, Owen, is what I see and understand and not what might or might not have happened; fact and not fiction… I do not make things up. The word 'pathology' comes from the Greek meaning 'the science of disease'. Science is the key and you, young man, as an officer of the law, should be mindful of that!* I felt like a child getting a bollocking. Christ, I even made myself stand in the corner for fifteen minutes afterwards." He grinned and winked at Cyril.

"Evidence on the glass?"

"They're working on it. Should have it by late today," April answered.

"The drugs, granted not much but surely that counts?"

"Owen, if we arrested everyone who tested positive for drugs we wouldn't have enough courts or prisons. We live, sadly, in different times. ANPR records?"

"From what we saw he came straight into Harrogate or let's say that his car did."

"So we accept an open verdict because of some rogue readings within the blood samples taken from the brain showing rapid death through oxygen starvation… structural neural changes of hypoxia… to do with the rapid rate of death?" Cyril paused and looked up at each officer in turn. "Clear as mud but I know just the person to help me understand that mud."

***

Within the hour, Cyril was shown to Julie's office and was informed that she would see him in five minutes. He waited for the secretary to leave before walking round the room like a penniless child in a sweet shop. No matter how many visits he made, the objects that were either floating in some kind of liquid within sealed glass jars or standing on one of the many dusty shelves always intrigued. The one that caught his eye on this occasion was on Julie's desk and seemed, from a glance, to be quite ancient. A yellowing, hand-written label in fine copperplate Latin script was attached to the lower part. Inside the glass was a head; the face had suffered severe damage to the eye socket, nose and mouth. There was a large cavity where those parts of the face should have been. He was about to pick it up when Julie entered.

"You coppers can leave nothing alone! If you touch that I wouldn't go to the toilet without washing your hands." She bent and kissed his cheek. "The damage you see there is a result of syphilis, Cyril."

She watched as he moved away and looked as Cyril wiped his hands on his trousers. The look on his face said it all.

"I'm giving a talk to some college students and these exhibits tend to grab their attention. I've borrowed it. Now, let's focus on what you came here for. Caner's report is sound; I'd have come to the same conclusion. I can, however, see why there is a slight diagnostic anomaly. Caner found evidence of neural hypoxia prior to death. That means that the more rapid the death, the more changes can be seen. This is because sudden death occurs while life functions including enzyme activities are operating to the fullest. It's to do with the neural changes in relation to the duration of the agonal period."

It was evident from Cyril's face that he was struggling to understand. "Think of the agonal period as the short time during a person's last breaths or in some cases, the last gasps a dying person takes. This is a result of inadequate oxygen supply to tissue or total lack of oxygen. If that's the case, Cyril, it is then termed anoxia, it's complex but it's to do with the destruction of the cells through the action of their own enzymes. A heart attack can show the same results."

He scanned the notes she had handed to him.

"Keep them. You owe me dinner."

He smiled. "Always a pleasure, Doctor."

"May I bring my friend?" She pointed to the specimen jar containing the head.

Cyril looked down at his hands and said nothing.

***

Staff at the Bauhaus bar busied themselves cleaning and preparing for the lunchtime trade. Paul Ashton moved behind the counter and then into the back storeroom where he found Carla, the manageress. She was taking a quick stock check. He started to move a number of boxes.

"Lost something?" She didn't give him time to answer. "With the death of Mr Stephens is this place still viable? What the staff really wants to know is, are our jobs safe or should we all be looking for new ones, Paul? If you don't mind my saying so, we know that you were walking a financial tightrope before he came along… sorry… but we're all concerned about our future prospects here."

He stopped his search and dragged a large cardboard box to the centre of the room, suddenly noticing the item for which he had been searching. They both sat on the box.

"You're right and I hold my hands up. Spent too much on the place in the first instance and really took my eye off the market. If it helps, I've had a word with David's family, and things will continue just as they are for the immediate future. Mrs Stephens has spoken to her accountant and they believe the business to be viable. We'll be continuing as before. I'm confident we can make a go of it; you just have to trust me. Providing we all do our jobs, there should be nothing to worry about. Happy?"

Carla smiled. "That's a relief what with my new flat."

Paul put his hand on her arm. "Everything will be fine. If you hadn't asked I wouldn't have moved the box and found that."

"My mother used to say that my father always did a *man look,* not too thorough!" Carla giggled putting her hand to her mouth. "Thanks!"

Paul picked up the blue pot-bellied steel flask and returned to the bar.

Chapter Seven

The electric garage door slowly and quietly rolled up and the Jaguar F-Type moved onto the large parking area, set well away from the main house, the exhaust bark breaking the relative silence. Jonathan Stephens climbed out leaving the car rumbling on tick over and walked round the car. It had been his father's latest pride and joy but then all his father's cars were special when they were new but his interest soon waned. Usually within months he would be yearning for something else. It wasn't only cars either. He knew his father had a roving eye and the family had faced some emotionally difficult times. Things would be different, for according to his mother the car was now his and he was, for the time being at least, the male head of the family.

He turned and pressed another keypad. A second larger garage-style door opened to reveal the small Robinson 22 helicopter, also painted blue. He and his sister had been two of the youngest helicopter pilots in Britain qualifying just after their seventeenth birthdays. He pressed the button for a second time and the hangar door closed.

He ran his hand over the car's roof affectionately before opening the Jaguar's door. It was then that he felt as though someone was watching him. Looking around, Jonathan let his eyes scan the hedges and trees that lined the garden periphery and then the drive. There was nothing. He tapped the car and smiled before climbing in. The engine revved and the rear wheels spewed loose gravel that clattered under the wheel arches as they churned the driveway. From the bridle path that ran alongside the house, a solitary figure emerged and watched the

Jaguar speed away before hands moved towards the hooded, covered face.

***

"A watched kettle never boils, Mum used to say." The words tumbled from Carla's lips in an attempt to reassure herself as she walked down Victoria Avenue towards the entrance to the Harrogate public library. Checking her watch she was disappointed to see that her forty-five minute break was slowly eroding. She had looked at all the parked cars on both sides of the road, hoping her boyfriend had found a parking spot but his car was nowhere to be seen. He was never late. Had she looked more carefully she would have noticed that she was not the only person impatiently scanning both sides of the road.

A horn blasted, causing a few pigeons to scatter from one of the nearby buildings. Both anxious observers turned in the direction of the horn. Carla chuckled and ran towards the black VW that had clearly seen better days. As she approached, her boyfriend pushed open the passenger door and she quickly jumped in to be met with a smile and the aroma of fried chicken.

"Sorry, lovely, late with traffic." He leaned over and kissed her. "Let's find somewhere to park and eat. I'll drop you back at the Bauhaus on time, don't worry, unless of course you get carried away and have wicked plans!"

She slapped his thigh as the car accelerated. "I need food," she whispered. "Food!" She exaggerated the vowel sound.

The person across the road had watched the whole street drama unfold. For some inexplicable reason it had brought a smile to his face but he turned to concentrate on the other cars coming and going. He rested his large rucksack on the pavement, lodging it carefully against his legs. It was getting heavy. He checked his watch again. The car for which he waited was normally parked at this time. Maybe, like the VW, it too was delayed by traffic or an accident. He would wait another hour and if it had not arrived by then he would try again the next day.

It would be another forty minutes before his patience was rewarded. The Volvo approached and parked in the central area of Victoria Avenue; it was one of the few roads in Harrogate that allowed parking on either side and along the centre. The driver climbed from the vehicle, collecting his jacket and bag.

The observer approached quickly removing a simple handheld jamming device from his pocket. Even though the driver had walked away from his car believing it would automatically lock with the press of his thumb, the signal had been blocked, the car remained unlocked.

Within minutes of the driver leaving, and in broad daylight, the observer opened the driver's door, found the vehicle's diagnostics board and downloaded the key code to a blank key fob. His research had been accurate and it had proved to be a simple and quick procedure. The passing vehicles neither distracted him nor caused concern.

On completion, the door was closed and as he walked away from the vehicle he turned to see the lights flash once as his thumb hit the button on the remote key fob. The initial stage of the job was completed. He checked his watch. If Bill Baines, the owner of the Volvo, were to keep to his normal timetable, something he had just failed to do, he would not be returning to the car until 6pm.

After putting the fob into his pocket, the observer rubbed his hands and blew onto them before moving towards the library. The object held securely within the rucksack would be placed in the car a little later. He could spend his early afternoon enjoying peace, quiet and a good book. Later, however, would be reserved for a far more guilty pleasure. He just needed to calculate the timing of his next deposit accurately.

***

At 5.45pm, Bill Baines, the Volvo's owner, left his office after packing some files and his laptop into a briefcase. He glanced out through the office window onto Victoria Avenue. The sun still cast dappled shadows and it appeared warm. Already sitting securely just behind the passenger seat of his car was a quilt-wrapped flask. The safety latch had been released, the lid fully opened. The car doors were locked. The observer waited a safe distance away.

It had been three hours since he had pressed the key to release the lid and he had walked past to ensure that everything was as it should be. It was. This was the crucial stage.

***

Cyril checked his watch; 5.50pm. The day had been relatively mundane. The mountain of paperwork seemed to have grown in direct proportion to the amount of time he had been away from his desk, making him question when the promised paperless workplace would arrive. Somehow, however, staring at the small forest of files, he knew, like flying cars and ray-guns, it would not be any time soon. He was relieved to see six o'clock come round.

The day ended with his usual, some said anal, desk tidying routine. Unplugging the charging electronic cigarette that dangled from the wall socket like a dead rodent, he popped it into his top pocket. Owen had left an hour earlier and the office area seemed quiet. The glow from one of the computer screens was clearly visible illuminating April Richmond's face with a ghostly blue-white glow.

***

A gloved hand carefully opened the passenger side door of the Volvo as wide as possible. The collapsed body of Bill Baines was visible, his head resting across the gear lever, eyes vacantly staring into the foot well, his upper torso contorted over the central arm rest. Leaning in, the observer moved the back of the passenger seat forward as he had done earlier and grabbed the padded flask. He left the door slightly ajar before walking round to the driver's side. He opened the door a fraction and turned to leave.

***

"Don't work too late!" Cyril instructed before he smiled and waved.

"Straight home, sir?"

"I've an appointment with a Black Sheep, April, it's been a long day. In fact, if the truth be known, it's been a very long week. Fancy a beer?"

She made a sad face. "Here until eleven, late start this morning. Have one for me." This would be the second time that she would miss out on an after work drink.

***

Within half an hour, Cyril was just turning across The Stray. The Coach and Horses, his destination, was visible in the distance when the wail of sirens burst over the noise of the traffic. A police car approached, blue strobe lights pulsing, a clear warning beacon to pedestrians and road users alike. Moses-like, it magically cleared a path and brought the stream of cars travelling along Otley Road to a standstill. Some mounted the pavement to allow the emergency vehicle a clear route through. It sped down to the roundabout before turning left onto West Park. As if on cue, Cyril's phone rang.

"Bennett." He listened, his eyes following the police car, as it turned right onto Victoria Avenue. "Close it down. No one near until the Forensics Team arrives and I want any witnesses held. Call DC Richmond, tell her to meet me there. No, I don't need a car…" He watched another blue light come into his peripheral vision; this time a paramedic… "I'm nearly there."

His pace had quickened since taking the call and he found himself nearly breaking into a run. Fortunately, the path across the grassland stretched from Beech Grove to Victoria Avenue keeping him well away from the roads. As he approached the scene, two police vehicles blocked either side of the avenue and an officer was rolling out blue and white tape preventing access to pedestrians and inquisitive onlookers.

Cyril breathed heavily as beads of sweat formed across his forehead. He showed his ID to one of the PCSOs manning the tape.

"Blue Volvo, sir, parked centrally. The traffic warden who reported it suggests there's no damage to the car nor signs of a struggle or theft. He's with the paramedic. I imagine he's a bit shaken."

Cyril nodded his thanks as he moved under the tape and approached the paramedic's vehicle. The traffic warden was sitting on a red blanket with his back against the side of the estate car, his head in his hands.

"Hello. DCI Bennett." He smiled, tilting his head to get a better view of the patient as the medic busied himself unfolding a foil blanket before wrapping it around the man's shoulders. "Is he in any shape to answer some questions?"

The medic nodded as he looked down at his patient. "He says he's okay but to be on the safe side I'll just keep an eye on him. Shock's a funny thing. This is Mike. Keeps telling me he's fine but I need him to sit there quietly until I've checked him out properly."

Bennett crouched in front of the man. "Mike, I'm DCI Bennett. Can you tell me what happened?"

There was a pause as Mike focussed on Bennett before protesting that his name was Michael. He stated that he was fine and did not require all the fuss, after all he had seen plenty of bodies in Afghanistan so seeing this one dead and in one piece was no big deal.

"Sorry, Michael. What regiment?" Cyril asked, a genuine tone of admiration in his voice as he tried to keep him sitting down.

"Royal Green Jackets."

"So you'd have remained calm when spotting the body. Can you describe it?"

"I told him." He pointed to the officer standing by the far tape. "He was the first here, came from Craven Lodge just up the road, he told me he's the beat manager for this area. Said his name but I can't recall."

Craven Lodge was the town's police office situated on the avenue. The two PCSOs manning the tape areas were from the same office. Cyril did not fail to see the irony of having a potential murder committed right under their noses.

"So tell me, as I'm likely to be in charge of this and I'd much prefer to hear it first hand," Cyril insisted. "May I?" Cyril pointed to the piece of pavement next to him.

Michael said nothing but stretched out the blanket. Cyril sat down next to him and removed his e-cigarette. "Do you mind if I vape and listen?"

"Make yourself at home." He chuckled. "Vape away!"

They both laughed. Cyril listened as Michael described the events again. He was reassured by the detailed response.

"The car's a regular, has a permit, as some of the businesses do along here. I see it most days. Met the owner a few times too, nice chap. Can't recall his name either, did tell me once but he always seemed to remember mine. Looked fit and healthy too but I guess as we used to say, when your number's up, it's up!"

"So you saw nobody else?" Vapour leaked from Cyril's nostrils as he spoke.

"Plenty of traffic and a few pedestrians but they were some distance away from the car, too far to really see anything. Once I saw the body I didn't want a fuss so acted as we are trained to do in circumstances like this, not that there are too many here in Harrogate. Break-ins and vandalism, yes, latest spate is wing mirrors being torn off, bloody mindless. I called it in, and within minutes the officer from Craven Lodge arrived along with those two." He pointed to the officers who were manning the tape at different positions.

"Has anyone been to the Volvo since you left it?"

"The bobby there, first chap on the scene, went over with the paramedic. The car's open so he checked the guy to see if he had a pulse; he was clearly dead. Strangely, both doors were open, I don't mean unlocked, they were ajar."

"And you were the first there?"

"I thought I was, unless someone else has reported finding a body in a car."

"No. Thanks, Michael. Do we have your details? We'll need your prints too."

"No problem," he said holding up his hand and waggling his fingers. "And yes, my details were the first thing they asked for. Will I be able to get on with my job?"

Cyril stood. "When the paramedic says so."

He moved away allowing the paramedic a few minutes with Michael who was soon on his feet. The avenue was quiet.

Chapter Eight

"What do we have, sir?" April Richmond approached Cyril with her usual enthusiasm.

"Looks like another heart attack or stroke and of all places bang in the middle of the avenue right under our bloody noses, what with Craven Lodge being so close. Another blue car too. What are we, five minutes' walk from the location of the other death?" Cyril paused and looked directly at the Volvo. "I sincerely hope that someone's not leaving their signature at the scene in the form of a catalogue of coincidences, April. Tell me I'm just an ageing, suspicious copper who doesn't believe in such things."

April looked at him and frowned. "Possibly less than five minutes to Tower Street. You're connecting this with Stephens's death because of the similarities?"

"I'm saying nothing at the moment, only thinking out loud. There's something else too that's gnawing away at me. David Stephens kept his aircraft at Yeadon Airport. Did you know that the road running past the airport where his hangar's situated is also called Victoria Avenue and here we are… " He left the sentence unfinished and waited for April to end it.

"Victoria Avenue!" She instinctively laughed more from surprise than humour. "You're joking, sir, surely that's a coincidence. There's no connection?"

"Do I appear to be trying to make you laugh, DC Richmond? A tip, I gave it to Owen when we started working together and I'll share it with you. Always keep an open mind."

April's facial expression quickly changed along with the immediate atmosphere. Although she was new to this team, she had never seen Cyril seem so immediately perturbed. Two CSI vehicles arrived and Cyril watched as they pulled to a stop in concert. It seemed that it was going to be a long evening.

Within ten minutes, privacy screens had been erected protecting the vehicle from any observers who might be in the buildings on either side of the road. The number of curious spectators had quickly swelled; the police tape that blocked the entry points to the avenue seemed to attract them. Cyril could see the local journalists congregating nearby also and already a television crew was positioning a reporter in order to get the best shot of the forensic activity. It was then that Cyril saw Owen.

"What are you doing here?" Cyril asked, surprised by his attendance.

"I was round at the Coach and Horses, thought you'd be popping in and then I heard the gossip. After ten minutes the whispers had grown out of all proportion and from all accounts a mass murder had taken place." He chuckled. "It's true. So I thought I'd see for myself. Knew where you'd be and now that I am here, what can I do?"

"Get pictures of all those standing by the tape at every junction and then organise a house to house. I want people knocking on doors along here and there initially." His pointing finger tracked along either side of the avenue from Station Parade, down towards the West Park. "And Owen, don't forget the Justice Centre and the library. Find out when the library closed, who was last in and see if you can get a list of people who exchanged books there today… you never know. Does it have CCTV?"

"Sir."

April approached, her hand over her mobile. "We have a name. A William Baines, thirty-eight years old, married with one child." She returned the phone to her ear. "He was an independent Health and Safety advisor working for *Firm Foundation Health and Safety*, just down the avenue, number thirty-six."

"Do we have a home address?" Cyril kept an eye on the journalists who had congregated along two of the tapes.

"Tadcaster, commutes. Forty minutes on a good day—" She did not get time to finish. It was as if she had trodden on Cyril's toes.

"I know where Tadcaster is. Who's attending?" His words were short and sharp, his expression leaving April in no doubt that she needed to be more alert.

"Next of kin have yet to be informed. Officers and Police Family Liaison on their way now, sir."

April was relieved to see Dr Julie Pritchett's car pull up just behind the CSI vans. She was also reassured to see it brought a slight smile to Cyril's face.

"Thanks, April. Busy day." He winked at her and she interpreted it as his way of apologising.

Turning away, he walked down towards Dr Pritchett's car.

"Anything, Julie. If you can get anything at all, no matter how small that says it's not natural causes, I'd be a happy man. I can't live with two deaths within a week with so many similarities to be told they're both coincidences. As far as I'm concerned right now, lightning doesn't strike twice so close together and it certainly doesn't strike twice on my watch without a fuss!"

Hannah Peters, Julie's assistant, came round the rear of the estate car and pulled on a protective suit. She smiled, lifting her hand as if to wave.

Julie simply looked at Cyril without saying a word, a look he had seen before. She could see what frame of mind he was in and simply took her leave walking quickly towards Hannah before calling back.

"Patience, DCI Bennett, patience. We can only find what's there."

***

Julie's inspection seemed to take an age. Cyril could have done with a pint but he also needed to wait, even though the potential crime scene was out of his hands. Something was gnawing at his insides. All he wanted was for Julie Pritchett to emerge from behind the screen like a modern-day Neville Chamberlain climbing down the aircraft steps brandishing a piece of paper, holding aloft some kind of incriminating evidence that shouted foul play. Cyril waited. He checked his watch, shook his wrist and looked again.

After twenty more minutes, his patience was rewarded when Julie emerged from behind the screen. She walked directly towards him, dropped her case and removed the face mask allowing it to dangle at her throat.

"He's definitely dead but then you knew that, probably all of Harrogate knows that by now too. What they don't know is that there appears to be no external trauma, no struggle nor fight, no damage to the car and as you know, his belongings appear to be intact, including his wallet. Sorry, not what you wanted to hear, I know. When I get him back on the table, you can be assured that I'll be very thorough, Cyril, very thorough indeed. I share your concern."

Even with her reassurance and words of support he could not hide his disappointment. "Thanks, I know that. Please phone me when you get home." Her smile said everything.

Chapter Nine

The national as well as the local Harrogate papers' front-page pictures and the coverage of the two deaths left Cyril in no doubt that the reporting was creative, far from accurate and certainly not at all helpful. The press release he had issued might have been at fault. Even after years in the job it was sometimes difficult to hide one's inner feelings. He made a note to get Communications to review what had gone out on the North Yorkshire Police social media sites. He needed to find someone who saw or heard something. Maybe someone had opened both car doors, maybe taken something — an opportunist. It had certainly happened before.

Cyril had organised to meet in an incident room after the general daily briefing. DC Smirthwaite, DC Nixon and Owen were already waiting. Cyril simply followed the splashes of tea that spread across the corridor from the kitchen to the incident room to know Owen was already present.

"Gentlemen, you've already read the newspapers and if, like me, you feel there is more to these cases than meets the eye, I'd like to get at least one step ahead to justify the time and money we're committing. There's likely to be an inquest as Baines, according to his latest medical report, showed no evidence of heart trouble or any other ailments that could bring about sudden death. There will be a quick collection of the evidence found to date which, quite frankly, is like the well-known stately home… Bugger all. However, the post-mortem is timetabled for this afternoon, Owen has kindly volunteered."

Cyril looked across at his colleague and smiled, watching Owen nearly blow the mouthful of tea he had just sipped onto the table. Owen managed to cough and swallow at the same time sparing those opposite. He looked up at Cyril and returned the sardonic smile.

"Did I not mention it last night? Sorry. Thank you, Owen."

A ripple of laughter followed as a hand slapped Owen's back.

"We know you enjoy attending them. Caner has informed us on many an occasion, *Right man for the job, constitution of an ox has the lad.* So as we say, if the cap fits…"

Caner's compliment made Owen sit up and feel a little better about the request.

It had become common knowledge that he had the stomach and seemed always willing to attend an autopsy. Importantly for Owen, it was good to know that he was better at one thing than his boss.

"The latest victim is William Baines, works as a private Health and Safety Officer, in partnership with a Colin Strong. According to Strong, before they established the firm together, Baines worked independently from home specialising in health and safety training within the renewable energy field and the brewing industry. You might expect that with his home being in Tadcaster, what with its three breweries. Before this he specialised for a number of years as a Health and Safety Manager working on the construction of offshore wind farms. He gave that up when he married, wanting to spend more time at home. I've made notes on the board showing what I perceive to be the coincidences between the two deaths. We have car colour, similar death circumstances and now a tenuous link to the licensed trade. All common sense really and that's a big worry. What have we found from the house to house?"

"Nothing apart from Strong's statement. Nobody saw anything untoward. I've spoken to the librarian and we're checking names of the borrowers from yesterday. There are cameras too and they've sent the recordings to our tech people."

Smirthwaite was the next to contribute. "I've run the photographs of those standing along the barrier tape through facial recognition but nothing."

"What about the car?" Cyril looked at Nixon.

"With Forensics. Just checking for updates. They've retrieved a number of loose items. There's a couple you might be interested in." Nixon flicked the switch and the large blue wall screen containing the image of the North Yorkshire Police crest faded away to be replaced by a photograph.

"Firstly we have a potato."

Everyone leaned forward together and a couple chuckled. Before them was a photograph of a very clean new potato. It looked for all intents and purposes like a small egg.

"Where was that found?" Cyril enquired, turning to look at Nixon.

"Under the driver's seat. They're checking for trace evidence. Secondly we have this. It's a beer mat, also found under the driver's seat."

The mat looked new and depicted one of those yellow smiley-type faces comprising a circle, two dots and an open mouth. There was no advertising on either surface.

"Other things found on the floor of the car are…" He flicked through the images. "… An empty energy drink can, two pencils, two paid receipts for parking and a child's hair slide. All the items retrieved so far have Baines's fingerprints and DNA along with those of people yet to be identified but we are at the moment assuming they're family members. We're holding off on DNA checks until we have firm evidence of the cause of death. Costs I'm told." He raised his eyebrows.

"The beer mat?"

"Yes, sir. Just as the cocktail glass contained David Stephens's prints, the mat has one clear print. It's invisible to the naked eye but they've given us a positive result. It's definitely belonging to Baines."

"But no further prints like those found on the other objects?"

"No. The mat is quite new as you can see."

"No other prints on the cocktail glass and now no other prints on this?" Cyril tapped the table with his pencil before Nixon spoke again.

"Further tests are continuing on the car but there's no signs of door or lock damage. What's rather strange, according to the report, is that the air vents on the dashboard were closed, pushed shut. Considering the weather on the day you'd naturally assume they'd be open and yet, when the body was discovered, both doors were fractionally ajar. I decided to check the photographs taken at the time the body was still in situ in the Jag. There are four adjustable dash vents on that model, two to the centre and one at either end. They too were closed. I spoke with a local dealer and he suggested that in summer, if we have warm weather, the interior temperature in the Jaguar F-Type coupé gets very warm and the climate control would be needed unless, of course, he drove with the windows open. Both doors on the Jag were found ajar like those on the Volvo. Seems to contradict my theory but from experience there must be a logical reason."

Cyril looked at the faces sitting around the table. "Another unexplained coincidence. Owen, just add it to the board. Let's see what the inquest on William Baines tells us."

Chapter Ten

Cyril removed an auction catalogue from his desk and flicked through the pages. He was grateful that he could use his lunch hour to attend the fine art sale viewing at the town centre auction house; it would help to distract him. He desperately needed to see the Baines autopsy results.

At that moment, he felt like someone walking on thin ice, ice that showed small hairline cracks. As he walked he would not know if they would hold and enable him to cross successfully or if the cracks would get bigger causing all hell to break loose. He had that nervous feeling of uncertainty fluttering within the pit of his stomach.

He turned onto Albert Street, stopping to admire the hanging baskets on either side of the black door to the auction house. He entered, glancing at the items presented in the passageway. The reception desk was at the far end. Cyril waved and smiled at both receptionists before entering the main room. Removing his catalogue and his glasses, he started his search.

***

Owen was an old hand at watching the anatomical investigation. It was the whole ambience, the stainless steel and clinical perfection that he loved, he knew the procedures too. He would utilise the screen suspended just to his right to see a more detailed view of the autopsy. The small camera attached to the pathologist's visor brought her field of vision directly to him. It was also recorded for evidence and teaching. Owen listened and took notes as Dr Pritchett carefully made the first detailed inspection of the body.

"The weight and height tell us that he was relatively fit. BMI is good. There are no immediate marks or contusions that might be linked to the day or time of death." She sampled under each fingernail. "No identifiable damage to the nails or knuckles."

Julie cut her usual U-shaped incision into the upper torso; some pathologists preferred the Y incision before inspecting the inner organs but both procedures did the same job. Hannah continued to photograph as Pritchett inspected and directed before she removed the internal organs. Each was extracted with care.

"All seems in order."

She weighed the heart before inspecting it closely.

"Appears to show some signs of right heart failure but… it looks fine and the arteries look healthy, I'd say no coronary disease from this first inspection but we have to perform a standard examination and I'll tag for a more focussed inspection of the cells. However, Owen, we can't see if he suffered from arrhythmia and this condition, ventricular fibrillation, can bring about sudden death but…" She paused looking again at the condition of the organ. "I doubt... As I said, arrhythmia is something we can't detect after death."

There was another pause as she moved her hands containing the heart under a large illuminated magnifying glass.

"Signs of petechiae."

"Sorry?"

"Minute burst blood vessels the size of pin heads that are ruptured. That could be due to asphyxiation." She paused turning to look at Owen, noting the optimism on his face and quickly qualified her statement. "This damage can occur in over thirty-three per cent of all deaths so don't read too much into it. It's evidential and that's all." She turned back, placing the heart into a stainless steel container before returning to the body in order to look again at the cadaver's eyes. She took a hypodermic needle and inserted it into the left eyeball before withdrawing some vitreous humour. Owen shuddered a little.

"So there's nothing to indicate sudden death through heart failure or stroke?" Owen's tone was a little subdued.

"As yet, no." Julie looked up at Owen, her face protected by the Perspex visor. "We have more to investigate. You'll have to be patient. I've noted prominent areas of lividity, demonstrating severe petechial haemorrhaging."

"That's where the blood has settled after death because the heart isn't pumping if I remember correctly," Owen said proudly. He noticed Hannah look up and smile.

"You have been listening, Owen." Julie nodded slightly and then removed the lungs. She held the organs to the light balancing them in her hands, the oesophagus trailed to one side like a limp neck. She weighed them as she had done the heart. She looked again. "A little heavier than expected. This can be an indicator of death through asphyxiation too, Owen."

"Could he have choked on a sweet or something, maybe one of those shocks that kill you when a bee stings you?"

"His airway was clear, one of the first things I checked and there seems to be no marking or damage to the back of the throat and certainly no sweet lodged."

"A possible anaphylactic shock?"

"Good question. Difficult to tell at this stage but we have his medical history so that should be easily identified. The victim dies of shock rather than asphyxia. I'll be sending peripheral blood for analysis and the outcome will tell us the answer to that question."

There was a pause as Julie looked carefully over the other organs.

"Nothing to do with the car, certainly not carbon monoxide..." She looked up at Owen. "We'd have seen clear signs."

Owen heard Julie switch on the 'Stryker' saw. It made the hair on his neck stand up and also brought an involuntary shiver. It seemed to him to have the same effect as hearing the dentist's drill as a child; he knew she was about to remove the top of the skull to access the brain with the high-speed oscillating saw. He stood slightly on his toes and avoided looking directly at the screen.

***

Cyril had marked a number of lots he wanted to take a closer look at but felt his concentration lapse on more than one occasion. It was when he approached a painting of a horse and cart trudging along a cobbled, terraced street that his interest became more focussed. The sketches and paintings of Norman Cornish had always attracted him, particularly those featuring interesting characters, characters who seemed to have vanished from most local communities.

"Beauty is in the eye of the beholder, Cyril Bennett," a friendly voice whispered over his shoulder. "Surely you're not taken by that, it's so simple."

Cyril did not need to look round, he knew it was Linda, the main receptionist. He did not turn immediately but simply tilted his head to one side. "For real beauty I need to turn round." He turned, smiled and looked directly at her and she blushed as usual. "But you're not for sale, I know you're spoken for."

Linda was middle-aged, attractive and Cyril knew she had a soft spot for him.

"We have a fire bucket somewhere near here for occasions like this! You charmer but then from what I hear you and certain bodily fluids don't mix," she giggled openly. They both then laughed as Cyril leaned and kissed her cheek.

"Touché!" He turned back to the painting. "I love it! Like all his work, he captures a time and place that was, I feel, a time more civilised… the good old days. The rag and bone man, the milkman, the bobby on foot patrol. Who wouldn't want these characters to return to our streets and communities? They're statements about things that were considered unimportant at the time, maybe even commonplace, yet now they're gone their true value is appreciated and therefore missed."

"What like rickets and diphtheria, Cyril?" She laughed. "Scarlet fever's making a return but I don't hear many people cheering. You should have been an estate agent, Cyril Bennett, the way your words of flattery paint pictures in my mind's eye, not only about paintings either!" She looked directly at him, a deliberate act that made Cyril a little uneasy. She read its title out loud. "'The Horse and Coal Cart'," before pulling a face exaggerating her dislike of the painting.

"In my job, Linda, the secret is to get those two things in the correct order and believe me, sometimes with the evidence we work with we'll often get the cart before the horse!"

They both laughed, Cyril more from relief that she had averted her gaze to the picture. "So what will it sell…?" He did not finish the sentence as his phone rang. "Excuse me. No peace for the wicked. Work calls as always."

Linda moved away.

"What have you found, Owen?"

"Nothing. No heart problems, nothing. No reason he should be dead." He could sense Cyril's disappointment. "She did say one thing but said that at the moment she'd not bet a fiver on it."

"And that is?"

"Hypoxia."

"Strangled?"

"No, nothing like that. She found some evidence… just a sec… petechiae… which are burst blood vessels, minute ones just visible to the naked eye. They were on the outer layer of the heart and also within parts of the eyes and the brain. Following on from David Stephens's findings, they're looking to see if there are any similarities within the blood tests."

"Asphyxia?" Cyril asked again.

"It's one theory but as I've said before, the evidence doesn't guarantee that outcome as these petechiae can appear in a higher percentage than the quoted thirty-three per cent of all deaths. There are different ways a person can die by asphyxiation too but there's nothing to suggest that he was murdered. She'll need more time. She says that she can only work on the evidence found but there are a number of speculative possibilities."

"Speculative?"

"Unascertained was a word she used. The evidence is limited and therefore she cannot give a definitive cause of death."

"Well done, Owen. Are you still with Julie?"

"No, heading back to the castle on the hill."

"Meet me at The Harrogate Tea Rooms, the one in Westminster Arcade, in half an hour. You know the place? Need some peace and quiet to chat things through."

Owen hung up and Cyril turned to look briefly at the painting again but his enthusiasm had evaporated, much like the characters trapped within.

***

The tearoom was busy but Cyril found an empty table in the far corner and ordered his usual. Although there was music it was quiet and he found that he could still think. He was even more convinced the deaths were in some way related, although he did not have one ounce of evidence to back up his theory, neither did he have a motive, it was just his instinct. Even the autopsy seemed to be against his viewpoint. He rang Harry Nixon.

"Harry, Bennett. Anything from Forensics on the car?"

"They've discovered that something heavy was placed behind the passenger's seat. Circular. It's a deep depression in the carpet and they're trying to get a clearer 3D image of it. If successful, they should be able to determine what it might have been. They've run all the prints through the system but family, friends and a number of prints belonging to Colin Strong, his business partner, are all that's showing, nothing out of the ordinary. I've arranged for CSI to visit David Stephens's place and take a closer look at the Jaguar to see if there's a similar indentation and any trace evidence from the potato. Thought it was worth a look."

"Well done. Arrange for me to see Colin Strong. This afternoon if possible. Call me as soon as it's done."

Owen waved and smiled on seeing Cyril.

"You'd have hated that, sir. It's a messy business when they cut through the skull. It's the noises mainly that give me the heebie-jeebies, and then there's the stuff all over her hands, quite disgusting… I'm starving!"

***

Jonathan Stephens was washing the Jaguar when the CSI officers' van came up the drive following a police vehicle. He stopped, dropping the sponge into the bucket and dried his hands on his jeans. His heart fluttered momentarily.

"Mr Stephens?"

Jonathan moved towards the police car.

"Just routine, sir. These guys just need a moment with the Jaguar. We can do it here or take it away, the choice is yours. There's something these officers need to check.

"It's open."

"You said the glass and the potato were under the driver's seat?"

Jonathan nodded. "The spud was almost in the glass."

Only one CSI approached the vehicle and opened the passenger door. She crouched shining a coloured light parallel with the black carpet mat that filled the footwell. Pulling on the back of her nitrile glove, she allowed the underside of her wrist to rest on the mat. It was still damp.

"The carpet's damp. Did you know?" She stood, directing her question at Stephens.

He nodded. "I've just used the carpet cleaner on them." He pointed to the industrial cleaner to the side of the garage. "Spilled a coffee yesterday, bloody latte too. The milk was beginning to stink so it needed doing. The cup holders are useless for a car costing this much!"

The CSI turned and walked to the van shaking her head as she looked at the police officer. "Waste of time and money that," she mumbled to her colleague.

Stephens watched them leave as he retrieved the sponge from the bucket and tossed it onto the car's bonnet, releasing a number of spectrum-wrapped bubbles into the air. He simply raised his eyebrows, smiled and continued his task.

Chapter Eleven

Craig Gillan turned the key in the lock and pushed open the door, a task he had performed for longer than he cared to remember. The same medical odour welcomed him like a sharp slap but swiftly disappeared as his sense of smell adjusted to the confines of the surgery. He dropped his bag on the chair and looked at the day's appointments. His first one was in twenty minutes, just time for a tea and a flick through the paper. The autoclave clicked away in the small, darkened storeroom.

Finishing the last of his tea he tossed the newspaper onto the waiting room table, slipped on his white coat and went to prepare for his first patient. He felt sure the topic of the day would be the two deaths within a week but then it would be more stimulating than the usual fixation on the foibles of Harrogate's weather or the newly found practice of removing car wing mirrors.

***

Bennett was looking at the whiteboard when Nixon popped his head round the door. "Nothing from the Jag. Stephens's lad had washed the mats, spilled coffee on it, allegedly, so Forensics could do nothing."

The nag grew within Cyril. "Funny that, or convenient. Maybe it's me. Am I just a suspicious person, Nixon, or do you too feel as though someone's pissing up our backs and trying to assure us it's rain?" He looked up and immediately thought of Liz, a phrase she had often used.

How the time seemed to have flown since her murder but he knew one thing for sure, that all the coincidences would have chewed away at her just like they were gnawing at him. She would not have rested until she had come to a solution or a total dead end.

"I hear you, Liz," he said reverently as he turned back to look again at the board. "I hear you."

It was not long before Owen flung open the door. "Thought you'd be in here chewing the fat." He waved the full autopsy report. "Julie asked me to tell you, *Something is rotten in the state of Denmark* and said that you'd fully understand. She then mumbled something about a ghost and walls… talks bloody gibberish that woman when she thinks of you," he said as he grinned salaciously.

"Hamlet, Owen! Shakespeare, the Bard of Avon… words like… pearls and swine seem to follow this conversation so naturally."

"He should've been bloody barred, bard from the school curriculum. Christ, sir, hated his stuff, filled with disjointed English that I could never understand. Certainly didn't speak like that in Bradford when I was growing up. Give me Roald Dahl any day of the week, all snot and bogeys. I couldn't get enough of that!"

Cyril just sighed. "Somehow, Owen, you never cease to amaze me."

"Thank you, sir." Owen stood and thrust out his arms in an attempt to create a theatrical pose. "*Ay, but to die, and go we know not where; to lie in cold obstruction and to rot…* Speaking of dying and rotting…" He tossed the report on the table whilst keeping a straight face. "You need to take a butcher's hook."

Cyril looked across at his colleague convinced that he was winding him up but he could never be certain. "Thought you hated Shakespeare." He picked up the file. "So she's found something?"

Owen just lifted his shoulders.

Cyril went through the report as Owen hummed some unfathomable tune. "She's recommended that parts of the body be retained for specialist investigation, going to a histopathologist. The cause of death cannot be immediately identified and therefore the term *natural causes* cannot be ruled out."

"Do you think Caner saw something too and the coroner brought an open verdict because of either the drug misuse or possible uncertainties or irregularities but there wasn't enough evidence to request an inquest?"

"Maybe Julie's found something that will allow us to justify the allocation of resources."

***

Craig Gillan pulled up his surgical mask to cover his nose and mouth before the small drill, capped by a rotating sanding disk, shaved away the hard skin from the client's heel. A small tube positioned within the drill's handle vacuumed the powdered, dead skin as it was released. He had assumed correctly, the finding of two bodies so close together and within one week of each other had certainly got tongues wagging and the Chinese whispers had already started.

"To think he was found in a car on Victoria Avenue in broad daylight. I visited the library too on that day. Just think, Mr Gillan, the poor man could have been dying while I walked past. You just never know these days. Country's going to ruin what with the youth of today. They call them *snowflakes*, I believe, not like the youth in my day. Much more respect for everything including Queen and country," she finished with a heavy exhale.

Craig let the sigh settle before switching off the machine and removing his mask.

She continued. "People have said that he was murdered, shot with one of them silenced guns, just like the other chap, you know the one they found in the car park on Tower Street. I never use them myself." She noticed him look up and frown. "Car parks, Mr Gillan, I never use those car parks, not silenced guns." She chuckled realising what she'd said. "No, you never know who might be lurking in the shadows. I don't know what Harrogate's coming to what with the reports of drug fuelled *yobbery* and then there's the litter."

Yobbery, that was a new term he had not heard before. Craig simply lowered his head and concentrated on massaging cream into her foot as he let the last part of the sentence sink in… murder and litter. He knew which he would rather be dealing with.

"You can't believe everything you read in the newspapers, especially the local ones neither; should you listen to the Chinese whispers, they'd have you believe that the world is coming to an end next Tuesday. So you saw nothing I take it, Mrs Clements?"

"No, but I've heard that a neighbour has one of those cameras in his car and he drove down Victoria Avenue on the day in question. He's taken it into the police. I know that for a fact! They were asking for the public's assistance."

He simply smiled and helped her from the chair. "How do your feet feel now?"

"Like walking on air, as always after your excellent work. Thank you. Is my next appointment in six weeks?"

"Indeed, Mrs Clements," he said and then mumbled knowing she was hard of hearing. "If we all haven't been murdered in our beds or lost in the landfill of litter that Harrogate is about to become if your predictions are correct!"

"You mark my words, they usually come in threes unless you break a match after the second. Well, that's what my mother always said. You mark my words, there'll be another body found soon, you'll see!"

It's being so cheerful that keeps her going, he thought as he walked her to the door before taking the tray of used instruments into the storeroom and placing them on the bench next to the autoclave. He had thirty minutes before his next client, enough time for what he needed to do. He removed his protective gloves and rubbed his hands carefully before slipping off his white coat. He checked the front door was locked before returning to the storeroom.

Chapter Twelve

Cyril's phone rang. He listened before going to one of the computers. He tapped the keypad and the screen came to life. A few more taps and he found that for which he had been directed to search.

"Owen, come and see this. The appeal to the public for help in the Victoria Avenue incident has brought a reward. Some dash-cam footage."

Cyril popped on his glasses and could feel Owen's breath on the side of his face as they peered at the screen. The video was exceptionally clear.

Cyril gave an involuntary commentary. "He's turned off the A61, Station Parade. There's the zebra crossing… He's stopped to let someone cross. Polite driver."

"The Volvo should be just ahead on the right," Owen said as Cyril's finger hovered over the mouse in readiness to pause it.

"There… coming up… Bingo!"

Both men stared at the paused image. It clearly showed the driver's door ajar and somebody crouched behind it. "Look at the shoes, Owen!" Cyril exclaimed as his fingers touched three keys and he heard the sound of the activation of the screenshot facility. He immediately brought up the image and then enlarged it. They could see only the bottom of the door and the feet of the person next to the car. He was wearing a pair of black ankle boots and what appeared to be dark socks and dark blue trousers.

"What do you notice, sir?"

"The shine on the shoes, Owen. Now that's unusual." Cyril looked at the time showing on the original footage. "It can't be Baines; he didn't leave his office until much later. So who's this and more importantly what's he up to in broad daylight in somebody else's car?"

They ran the rest of the footage but there was nothing they could see that was of any relevance to the case.

"It's not much but it's a start and better than nothing, sir. Maybe the Forensic foot fetishists will be able to see something we can't. They'll certainly run checks with the National Footwear Reference Collection. We can then see who might stock the shoes locally and then we put two and two together…"

The Forensic Footwear Analysis Service at their disposal would certainly be in a position to investigate their findings but Cyril felt sure that there would be little to discover.

"What?" Cyril turned to look at his colleague. "Owen, I don't know who fills your head with these things but one step at a time eh?"

"Funny, sir, very funny."

"You made a note on the whiteboard that the indentation to the carpet mat behind the driver's seat was from something weighing approximately fourteen kilograms."

Owen nodded. "How they know this stuff is beyond me. Whatever was put there had to be carried from the car so we're looking for someone with a large holdall, rucksack or cabin bag maybe. Nothing else was taken — phone, wallet — so what was in the back? Don't forget also that the doors were left ajar. Whatever it was, Baines must have left it visible and it was removed before his return. But there's no sign of a bag here unless it was on the driver's seat, and if that's the case there should be something for Forensics. But we can't commit to DNA checks until we have something concrete, it's unjustifiable."

"So theft is a possibility? Anything from CCTV for the area or the roads leading to and from the station on that day?"

Cyril immediately realised what he had asked. Harrogate was not only a major conference centre but also a favourite holiday destination with travellers coming and going daily. He was aware that the majority would not be in this part of the town trundling luggage, but they would either use private transport and drive to and from their hotel or venue. If they came by train or coach they would probably not walk in the vicinity of Victoria Avenue.

"CCTV from the library. We have an image of one person coming in carrying a large rucksack, they left later and then returned. The way the bag was handled on the return suggests that whatever had been in it had been removed between these times." He looked over the notes.

"That fits the dash-cam times."

"We're checking the names of those returning books, it's computerised now but from all accounts the person wasn't recognised by the librarians. It appears that he just picked something and read there. Just killing time probably."

"After preparing to kill Baines?" He hoped the question would remain rhetorical and immediately continued. "Do they know what he picked up? DNA or prints might be possible."

Owen just looked at Cyril and his facial expression clearly answered the question.

"Can we get a height and weight reference from the images, Owen?"

"Five eleven with normal build. He knew where the cameras were and was able to avoid facial recognition. Been there in the past probably, sir."

"See what else the technical people can get from them. What did you say April was working on?"

Owen replied, "A cold case. Stolen cars, bloody expensive ones too. None has been recovered. If you recall there was a spate of robberies, about a year ago, they were taken from people's drives. The gang who did it broke into the houses and took the keys before making off with the cars. It was also believed that some keys had been cloned. We didn't know if there was a link to an increase in vehicle vandalism at the same time; the vandalism's started again and the powers that be want it investigated and the perpetrators prosecuted. You can see why pressure has been put on us after a number of cars were vandalised because one of them, can you believe, was a marked police patrol vehicle! Suddenly, with that, there's a need to see some action and according to the press, *If we have all this technology at a cost of millions and still we can't find petty criminals....* It went on a bit. I'll show you the cutting. Published when you were away."

Cyril stood and left the room, indicating to Owen that he was not best pleased.

Chapter Thirteen

The safety latch was flipped over the top of the flask and the last tendrils of escaping gas dissipated magically around its base. The black quilted blanket was wrapped around the potbelly shaped container. He removed his gloves before rubbing his hands.

He stretched and switched off the extractor fan that had been buzzing in a way that was intrusive but as he flicked the switch all went silent. *If only every annoyance were as easy to eliminate,* he thought. He lifted the container and placed it alongside the yellow gas detector, the reading now showing normal.

***

April Richmond drove as Cyril glanced across The Stray.

Within ten minutes they were parked on Victoria Avenue. "You've glanced at the file? Baines worked with a Mr Strong. When we've interviewed him we have an appointment with Mrs Baines."

Colin Strong was welcoming and was clearly shocked by Baines's sudden demise.

"He was absolutely fine. In fact, he'd just had a medical, something to do with an insurance policy. I didn't realise they did that any more and you'd think I'd know being in this profession." "When was that?" Cyril asked.

Colin Strong glanced at the calendar. "Last Wednesday afternoon, one of those private health centres. One thing that did show up was mild arrhythmia, they detected that his heartbeat had a slight irregularity. They assured him that it was only minimal. Suggested he see his GP. They recommended he take Apixaban, a drug to aid blood thinning to prevent the possibility of a stroke. They advised him not to be fobbed off with Warfarin as it needed more monitoring as the drug's efficacy can be affected by diet."

Cyril glanced at April who quickly brought up Baines's medical file on her iPad. There was no reference to the described medical condition. She checked again before turning to Cyril. "Nothing showing."

"Was he concerned? Had he booked an appointment with his GP?"

"A little, said that his heart rate monitor on his fitbit had been playing up recently and that he wasn't getting accurate readings. He put it down to the thing being faulty. I tried it and it was fine. Said he'd make an appointment with his GP but whether he did or not, I can't say."

"Did he have any other worries, home, financial, this business?"

"Ups and downs at home like all relationships. I can't answer for his financial state, Detective Chief Inspector, but I can tell you that professionally he was fine. To be honest, we're struggling at present but we anticipated that when we started the business. We were under no illusion that the first years would be tough but we could never have imagined this."

He paused as if trying to take control of his emotions. "Can you believe that he's just landed an account with a large food processing and distribution company out York way. *Clear Foods,* we've been contracted to run a number of Health and Safety lectures and training. He has a good reputation in the industry." He suddenly stared at Cyril. "Sorry, can't get it to sink in… had."

"Was there stiff opposition for that contract?" April asked not lifting her head from her tablet. She had searched for details of the company as he had been speaking and had located it on Google Earth.

"There's always competition but that's healthy."

"What happened to the previous provider of health and safety support, Mr Strong?" April still did not look up from her pad.

Strong appeared to be rather taken aback by her question and the lack of eye contact and the resultant pause made Cyril's stomach lurch. He glanced at April in admiration. If Cyril had been looking at a pair of sparring boxers he would have seen that one had just landed a body blow of some force.

"Failings."

"Can you be more specific?"

"They had a snap inspection after an incident, and a number of issues were identified that should have been clearly addressed."

Cyril just looked at Strong encouraging him to say more.

"Management of forklift trucks and warehousing, dangerous storage concerns, questionable practice regarding water purification, inappropriate organisation and control of the atmosphere and working environment within their freezer area too; that was a major problem for them but as you can see there was quite a list. There was even an issue with safety equipment, and believe me, in this day and age, that should never apply as everyone seems to be wearing Hi-Vis jackets. I'm surprised the army doesn't have to wear them over their camouflage clothing!"

Cyril simply smiled. "This might sound like a strange question but was the previous health and safety company local?"

"Newcastle based. Been a serious blow to them losing that specific contract; once your reputation is knocked, others might look more closely at their practices. You win some... They were obviously just not good enough and in this game you have to be. Lives can be lost, resulting in compensation claims."

Cyril felt that churning return to his stomach. "Thanks, Mr Strong."

***

Craig Gillan marked each of the three verrucas before bringing the laser towards the foot. A flexible pipe, positioned just above the big toe, provided a strong vacuum that extracted the smoke and aroma of singed flesh away immediately as the laser lit and burned each targeted area.

"I thought you'd have frozen them off, Mr Gillan," Owen asked. "I spoke to a doctor friend and she told me to get them removed. They were getting a bit sore."

"We try to keep abreast of technology, Mr Owen, and as you will discover, a laser is far more effective. We did at one time use liquid nitrogen and other cold inert gases. I believe you're a police officer."

Owen simply smiled.

"A lot of my patients have been talking about nothing other than the two shootings. You wouldn't believe the things I hear whilst clipping toenails but these last few days… What you need is a couple of the old ladies I see, they'd have the case cracked and the man hanged from the lamp post on The Stray before afternoon tea. They all think they're Miss Marple!"

Owen looked directly at the chiropodist eager to put him right but he just remained silent, besides, he wasn't too sure who Miss Marple was and didn't want to appear ignorant or stupid.

Within minutes, a large padded dressing was placed on the affected area.

"It might be painful a little later. Please keep the dressing on. I'll see you next week."

Owen tentatively put his weight onto his treated foot and felt no sudden discomfort.

He presented his appointment card and paid the bill.

"Good luck with the murders. See you next week."

***

April rang the bell. A young woman answered the door.

"Mrs Baines?"

"No, I'm her sister."

April showed her ID. "We have an appointment to see your sister. Is it still convenient?"

April and Cyril were shown into the lounge. Two children were playing in the corner and the television was on.

"My sister's little girl isn't ready to go back to school what with… anyway I brought my daughter to help normalise things. My little girl was upset for a while." She smiled as if trying to lift the atmosphere. "I suppose all kids are like that at this age."

One of the girls, wearing a princess mask that covered only the eyes and forehead and a pair of her mother's high-heeled shoes, looked round and smiled before returning to the make-believe game they were playing. Mrs Baines came into the room.

"We'll not disturb the girls. Let's go into the kitchen."

April and Cyril followed.

Cyril offered their condolences. It was evident she was dazed by the suddenness of it all and was only there in body. Her eyes were red and dark rings seemed to encase that sadness.

"Are you sure you want to talk to me today, Mrs Baines? This can wait."

"I'm fine. The sooner it's done the sooner I can go back to my daughter."

"Your husband had a recent medical?" Cyril deliberately left the question in the air.

"Yes, he wanted to increase his life cover for the sake of me and Tilly, the house being heavily mortgaged on account of starting up the business. He drives a good deal too and he thought it was wise what with the traffic. *You never know what's round the next corner* he always said, and that's why he insisted we get a Volvo, had it for a few years now, built like a tank according to Bill." She stopped and hung her head and Cyril watched as April slipped her arm comfortingly around her shoulders. "Probably overly cautious too with the job he's in."

Cyril waited until Mrs Baines regained some of her earlier composure. "Did he talk about the results?"

She laughed, a mechanism to mask her deep upset and April could sense that Mrs Baines was right on the edge.

"We can do this again," she reassured. "There's no urgency."

"No, just bear with me and I'll be fine. The medical, yes, he was diagnosed with a slight irregular heartbeat. It had never been detected before and they suggested that he should get it checked out again in a few weeks. They said it could be stress related and what with the new business and everything…"

"And everything?"

"He always pushed himself even in business; ever since I've known him he's been driven to succeed, to be the best he could be. He became more anxious though after he successfully won the new contract. Anxious is probably not the right word. He was more protective, checking where and when we were going out, where Tilly was and who she was playing with." She laughed. "He was always so protective though where she was concerned. He'd have wrapped her in cotton wool if I'd let him. He was working long hours too, he'd just ring and say he'd be late."

April again was a step ahead, her intuition telling her that there was something behind those comments. "Did he have an office here in the house?"

Mrs Baines nodded. "Yes, just along the corridor."

"Would you mind if DCI Bennett had a look round?"

"Has Bill done something wrong?" There was clear anxiety audible in her tone and her eyes immediately looked directly into April's.

Cyril did not speak but they both smiled. "It's sort of routine," April lied.

She nodded and once he was in the corridor, Cyril put on some gloves.

It was a while before he returned. The women were sitting with the girls on the floor in the lounge and for the first time he could hear laughter. There were toys spread haphazardly and April was wrapped in a shawl.

"I have two lovely *nurses* who are making me better."

The girls turned and looked at Cyril.

"Is she well enough for me to take her home?" he asked as he crouched and felt April's forehead.

The girls looked at each other and nodded. "You must look after her. She's very special."

"She is indeed and I shall, I promise."

April looked at Cyril and blushed slightly.

He held out his hand before helping her to her feet.

"Just one more thing, Mrs Baines. Your husband's personal belongings were still in the vehicle: his case, phone and wallet. Will you just look at this list of items and let me know if he had anything else with him that day?"

She scanned the list. "No, no that looks fi…" She paused and went over the list a second time. "He has two phones, one belonging to work and his personal mobile. They're both identical so how he tells them apart I don't know."

Cyril looked at April. Within minutes they were heading back to Harrogate.

"She's worried he was seeing another woman, the sister mentioned it when she went to put the kettle on. It was just a feeling Mrs Baines had, no evidence. She's struggling though so she might believe anything." She paused. "Those were kind words you said to my two young *nurses*, Detective Chief Inspector."

Cyril just smiled. "His missing phone. I wonder if he left it at the office."

He took his mobile from his jacket and looked through a number of images. "I think we can now justify the expense of DNA testing of the items found in Baines's car." Looking at his phone whilst travelling suddenly brought beads of sweat to his forehead and the feeling of nausea to his stomach. He swiftly opened the window to allow the cooler air to hit his face.

"Stop at his office, April. I want to check to see if his phone is there but from what I've found today, somehow I doubt it."

Chapter Fourteen

The evening was warm as Claire Baldwin parked the car but left the engine running. She welcomed the air conditioning, its constant blast of cooling air relieving some of her anxiety. She had decided not to put the top down for fear of blowing her hair into a tangled mess. The house was set some way back from the main road along what appeared to be a private lane. She looked again at the address on the card before glancing at the satnav. It was correct. She flipped down the sun visor and the lights on either side of the vanity mirror lit up. Moving a hand to each ear she checked that her earrings were still in situ. For some reason she had never summoned the courage to have her ears pierced and therefore could only wear clip-on earrings. On many occasions she would often return home with only one! Today, however, she wore some that her aunt had given to her, made from fragments of ancient Chinese pottery, ringed in silver, and as a gift, were worn only on special occasions. This afternoon's meeting was special for Claire, and the reason for the earrings and the fluttering in her stomach. She glanced at her hair, adjusted the front and closed the flap over the mirror. She was ready.

Moving up the pathway she admired the well-tended garden. The smell from the lavender bushes that formed a continuous purple border was aromatic and heady. It wafted into the still air as she deliberately brushed past, its luscious scent lingering long after she had mounted the two steps set before the blue-green door; the words eau de Nil immediately came to mind. She took a deep breath and lifted the knocker before allowing it to crash against the striker.

Within minutes, the door swung open and a familiar smiling face greeted her.

"Ms Baldwin, welcome. How lovely to see you. No difficulty finding it?" he asked as a welcoming grin spread across his face as he showed her through to the conservatory. "I thought you'd be more comfortable in here on such a pleasant afternoon."

The hallway was cool and she immediately felt the contrast as they moved towards the back of the house. As they walked down the corridor, he checked the toilet door was closed securely.

She was initially struck by the size of the room. It was light and airy. A ceiling fan slowly rotated bringing a cooling disturbance to the air; it was warm but comfortable. Wicker chairs and small tables stacked with colourful magazines sat elegantly filling the space. It was as if the scene had been lifted from a *Home and Garden* magazine; nothing seemed out of place. Whoever had furnished the room had a good eye.

He slid his hand into his pocket and pressed the remote switch. In a toilet down the corridor behind the secured door, the lid flipped automatically open on the large concealed flask.

"Refreshment?" he smiled. "We can then sit in the garden and chat, we have much to thank you for. Homemade lemonade… or would you prefer something a little stronger perhaps?"

***

For the first time since the two deaths, Cyril felt as though he was justified in organising a full briefing. After speaking at length with Cyril, the coroner had requested more evidence before the cause of death could be stated. The nag in the pit of Cyril's stomach had not only increased but the discovery of three items in Bill Baines's home office had convinced him that, as Julie had said, *something was definitely rotten…* It was not in the state of Denmark but it was there, right under his nose and he did not like the stench. He felt sure the deaths were not isolated incidents and although there was no evidence to think David Stephens's death was anything other than natural causes at this stage, Cyril was determined to investigate both further.

The room buzzed with a degree of anticipation. He had said nothing to anyone, not even Owen. Cyril wanted them all to see what he had found at the same time so he could judge their responses. Dependent on that he would know whether he could justifiably release his hounds to scrutinise and investigate the lives of both dead men. He appreciated that, at this stage, he had more questions that required clear and defined answers. He needed Forensic help and for that to happen he needed resources, valuable and expensive resources.

Cyril looked around the room at the familiar faces and reflected on their past successes. He felt proud of what they, as a group, a team of professional individuals, had achieved in their time together. He was also aware that one of his key members of the team, Shakti Misra, was due back from leave in four days' time and that Smirthwaite would be commencing his.

Cyril tapped his e-cigarette on the table and the chattering and laughter ceased. Suddenly conscious of the sea of inquisitive faces looking in his direction, he felt a surge of adrenalin and knew in that instant why he loved his job so much; it was like turning a switch, it was *game on*. He let the anticipation hang, soaking up the moment like the final seconds before the starter's gun rips away the silence. Cyril turned to look at Brian Smirthwaite.

"Brian, whatever elements you work on with this case you'll be liaising with Shakti on her return. You'll have twenty-four hours to overlap. Keep it tight, and please enjoy your holiday when it comes, you've earned it. Sorry you'll miss this one."

A rumble of laughter ran round the room as Brian showed disappointment on his face but then broke into a huge smile and pumped the air with his fist.

Owen came in with a number of identical files and handed them out. "Hot off the press," he mumbled. "Read and inwardly digest."

"Thanks, Owen. Page one. April and I went to visit Mrs Baines a few days ago and we managed to get the chance to look in her late husband's home office. What we discovered has now been officially cleared with the family and they're aware that the circumstances surrounding his sudden death might not be as was first thought. His wife said that he'd been a little over-protective prior to his sudden and unexplained death. He'd also had a health check as he was taking out extended life cover. Which came first? I can't say at this moment but one must have begotten the other. The insurance was to cover monies raised for the business on his mortgage. It made sense considering his family commitments and circumstances.

"It was discovered during the medical that he was suffering from an irregular heartbeat, arrhythmia. The report is there, item 1C. This medical condition cannot be detected after death and so it's only just come to light. Speaking with the pathologist, arrhythmia can result in sudden death but I'm assured that this condition was not the cause in this case."

"I see that the insurance company still agreed to provide the life cover even after the diagnosis so they themselves were not overly concerned," Nixon added.

"There may have been a financial consequence," a voice from the far side piped in. "They don't give owt for nowt."

"Let's not go off piste just yet. We need to focus on what we have here." Cyril's tone brought back their focus. "We also see that he was responsible for winning a new contract. He received a note from a Claire, no surname, no date, no address, and so no trace details. It suggested that management of *the atmosphere and environment within chill and purification area* was *bordering on criminal negligence,* her succinct words, as the food factory had caused a number of health issues within the specific plant. That these factors had initially been concealed. There was also a need to shut a line, but she doesn't go into detail. What we do know is that this came before they appointed Baines's operation as new health and safety advisors. We should know when this occurred from the factory records providing it was declared or from the findings from the Health and Safety Executive. There's nothing here to suggest that Baines had any involvement officially or unofficially around that date. There's more, something a little more cryptic. She adds a note at the end. *I've seen the face again!*"

"Seen the face again? Who? What? Where? And why?" asked Owen.

"She was specific, using the definite article."

Sitting next to Owen, April wrote down the word 'the' and slid it in front of him. He quickly reciprocated with the word 'Ta!'

"Right! So why write the note? Does it suggest that this Claire must work at the factory?" April asked this specific and open question to draw further thought and comment.

Cyril raised an eyebrow, knowing that she had just baited a very large hook.

Smirthwaite came in immediately. "What about the previous advisors, the ones losing the contract, the experts whose lack of action brought in the damning inspection from the Health and Safety Executive?"

"According to that report, certain failings brought part of the factory to a standstill. Says here in the HSE report that it was specifically to do with a negative pressure room, whatever that is, and that it was in use when the necessary safety equipment was neither maintained nor working. If it were closed down for days you can imagine the losses and the trouble that would bring. No wonder their contract was revoked. However, we cannot be certain that the note we found refers to this specific incident and we shouldn't immediately put the two together."

"What we do know," Cyril interjected, "just like the note implies is that these serious failings were with part of the water purification and freezing process that require the use and safe storage of inert gases. Brian that's for you. Names and checks on those working for the Newcastle firm who have just had their contract cancelled.

Find if any lost their jobs just before or immediately after that date. Get addresses and pictures, you know the score."

Brian lifted his pencil, acknowledging the request.

"Who was the responsible person on site?" Owen asked.

"It's in the file. Arthur Thorndyke was off sick at the time of the inspection and a deputy was in charge. The names are there, Owen, that's for you to check. If you can question both, please."

"Sir."

April raised her hand. "It was also suggested by the sister I spoke with at the house that Mrs Baines had expressed concerns that her husband might be having an affair, she was worried because he was working late and seemed anxious. There was no evidence of that, and Claire may well be a legitimate work contact but it's worth bearing in mind."

Cyril brought the discussion to a close on that issue. "There are two further things. Number one, we need to identify this person named on the note. Who is Claire? Secondly, I said that we found a number of items in his office but then there was this…"

Like a magician, Cyril had saved the best until last. He pulled on a pair of gloves before lifting a plastic carrier bag he had placed beneath the table. He extracted a bundle that was wrapped in a sheet of newspaper. He carefully unwrapped it revealing notes smothered in cling film.

"We can only guess as to the value but if these are all twenty-pound notes you're looking at the thick end of five grand. Mrs Baines, as you can imagine, was shocked when she found out. Said money was tight and that she'd no idea it was there."

"And the newspaper headline on the wrapping?" April asked.

Cyril held it up.

Huge Fine for Local Food Processing Plant

There was silence.

Owen was the first to speak. "Forensics on it?"

"As yet, no. This is how it was found, apart from the sealed, protective outer carrier bag."

"And we don't know if Baines was about to donate it or had just received the money I take it?" someone asked.

Cyril just shrugged. "What it does do is provide us with a justification to look into his death in more detail. You'll read from the autopsy that we're awaiting a report from histopathology on certain samples. I also want to investigate further Stephens's death and his businesses. There are, for me at least, too many similarities. Lastly, we have a missing mobile phone. Baines had two, one for personal use and one for business. To make matters worse, they were identical. His wife knew the passcode to his personal phone but the tech people have tried the code without success. So the one found in his car may well be the one used for business."

Turning to DC Dan Grimshaw, who was leaning by one of the whiteboards, Cyril instructed, "Dan, you're into this techy stuff. Chase that up and get hold of both phones' histories."

Dan smiled. Cyril's unfamiliarity with technology was well known within the team. "It's impossible to get into an iPhone if you don't have the passcode or the correct finger as the passcode encrypts the contents. The same happens with a laptop if the owner has set up encryption using something like BitLocker…" As it was clear that the technical information was drifting over Cyril's head, Dan said, "Leave it with me."

Cyril suddenly felt old and disinclined. He said nothing, only nodded his thanks. He was aware so much police time was taken up trawling through phone and Internet files and records. Ensuring that vital evidence was neither missed nor lost, brought with it additional burdensome cost implications. On the other hand, he was also aware that a number of national criminal cases had failed through not pursuing this kind of evidence sufficiently. If he were to be honest, this part of policing frustrated his natural curiosity.

Chapter Fifteen

Claire stood by the open French windows admiring the view, as she carried on the conversation with a distant voice that seemed lost somewhere in the depths of the house. They chatted about the usual mundane things, the weather and the view she was now enjoying. Providing he could hear her from afar, he was happy with that for the present.

On the patio was a small mosaic topped table. The wrought iron legs, once painted white, were showing signs of rust. In places the paint was cracked, strangely giving the table an attractive antique look. On the top was a glass dome, an old type cloche. Her curiosity drew her towards it. Trapped within its amber surface she could see hundreds of what appeared to be bubbles encased within the glass. It was then that she focussed on what it covered. It was a bundle of currency, twenty-pound notes secured within a broad band of paper on which was written her name. She looked more closely. Next to it were three potatoes.

"Walk to the tree, you get a wonderful view of the water down in the valley," he announced, his voice still distant. "The grass will be dry."

Gratefully, she moved away from the patio and the final part of his sentence drifted away as if caught on the light breeze. Occasionally she looked back at the glass cloche, her stomach tumbling, a mix of excitement and uncertainty. She knew that she was to be rewarded but the money trapped beneath the glass seemed more than she could have hoped for.

***

He emptied the sachet into a glass and then topped it up with cloudy lemonade. Checking his pocket to ensure the key fob was there and secure, he pressed it again just to be on the safe side. He moved through to the garden.

"So you like my view?"

Claire turned and smiled. "It's beautiful and I bet it has a certain attraction during all the seasons." She returned to the patio.

He handed her a glass. "Cheers. Thank you for coming to see me at such short notice." He drank over half the glass. "I do like lemonade when it's home-made. Drink up and I'll get us another and then I'll give you a tour around the garden. We can chat and I can thank you properly." He emptied his glass and Claire followed suit.

***

"Stuart!" Cyril turned to DC Stuart Park who was flicking through the file whilst waggling his pen in his fingers. "Get onto Mrs Stephens. I want to look at all the logbooks for the two aircraft. I need to know when they were used and by whom and their destinations. The logbooks may well be stored at the hangar. Then get onto the club where his plane's kept. Usual stuff; when it flies and with whom. Talk to his son…" Cyril paused trying to recall the name.

"Jonathan," proffered Owen.

"To be honest, I really don't know if you'll detect anything apart from what you find in the journey log. The aircraft records give few details other than the hours flown but you could cross reference for anomalies. I just need to close down all potential avenues of investigation. I was concerned when I heard he'd given the Jag an internal valet."

"He also brought in the glass so he may have nothing to hide, sir."

Cyril smiled. "That may well be, Stuart, but in my experience, when someone comes forward with one hand open their other might well be closed. Who knows what might be concealed there?"

"Can Forensics procedures now be done on the contents of Baines's car?" Owen asked as he fumbled through the file.

"Yes, and I also want the Jag in for a thorough vetting too. We're doing a full search of Baines's home office and his place of work on Victoria Avenue."

***

Claire sipped the second glass of lemonade as they stood before moving further out into the garden. The sun was warm.

"You like it?"

"The lemonade is lovely, thank you."

"I meant the view, my dear."

"It looks beautiful and the lake or reservoir view from the tree is stunning. The sky is huge. At night the stars must be so beautiful." She looked again. "But the garden also looks like hard work."

"That's not my worry I'm delighted to say, comes with being rented." He smiled. "The reservoir, it reflects the sky like a tiny jewel. If you look in that direction you can see the wind turbines just over the hill. Why I was angry when they planned to erect them there, I'll never understand knowing fully their true benefits. I enjoy watching their blades' monotonous rotations. There's something soporific about their speed and gentleness, they're not like machines at all." He then pointed to a stone outbuilding. "I'll show you what's in there later. You'll be surprised. However, Claire, that's not why I asked you here. I'm sure you're not fully aware of just how grateful we are for your co-operation, your help and shall we say, your persuasive words in the right direction. It made a huge difference to us. I know David was very taken with you and as a sign of our gratitude, I have a generous gift for you. It's on the table under the antique glass cloche."

Claire felt her face flush and as she walked towards the table, a sudden desperate need to urinate seemed to overpower her.

"I'm sorry but may I use your bathroom?" She placed her glass next to the cloche and moved towards the French windows.

"Just up the corridor on the left." He pointed with his free hand. Time had passed so quickly.

Claire walked briskly through the conservatory.

"Claire!" he called, making her pause momentarily halfway along the corridor. "The light if you need it is outside on the left. Everyone struggles to find it."

"Thanks." Her voice trailed to nothing the further she dashed up the corridor.

"Three potatoes… mort," he whispered in a French accent.

The concentrated Furosemide, a strong diuretic he had added to her first drink had worked more quickly that he had anticipated. He heard the door open quickly and then close. Listening to ascertain if the lock would be turned, he heard nothing until after a few seconds a dull thud sounded and then a clatter, not dissimilar to that of a body collapsing against a wall. The sound of loose-standing objects being knocked over echoed down the corridor. He looked at his watch again. His timing had been perfect. He would simply move her car away, leave it in a remote location and set fire to it.

He looked at Claire's bag. *Unusual for a lady not to take her worldly goods to the loo with her but then,* he thought, *she was in a hurry*. He put on a pair of gloves before opening the bag. Amazed by the number of items confined in such a small space and by how many zip compartments there were, he methodically searched for the specific items. "How you locate your phone when it rings in this bag of junk is anyone's guess," he said out loud. He removed the phone and her car keys before walking along the corridor to the toilet.

Knowing that the pressure must have built up behind the toilet door, he pushed it open a fraction feeling the cold air escape rapidly. Wisps of dry ice curled catlike around his legs. *She had obviously seen the telltale mist but had been so desperate that she had ignored it,* he surmised. He opened the door as widely as possible to allow nitrogen-rich air to flood out of the confined space and to be replaced by the surrounding air.

Even with the extractor fan working, he knew the danger. From the cupboard at the top of the corridor he collected and fitted a self-contained breathing mask. One could never be too careful. Leaning down, he lifted her dominant hand before using her index finger to activate the security device on her phone. Once unlocked, he would then change the passcode numbers. He bent across her slumped body in order to close and lock down the lid on the flask just to be on the safe side. Experience told him that there would be a quantity of liquid nitrogen still evaporating within the Dewar. All he needed to do was to dispose of her car. He removed the mask and propped open the door to the toilet before collecting her car keys.

Chapter Sixteen

DC Stuart Park sat at David Stephens's desk; the office was small but organised. A number of photographs dotted the walls depicting either cars or aircraft. There was even an aerial photograph of the house, probably taken by Stephens. Two models, one a Piper Archer and the other a small blue Robinson helicopter, were positioned directly in front of him and it made him realise the extent of Stephens's wealth.

He carefully thumbed through the first of the logbooks. At this stage he had little idea what he was looking for but he had performed similar operations many times and knew that something would grab his attention. He made the occasional jotting adding a post-it note to the relevant pages. He was particularly interested in the landing airfield noted in a specific column for every log entry. The majority of flights were out and back to Yeadon without touching down at an away airfield but on occasion there were a number of stops, some overnight.

There was a knock on the study door and Jonathan Stephens popped his face tentatively round. "Sorry to interrupt, but Mum says you might need me."

Stuart pointed to the chair opposite and smiled. "It won't take long, just a few questions."

"Has my father done something wrong?"

Park shook his head. "No. As you may know we're investigating another death. You've probably heard about it, similar to that of your dad's, so we check, it's what we do." He could not believe he had said that but it was the first thing that came into his head. "Did your dad use his aircraft for business?"

"When he could. Helps to set the cost against tax he used to say. To France mostly, but we've flown to Italy and Spain. He bought wine for the business. He liked exclusive vineyards, something different. He told me there was more profit in that. Also he could visit the smaller Champagne houses. Many had the facilities to accommodate the landing of light aircraft."

"So he'd fly into France, clear customs at a specific airfield, and then be free to fly and land anywhere?"

"In a nutshell, sir, yes."

Park was rather taken aback by his sudden formality. "Did you go?"

"On occasion. He let me do the flying. Loved it, especially the challenge of landing at the shorter farm strips. I see you're checking logs. Those flights will be classed as P1 in my logbook. I think he stopped adding P2 to his a while back."

"P1 and P2? Can you explain?"

"Sorry, yes. If two private pilots fly they elect who is lead pilot, pilot-in-command. He signs P1. The second pilot is exercising the privileges of his licence as a required member of the crew and is allowed to record the hours as P2. It means nothing really and these days you'll not see many pilots doing this. There's a description in the front of the logbook. May I?" He leaned across the desk, opening one of the books to the relevant page.

Stuart Park nodded as he quickly scanned the details.

"I see the majority of times you landed back at Yeadon, even when coming from abroad."

"By law, you land at a customs airfield. You clear customs and then either fly on to your home field or as we do, hangar the plane. We'd then use the helicopter back to here. Again, sometimes customs would be waiting and at other times not. You never really knew. The same when flying to France. You complete a flight plan notifying Special Branch and customs of your intended destination and route but whether you see anyone is pot luck!"

"Were there occasions where he'd take other passengers?"

Jonathan frowned a little giving the impression that he was reflecting on the type of answer he should give. "Dad would take the staff from the businesses, as a gift, presents, rewards, like. It could just be a flight around Yorkshire or a helicopter trip to a restaurant. He liked flying in to land at a hotel near Bolton Bridge. Always impressed them. He'd also take managers with him when he went abroad, buy the wines and other products."

Hearing the word *products* made Stuart Park sit up but he said nothing, just made a mental note.

"Did he ever take Paul Ashton on one of these trips? You said managers but not partner."

"Paul wouldn't fly, he had some kind of phobia."

Stuart made a note before asking. "Do we have names and dates?"

"Dates are in the flight log. Maybe the names will be in Dad's diary. They were always kept on his computer and his phone."

"They were returned to you, the phone and laptop found in the car?"

"Yes, that was his business phone but his personal phone we haven't been able to find. We did ask your lot but that wasn't on the list of items found in his car that morning."

"Are these passcode protected?"

"Probably, I don't know them."

Stuart picked up the phone and it requested a touch ID or passcode.

"My father used his print, he found it magical. That's what he said every time he did it. Same with the laptop."

"What about the logs?"

"They're kept with the plane at the service hangar. They are never in the aircraft for obvious reasons."

Park thanked Jonathan and watched him leave. He rang Cyril. "Sir, think it might be wise for Stephens's IT equipment to be checked either here or at the lab. Would suggest back with us."

"I'll clear it."

"There's a mobile phone missing too… Stephens's personal one."

The line went quiet.

"Another coincidence, sir?"

***

Once the wide top of the flask was opened, the evaporating nitrogen gas from the liquid nitrogen flooded out of the vessel forcing the oxygen from the enclosed confines of the room. The fan had been rigged to help extract the air and ensure that oxygen, normally twenty-one per cent of the air we breathe, fell swiftly below five per cent, as the increasing pressure building within the small space forced the oxygen through the fan and any gaps in the window frame and the door. Anyone entering this oxygen-starved space at this stage, as Claire had, would be rendered unconscious by the third breath and dead in less than a minute. She would neither have felt alarmed nor anxious. She would simply die.

***

Claire had collapsed behind the door. She was folded like a crumpled marionette; arms and legs seemed to be arranged at the most impossible angles. Her head had collided with either the towel rail or radiator, peeling a deep, triangular flap of flesh from her forehead, but as her heart had stopped pumping, there was little by way of blood loss, a weep, a streaked tear of red and that was all.

It had been three hours since she had entered the house. Her car had been disposed of and fortunately, the recent spell of dry weather had made leaving the dumpsite relatively simple. There would be few clues left and by the time the fire brigade had extinguished the fire, any tracks that were made would be awash. The incendiary device, dropped into the fuel tank, had been programmed to delay the incineration process, allowing adequate time to move well away from the site before the burning car attracted attention, yet not long enough to have it discovered and reported. Like all his work, it was based on accurate timing. He was aware that the man-made electronic fuse might be located after the event, but the heat of the burning fuel would, he thought, destroy most of it. Cars are stolen so regularly, and what with the recent spate of vehicle vandalism he had read about in the local paper, it might simply be a statistic; that is, of course, until they discovered that the owner was missing too.

Having first brought her to a sitting position on the toilet seat, it was less difficult to move the body. The dead weight of a cadaver, no matter how slight, can never be overstated. Once the door was fully opened he could stand, lift her vertically and manoeuvre her through the opening. The next step would be a simple fireman's lift.

He carried Claire's flaccid body through the conservatory. He glanced at the half empty glass, the cloche and then towards the stone outbuilding.

"I told you I'd show you what was in here. Do you remember?" he gasped, breathing heavily under the load before turning so that he could push open the wooden door with Claire's head. "Good to see you using your noddle, if you'd used it before you would have realised that we'd know just when you put your pretty fingers into the sweetie jar and all of this could have been avoided. Never mind, nothing we can't cope with. Stiff upper lip, my girl… or you will have when rigor mortis begins to set in. Starts in the face, I believe, but they also say that moving a body can change the time it sets in. Fascinating isn't it? However, once you're in here it'll make absolutely no difference."

With his free hand he opened the chest freezer.

A frozen face stared up at him; a potato lodged in the open mouth, making it resemble a wild boar dressed as a centrepiece at a medieval banquet.

"I've brought you a woman. This is Claire. You'll recognise one another as you've recently met."

He let the body roll from his shoulder so that the corpses lay head to toe. It flopped heavily into the cavity with a dull thud, a noise that brought a smile to his lips. He witnessed a layer of ice particles fly upwards like fine rainbow crystals from the frozen, rigid figure that was half covered beneath the body of Claire Baldwin.

"I don't think you'll get up to any hanky-panky, Arthur, do you? You're a tad frigid, I see. Besides, it would be so wrong for you two, so very wrong."

Claire's head was at an angle and her milky blue eyes stared back. He noticed the one earring that was visible. "Match your eyes them, love." He stood for a moment taking in the scene before he stretched over to a shelf and collected a small potato. He leaned in and placed it partly into her gaping mouth before moving her hands to the side of her face thus mirroring the other corpse trapped within the freezer. He scattered a tendril of ivy across her neck. "Just like brother and sister. What do we say? One potato, two potatoes, three potatoes, four… you know the rest, your rhyme may well be the same but end with a different connotation. You've been chosen. Well, my dear, you chose yourself really."

Removing a phone from his pocket, he took a photograph of the face of the frozen corpse with which Claire had just been placed. He moved close enough to capture the whole upper torso and the frosted tendril of ivy.

"A picture of you literally frozen in time, Arthur. No smile? Perhaps not. We'll have one of you later too, Claire, but only when the ice crystals form."

Slowly he put his hand onto her face and straightened it before looking at her other ear. Furious, he realised that the earring was missing. "Shit! It could be just about anywhere." He tried to recall if she had been wearing both on her arrival or during the conversation but he could not. "Bloody clip earrings. Jesus!" Slamming the lid, he quickly slid the steel retaining bar through the hoops before adding three padlocks onto the steel hasps.

Only then did he allow his eyes to scour the steps he had taken. There was nothing.

Even in the toilet there was no trace. The car, was it in there? He felt nausea rise from the pit of his stomach. "Shit! Bitch!" He crashed his fist against the wall.

Chapter Seventeen

Jonathan Stephens looked across the kitchen table at his mother and sister, his hand cupped around a mug of coffee.

"There's something not right, I know it and I've had a feeling about it for some time."

"Jonathan, I know what you're about to say but don't, change the record, just stop it. He was a sick man, he drove himself too hard, drank too much and goodness knows what else. The business always came first. We've tried to get him to slow down, get a proper business partner to share the load but he was stubborn. He just couldn't let go. He wouldn't trust anyone, either that or he didn't want people to get a glimpse of what was going on. Don't you dare say that! We're family and we look after each other, more so now!" His mother started screaming. "Don't you bloody well dare!"

"What about the chap he said he used to see, the mystery figure, the *nosy bastard* he used to call him? It used to worry him. You both know it. Someone realised that something wasn't right and Dad did. I believe you knew too."

His sister stood and shook her head. "Jesus, Jonny, just let him rest in peace for Christ's sake. You've gone on and on… tell the bloody coppers if it'll shut you up but do it quickly, say what you have to say and then just shut the fuc—!" she yelled, not finishing the final expletive before storming out, her elbow knocking the table and spilling her coffee.

Moving to mop it up, his mother looked at him, tears in her eyes. "We've suffered enough. I've been through enough. Your father drank too much and, well, you know. He was going to stop. He'd seen demons in the bedroom before now, screamed out loud. How he ever passed his medicals I'll never fully understand although I have an idea." She sat down and wept.

Jonathan came around the table and consoled her.

"You know just how hard he worked; it provided all this and more, he was a generous father to you and your sister. Be thankful and just let it be. What did he use to say when you were little? *Watch the wall, my darling, as the gentlemen go by...* As your sister says, let him rest, darling. Please."

***

Stuart Park found Cyril in his office, a cup of tea in one hand. He was swivelling to and fro on his chair as if in deep thought. Stuart tapped on the partly opened door. Cyril stopped the chair's movement and turned. Seeing Stuart, he smiled.

"Come in! Tell me something, Stuart; advise me. What would you do if someone were to give you this?" Cyril picked up a photograph from his desk and passed it over, it was of the Bentley his father had bequeathed him.

Stuart looked at it enviously. "I'd thank my lucky stars, sir. Bloody gorgeous that is. A Rolls?"

"Bentley."

"Same thing really in my eyes. Great colour too! Which lucky bastard owns that?"

"Unfortunately, right at this minute..." He paused before collecting the photograph, glancing at it and then back at Stuart. "Me!"

Stuart smiled and pulled a face. "Nice! Please may I have a ride?"

Cyril could not help but laugh. "Only if you come to look at my puppies first!"

They both chuckled.

"On a serious note, sir, I've been going through the flight logbooks of the Stephens family. They used the aircraft for flights to the continent, France mainly, linked with the business when visiting vineyards, and the like. I want to get someone to go through their business accounts to see what was purchased and what was personally brought back into the country."

"If we do that, the family will have to be informed that his death is being investigated. It's a serious move."

"I think they're already aware of that." Stuart added, "Jonathan wanted to know if his father had done something wrong so I told him we were looking into his father's death owing to the similarity with another death. He's not stupid and he wasn't surprised."

"Do they have sole use of the aircraft?"

"No, he allows it to be rented by the flying club on occasion. Helps with hangar and running costs. Happens all the time in the private aircraft industry, I'm led to believe."

Cyril nodded knowing that from his past experience. "Have you seen the aircraft and logbooks?"

Stuart frowned shaking his head. "Father's, son's and daughter's but she flew very little. The aircraft logs are with the aircraft."

"As soon as."

Stuart Park stood. "Yeadon here I come. I could do with that R2 helicopter that's in Stephens's garage, or that Bentley." He leaned over and tapped the photograph.

The call came through from Julie fifteen minutes after Park's departure from his office.

"I have some results from the pathology lab. We need to chat."

***

Julie was already at her desk when Cyril arrived, denying him his usual time with the objects dotted along the shelves.

"Hypoxia, Cyril, but in the end it's up to the coroner and your evidence as to the exact reasons. The results are convincingly similar to a case in which two engineers died from immediate oxygen deprivation. They were working in the brewing industry about six years ago. They were repairing a faulty release valve at the top of a tank that held vented inert gas produced by having liquid nitrogen stored under pressure below."

Cyril's expression conveyed his confusion. "Think of it as a shallow chamber that collects any gases that are released so that they can be controlled and monitored before they're vented into the atmosphere. Today, you just can't put gases, even inert ones, into the surrounding environment without monitoring them. Anyway, to get to a part of the valve, the engineers had to remove the top seal. It was believed that the tank had been purged of any residual gas before this operation took place.

"When the lid was removed, one of the engineers was suddenly overcome and dropped into the upper chamber. His colleague, seeing this, used a stepladder to climb into the chamber to rescue him but he too was immediately rendered unconscious and died within minutes. It appears that errors had been made on both sides. The engineers had received training within the last six months and there had been warning signs instructing that the use of self-contained breathing apparatus was mandatory within the chamber but not when working near and in the area."

"Do we know the type of gas that killed them?"

"It wasn't a gas but the total lack of oxygen. After very few inhalations, maybe three, they would be unconscious and within a minute or two they'd be dead. They would have had no warning signs at all."

"You mentioned that they'd removed the seal and the lid or am I missing something?"

"What was stored deep within that tank, below this chamber, would have been liquid nitrogen. It can be referred to as LIN, Cryogenic liquid nitrogen or simply liquid nitrogen and it's used in a variety of industries for myriad reasons. In some ways that's immaterial right now. I'm trying to keep this simple, Cyril. When it's stored in a pressurised container, no matter what the size, it needs to have a safety valve. It boils at minus 195.8 degrees centigrade or Celsius, that's bloody cold. It's freezing enough to cause severe skin damage and frost bite, or cold burns as they can be described. It's colourless and odourless, but it's around us, we breathe it, it makes up seventy-eight per cent of that air so it's difficult to detect. Although on the face of it the stuff looks safe, inert and chemically inactive, it's exceptionally dangerous in certain situations."

Cyril scratched his head. "Please remember that you're talking to a copper and not a particularly bright one." He grinned and pulled a face, hoping for a complimentary riposte but none came.

"Pure nitrogen vented into a carrier bag over your head will be a way of shuffling off this mortal coil, Cyril, leaving it quickly and probably painlessly. Then there's nitrogen, kept in liquid form within insulated containers of any size, and maintained at a set pressure. The environment around the vessel has an ambient temperature, that heat warms the liquid nitrogen forming a vapour; unless that vapour is properly vented, an explosion can occur."

"Julie, what has the death of these two workers got to do with Baines?"

"Look, there's no reason why Baines should have died suddenly, yes there's evidence of an irregular heart rate but many people who kick a ball about at weekends have arrhythmia. The two guys who died in the tank were fit. We know how they died, and as a result, can compare the pathological results with those of Baines. It is my professional judgement that all three died of hypoxia, think of it as asphyxiation. They demonstrated the same degree of damage to their organs. Only by comparison with the pathology records of those unfortunate workers can we make a presumption of how Baines died. In cases like these we take the evidence we can to extrapolate the truth, the coroner will now ask for further evidence, your evidence, and then we'll see.

"I'd like to be able to state that the way Baines died is irrefutable. I can't. All I can demonstrate is that these three men may have suffered the same fate and that, Cyril, might just be the lead you need. And before you ask, we're looking at samples taken from David Stephens as we speak. You need to do some research into the world of liquid nitrogen. Two further points might interest you. The American government is considering using liquid nitrogen as a means of performing capital punishment after the difficulties they've had with the lethal injection and in this country, nitrogen-rich environments are used for the humane killing of poultry. Look it up!"

Chapter Eighteen

It was midnight when Cyril finished his search on the Internet. A large sheet of paper was full of jottings and sat alongside two empty bottles labelled *Black Sheep Ale*. The more he had read, the more he could see the possibility that Baines had accidentally killed himself or had been murdered. Had he committed suicide, one question would need to be answered? As for Stephens, that prognosis would have to wait until pathology results proved that he had also suffered from the same symptoms as Baines and the two unfortunate brewery workers Julie had discussed.

Cyril sat back and drained the remaining beer from his glass. He let his eyes drift to the wall and he stared at an Isherwood oil painting directly ahead. Its composition taunted him. The oil painting's blue and misty sky was streaked with yellow that had all the appearance of a poisoned gas. It hung above the buildings and the disproportional pedestrians who somehow seemed motionless, as if trapped in the petrifying haze. The more research he had carried out on liquid nitrogen, the more complex and confusing the task seemed to have become. This confusion was why he thought he saw gas and death clearly reflected within the haphazard brush strokes of the innocent painting or maybe it was the beer and the lack of food. There was one thing he had gleaned from his evening's labour, the ideas and the theories he had derived from his reading were full of possibilities, admittedly long shots at best, but they were certainly not lost pathways of investigation. In all his years of policing, he had learned not to dismiss the obvious or the obscure.

***

Walking into the station the next morning, Cyril paused and chatted briefly to the officer on the desk. He slipped the lanyard holding his security ID and key pass over his head before making his way to his office; the rolled up piece of A1 paper, like a large cigarette, was tucked under his arm. Owen had not arrived. Cyril checked his watch, shook it and looked again. He scribbled a comment on a lime green post-it note and attached it to Owen's computer screen.

Morning. We need to chat immediately when you get this.

Cyril rolled out the paper onto his desk before weighing down the corners with different objects. He read through the scribbled notes and the highlights he had made.

Liquid nitrogen is a cryogenic fluid that can cause rapid freezing of living tissue. If appropriately stored it can be kept and transported. It is maintained in this state by a slow boiling of the liquid and this evaporation process releases nitrogen gas.

Liquid nitrogen has become popular in the preparation of cocktails!!!

Used in the brewing industry/purging oxygen from water/food freezing and processing.

If liquid nitrogen evaporates it reduces the oxygen content in the air rapidly and can act as an asphyxiant, especially in confined spaces. It is colourless, without smell and tasteless and may kill quickly without prior warning. The victim may feel slightly euphoric and have no sense of the danger in which they find themselves.

Cyril had just finished reading the notes when the light suddenly diminished.

"Come in, Owen, and stop blocking the light. Take a look at this. Even at my time of life I've had homework."

Owen came over and stood next to Cyril before looking at the sheet of paper. Owen held a slice of burnt toast. A globule of molten butter dropped onto the paper but was swiftly smudged with his thumb which then travelled to his mouth to be cleaned. "Sorry!" He popped what was left of the toast into his mouth and wiped his hands on his trousers.

After a few moments he let his finger run along the highlighted sentences following each line in order before going back to the first one that referred to cocktails. "How does that work then?"

"New fad, I believe. It quick freezes the items going into the cocktail but also makes it look somewhat sinister, smoke or steam is seen tumbling out of the glass and down the stem. Although nitrogen gas is slightly lighter than air, when it's very cold, it's heavier and that is why you get the tumbling low floating cloud, a dry ice effect."

Owen looked up at Cyril, his face showing signs of puzzlement.

"When I was at the Bauhaus Champagne and Cocktail place, I noticed a purple drink doing just that. Looked for all intents and purposes like a witch's cauldron. Can't imagine anyone drinking it, bloody foul concoction!"

Picking up a pencil, Cyril made a note. "As things are getting colder, my friend, we might..." He emphasised the word might, "...be getting just that little bit warmer."

Owen's confused expression did not alter. "Really? Right."

Cyril's phone rang. "Bennett."

Owen watched Cyril doodle on a corner of the large sheet of paper for what seemed like an age. He might like art, but from what he could see, Cyril was certainly no Picasso.

"So why is it relevant, April?" He listened again. "I don't want it moved. Get it checked out thoroughly and I need someone watching the house, preferably plain clothes officers." Cyril wrote the word *Wighill* on the paper. "We're on our way." As he said that the force he used to add a full stop after the word made the pencil point break sending a small projectile across the paper.

"Car... burned out... Wighill."

"As I mentioned the other day, there's been a spate, that's why April's chasing up that cold case."

"Belongs to a Claire Baldwin. Turns out that Ms Baldwin hasn't been to work or been seen for two days and the car is miles from her home address."

It was apparent that Owen had not made the connection. "The note I found in Baines's home office. Claire. Remember?"

"Hell! I was just focusing on Baldwin. Got you!"

"We're doing a background check now. There's more to this than meets the eye."

***

Within thirty-five minutes they were turning off the A1M heading towards Dishforth Airfield. A black jet marked with yellow lightning flashes flew low over the road. However, its destination was RAF Leeming, not Dishforth. Cyril tilted his head and watched its slow turn, a trail of black from the rear, charcoal lining the blue sky.

"That's a Hawk. RAF training aircraft."

There was a sudden pause as Owen negotiated some roadworks.

"How come you get travel sick in a car but you can fly a plane? Don't you need a lot of those sick bags when it gets bumpy?"

"Turbulence? No, must be the adrenalin. It seems to be just your driving, Owen, that brings on the nausea especially when you think we need to arrive before we depart!"

"Right, sir. Wait until you get that Bentley. You'll be on cloud nine as they run like silk."

Immediately Owen realised he had said not the most tactful thing and quickly changed the subject. "So the burned out car's in Wighill, near Tadcaster, and she lives in Thirsk? Maybe it was taken by someone who needed to get home as there are no trains to Tadcaster. They removed the line, come to think of it, way back in time! You told me about the man who did it."

"Beeching."

"That's him. And the buses as well! Probably a group of lads pissed, possibly squaddies who'd spent up and couldn't afford a taxi." He turned to Cyril hoping to see that his theory might have a degree of credibility but Cyril simply stared ahead.

Passing Dalton disused airfield, Owen thought of a previous case but owing to the memories it held he tried to block the thought from his mind and concentrate on the road. Cyril said nothing for the next ten minutes and then raised a hand. The volume on the satnav had been turned off earlier in the journey.

"Next left, Owen. Just after what looks like a shop."

Owen turned. The row of terraced houses stretched for some distance both on the left and right. Cars were parked on either side of the narrow road, half on and half off the pavement.

"Park on the right where you can."

There was a blue Ford Mondeo positioned on the opposite side of the road about twenty yards away. The driver watched them carefully. The camera facing forward would have recorded their approach. It was then that Owen pointed to the satnav.

"We're on Victoria Avenue! This has got to be some kind of bloody joke, sir." He could see from Cyril's demeanour that he considered it neither a joke nor remotely funny.

"It's deliberate, Owen. You can trust me on that score."

Cyril flashed his ID and the driver of the Mondeo nodded.

"Nobody in or out, sir. A window cleaner came down the road and knocked but there was no answer. He pushed something through the letter box."

"Is there a back way in?" Cyril enquired as he glanced up and down the road.

"A narrow passageway, wide enough for a car, leads to the small rear gardens of that terraced row. I have a colleague round there. She's seen nothing, apart from the window man, or she hadn't up to five minutes ago."

"Thanks. Owen, check neighbours on either side. See if someone's home and find out who has a key."

***

April pulled off the road and into what was an extended opening of a farm track. A huge pile of dung stood sentinel like. A white wisp of steam rose from different parts of the heap accompanied by an even stronger aroma. The CSI van was further up the lane and two white-suited figures were just clearing away. There was no sign of a fire engine other than the mud it had left when pulling out onto the road that was now dry.

"DC April Richmond," she announced holding out her ID. "Anything?"

"Nobody in it, thankfully. Looks like a take and burn. Buggered that tree, well and proper!"

April looked up at the singed mantle that once held a bounty of oak leaves and then back to the car. There was nothing remaining of the tyres; in their place was a fine filigree of woven wire that had quickly become rust coloured in places. The car had changed out of all proportion as melted puddles of plastic and metal skirted the vehicle's edge, the glass had gone and the convertible roof was only a metal, exposed rib cage.

"Still too hot in places, even though it's been doused. Images will be with you now. Bonnet and boot are made from aluminium so there's little left and the engine parts have welded to sections of the body. It was some fire. From my experience the fire started in the petrol tank. That too is some kind of plastic. The car fire was out when the fire brigade arrived but as I said, they doused it mainly because the tree had started to burn too. It's always best, just to be on the safe side with all this grassland. Owing to the possible significance of this wreck, we're awaiting a transporter now."

April thanked them and went back to her car. She would need to notify Cyril.

Chapter Nineteen

Leaning against the Mondeo, Cyril removed his mobile and watched as Owen knocked at the first door. Cyril listened to the ring tone; it rang three times. "April, Bennett. What have you found?"

"I was just about to ring you. Car's up a farm track, half a mile from the village and quite isolated. It's completely burned out, Porsche Boxster, according to the chassis plate. It's registered to a Claire Baldwin, Victoria Avenue, Thirsk. Yes, I thought that a strange coincidence too. It feels there are too many similarities, right, sir? Who's playing games with whom is the question that's puzzling me."

"Was the fire brigade involved?"

"Yes, from Tadcaster, but once they realised it was a stolen and fired car they simply doused and extinguished it quickly and left. That was some hours ago. CSI have just finished with it. Looking at it, I can't see them retrieving much."

"Get a mail drop organised for the village, see if anyone saw the car before it was burned. Get an exact picture of the type of vehicle and colour from DVLA records. I would imagine it might have attracted someone's attention, kids particularly. See if anyone noticed any unfamiliar faces or cars, maybe some other vehicle, not the Porsche, left unattended for a period. With Baldwin missing, someone may well have planned this and if so they'd need some return transport. Ensure that the wreck's taken in and kept under wraps, at least until we find the owner—"

"As we speak, sir," she managed to interject.

"Good. Get someone back at the station. Dan Grimshaw was looking into Baines's phone so get him to check if our Claire

Baldwin is active on social media and if so, get them to retrieve what they can." Cyril made a mental note to chase up Grimshaw about the requested phone records. "I've asked for a background check on Claire Baldwin, usual stuff, parents, boyfriends, standard procedure. Chase it when you get back, please."

Owen waved to catch Cyril's eye from across the road. "This lady has a key!"

He moved quickly towards them and smiled at the elderly neighbour.

"She hasn't seen Claire for a couple of days. The car's not been here neither."

The lady quickly interrupted, as if frightened that Owen was going to steal her thunder. "She usually works from home, Internet stuff. If she's travelling into her office near Newcastle she takes the train and parks her car at the station car park or sometimes, if the weather's good, she uses her folding bike. On those mornings, I'm pleased to say, I'm not awoken by the roar of her sporty car. The noise bounces off the house walls you know and I always sleep—" She did not finish as Cyril managed to interrupt as politely as he could by holding up a finger and speaking.

"Thank… thank you, we'll need the key just to make sure she's safe."

"Sorry, yes. A minute." The neighbour returned inside.

Owen turned and grinned at Cyril. "Just like me gran. Salt of the earth."

Cyril and Owen slipped on plastic overshoes and gloves before opening the door. The hallway was dark but ordered. Cyril called Claire's name and waited but there was no response. He picked up the printed note and the mail. *Your windows were cleaned today* followed by a handwritten date. There were three other letters. Cyril looked at them all before placing them on the hall table and moving into the lounge. The same order greeted them.

"You go upstairs, Owen. Any photographs etc."

Owen mounted the stairs two at a time as Cyril moved into the kitchen-dining room. The house was tastefully decorated and Claire Baldwin was obviously an organised and house-proud woman.

"Everything seems in order up here, sir, strangely no framed photos."

"None down here either."

Cyril slid open the top drawers in the kitchen hoping to find the dump drawer. Everyone had a space where all the day's pocket and handbag detritus was stuffed, even he had one although he hated to admit it. There was a calendar propped up by the breakfast bar. He photographed the page showing the week before and read the appointments and notes that had been added. Behind it was a collection of other papers, notes and letters. He checked each one, photographing anything he thought to be relevant. Owen entered.

"Anything?"

"Nothing that stands out."

Owen opened the fridge. There was little in the way of food but in the centre of the second shelf was an egg box.

"Never do that. Always keep mine in a bowl. That's how I was brought up. Never lasted long enough to go off."

Cyril turned.

"Eggs! She keeps hers in the fridge, look!" Owen exclaimed.

Cyril leaned round the door and took hold of the carton. He carefully opened it. In each cavity was a small plastic box in the shape of an egg. They were coloured too to give that appearance. On closer inspection, Owen could see a thin hairline joint running round the upper two-thirds.

"It's in two parts, sir."

Cyril popped on his glasses and was surprised to see the joint. Placing the carton on the work surface he removed one and held it to the light. The bottom section failed to allow light to pass. Holding the lower part in one hand and the top in the other, he turned them in the opposite direction and slowly they unscrewed. He paused lifting his eyes to peer over his glasses at Owen.

"Will we be chasing the dragon, Owen? That's the question," Cyril said as the lid separated from the main body exposing what appeared to be a sealed packet containing white powder.

"Looks like you're right, it's the start of a dragon chase, sir."

Cyril came to the door and pointed to the officer in the Mondeo who came over to join him.

"No one in or out. It has to be checked." He handed the officer the key and called for support.

"I want a dog too, looking for drugs."

As he finished, the neighbour tapped him on his shoulder. "It might be nothing but the last time Claire and I had a chat she asked me if I'd seen anyone looking through my front window. I hadn't but she mentioned seeing a face at her window."

The hairs on Cyril's neck bristled and suddenly the neighbour had his full attention. Owen joined them.

"Face?" Cyril did not want to lead her.

"She saw it a few times, couldn't make out whether it was male or female. She said that she got the impression that she was being watched and when she glanced towards the window, she'd see this figure disappear out of view as if he or she were just walking past. She'd no idea of how long they'd been standing there, or if they really had. She was never sure."

"Have you seen anything?"

"Look at the avenue, it's not exactly a thoroughfare is it? As I told her when she asked me the same question, no!"

Cyril looked up and down the avenue. He thanked her and explained that the police were taking Claire's disappearance very seriously and that as a result there would be quite a lot of police activity. It brought a smile and a look of excitement to her face.

"Will the telly people come?"

Cyril smiled before turning away towards the car but then stopped. "One last thing. Do you know whether Claire had relatives locally or boy or girlfriends?"

"We only chat, Detective Chief Inspector and I'm certainly not one of those busybody neighbours who interferes in everyone's business I'll have you know." The neighbour slipped her arms under her bosom and shook from side to side whilst pushing out her chest as if in defence before she let slip that occasionally Claire entertained men friends but she could offer no names nor a useful description.

***

Brian Smirthwaite was adding details to one of the whiteboards. The incident room had been quickly adapted for the investigation of both deaths as well as the disappearance of Arthur Thorndyke from the food factory. At this stage there was little evidence to suggest his involvement. Brian was transferring the names of the employees who worked and had worked for the Newcastle-based Health and Safety consultancy. After each name was a list of qualifications.

It had quickly become apparent that the firm, although based in the centre of the city, had consultants who were dotted around the north east and west of the country and in many cases worked freelance. Brian bracketed the names of those who had left on or around the date of the loss of the major contract. They tended to be people directly involved with the York food-processing firm *Clear Foods*. Claire Baldwin's name had been added. Brian had also downloaded photographs of each consultant.

Chapter Twenty

Cyril studied the notes on the toxicology results as he sipped the red wine.

"You can have five more minutes, then you can ask me three questions and that's it. This is supposed to be a social meal where you stare into my eyes and I reciprocate whilst having an aperitif. We sit and eat dinner with neither talk of police procedurals nor pathology being mentioned once. You tell me that I look beautiful and flatter me about my new outfit. Are you listening, Cyril Bennett? Yes, you heard me correctly, new outfit, and then we see where that takes us!" Julie's voice drifted from the kitchen as an aroma filled Cyril's nostrils making his mouth water. Ironically, the strains of Richard Ashcroft singing, "The Drugs don't Work", coming from the sound system did not help his yearning for answers. Cyril quickly moved to the kitchen door and wolf-whistled. "Lovely, sorry!"

"Punishable offence now in France, whistling in a sexist and salacious way intimidating us poor females. Fortunately, we live in a country where some common sense still prevails."

Cyril smiled, realising the latter part of the sentence was clearly tongue in cheek. He went back to the notes Julie had written.

There was nothing from toxicology suggesting drug use for Baines but traces of cocaine were found in the blood and vitreous humor samples taken from Stephens.

He made a note to ask if drug misuse might have been the cause of Stephens's heart issues and added the question to the bottom of her notes.

Julie came in carrying a glass of wine. She draped the apron on the back of a chair, leaned over and kissed his head before sitting opposite. "Right, Cyril Bennett, ask away."

Cyril brought his glass towards hers. "Cheers and thanks. It smells divine."

"You're up to no good. I know you too well."

"I've been thinking."

Julie let out a sigh. "Never a good sign at…" She looked at her watch… "Seven thirty-three."

Cyril ran his finger round the rim of the glass as if hesitant to speak. "You don't fancy a Bentley, do you, not just to drive but to have and to hold from this day forth?"

She simply shook her head. "Bloody men!"

"Thought not!"

***

Owen was reading from the whiteboards when April came into the incident room. She leaned over and straightened the mug he was holding, its angle having allowed the contents to dribble onto the lower part of his trousers and onto the floor by his right foot.

"Thanks. Carried away by this riveting information. The money found is clean, no prints, none. How does that happen unless it's money from ill-gotten bloody gains? Claire Baldwin was working as a consultant up until they lost the contract. They have, according to Smirthwaite, not seen her since she was reprimanded. That's over a fortnight ago. Neighbour hasn't seen her for a couple of days. To cap it all, according to the neighbour Claire sees faces! It's getting like a bloody jigsaw puzzle and I hated them when I was a kid. My gran always had one on the go. I used to help her with the corners and the edges and she always let me put in the last piece. Spoiled I was. We'll know more when they finish house to house in the area. What did you make of the name of the road?"

April made a note on some paper attached to a freestanding easel:

Who did what to whom and when? Who has seen what? Should we be considering the street names a coincidence? A person by the name of Claire was in contact with Bill Baines or vice versa. If we assume it to be the same person as the one now missing, a huge assumption, one lived on a Victoria Avenue, one died on a Victoria Avenue. One lost a job, while one gained a job.

Another person, linked with Baines's death had a connection with a Victoria Avenue. Coincidence or is someone taunting?

To do: Check with Mrs Baines if she recognises Claire Baldwin.

April pointed to the photograph Smirthwaite had added to the list. Owen followed her finger and continued sipping what was left of his tea.

Check if any of the Stephens family or their employees know or recognise Claire Baldwin. Also check at Yeadon, the local flying club, for connections with Baines and Claire Baldwin.

Check of Baldwin's phone records.

Phone records already checked for Baines and Stephens?

Find the corners and edges of this jigsaw and the middle will follow!!!

x

She put the pen down and stood back.

"You after my job?" Owen said, only partly tongue in cheek. "As I said, hate bloody jigsaws."

April just smiled. "These things nag at me. Just can't stop thinking about them until I have the answers. I have to write them down as it helps my thinking process. Did you chat to the deputy at the food plant?"

Owen put his mug down. "Yes, appears that his boss liked a drink and he's gone to stay with a relative until he's feeling better. It appears that his direct line manager is happy with that. According to his deputy, he'd received a couple of written warnings. I don't think Arthur Thorndyke will be with them much longer. From all accounts he's stretching their patience but he knows they can't just sack him. He hasn't been in to see their medical officer and he's late with his fit note."

"Sick or fit?" April asked whilst underlining Thorndyke's name on one of the boards.

"People refer to it as a sick note but it's officially a fit note. Thorndyke's on long term sick. *Clear Foods* has tried to see if he could come back part time or in a reduced capacity but they're having difficulty getting in touch."

"As a matter of interest, Owen, did they have any health and safety issues, accidents or incidents whilst he was in charge?"

"Good question. Thorndyke suffered from an industrial injury and hasn't been back to work." Owen frowned. "Clearly he wasn't the most efficient operative on their payroll but possibly the clumsiest!"

Owen left the room.

***

"Who's written this?" Cyril stood looking at the flip chart. A number of faces turned away from computer screens to look and a couple of officers came to join him.

"April Richmond's writing that. I'd have a fiver on it."

Cyril looked at the clock. It was noon. He read the sheet again and then went to find her. She was in the kitchen finishing making some tea and collecting a plastic box from the fridge.

"A minute, April, before you tuck into…"

"Cheese and tomato, sir."

"Yes, lovely. I've just read the notes you added in the incident room. Do something for me will you, please?"

"Sir, if I can explain..." She did not finish.

"Write it out for me but this time add all your ideas. Broaden it taking each strand of thought to a conclusion. I know it will be conjecture but I think it would help focus the case. To extend your analogy, let's see if we can add more than the edges. Is that possible?"

"This afternoon? Should also have something back from Forensics on the burned-out car and the contents of Baines's car."

"Champion. Enjoy your lunch."

As Cyril left, DC Dan Grimshaw came along the corridor waving a piece of paper. *Peace in our time*, Cyril whispered to himself.

Chapter Twenty-One

Owen listened, the phone on speaker, as the details of the accident reports taken from *Clear Foods* were read to him. It was evidence held by the Health and Safety Executive and used during the case against them. There were four injuries pertaining to the period: three female operatives and one male. The most serious, the male, suffered severe breathing difficulties and skin damage to his hands. He had been hospitalised for a couple of days and had yet to return to work. The three female employees suffered minor breathing complications and emotional trauma. All were checked by paramedics and also at Accident and Emergency but none was detained. Even though he was injured, there was a case of gross negligence pending against Thorndyke since he was supposed to have been in charge. Owen tapped the phone to end the call. He could only speculate as to the amount for compensating the victims knowing the way the system seemed to work.

***

Dan Grimshaw looked more than a little flustered when he paused, slightly out of breath, in front of Cyril.

"What do you think I've found regarding the phone records and the social media accounts for the two dead and the missing woman?"

Cyril stood patiently, waiting for a punchline. "I don't know. What have you found?"

"They had not communicated with any of the others in the past. None had Facebook, Twitter or any other social media account, from what we can discover."

"And, your point is?"

"Who doesn't have some sort of social media account these days, even a lapsed one that you tried and gave up on? It's like not having a television. Who doesn't have a TV today?"

Cyril paused. Experience told him what Grimshaw's reply would be after he informed him that he did not have a television. He mentally bet himself a tenner. "I don't have a TV, Grimshaw… not had one for years."

He saw the frown develop on his colleague's forehead and waited as he watched the information sink in. "Really? I don't watch much, don't know why we have one, usually a load of the proverbial. The wife likes the soaps. Me? Can't stand them."

Cyril smiled inwardly. He'd won his bet. "Is that all you have to tell me?"

"No, sorry. Information on the two missing phones, they're their personal ones. We know the make of each and we know the calls made over the period of ownership. They're still receiving some calls but nothing outgoing. I've checked the numbers and Baines has received calls but they're from business acquaintances who are, as yet, unaware of his death. Stephens's personal account dried up pretty quickly as the news hit the press. That gives us an insight into their address books but from experience it will be impossible to get any further. There's no co-operation by the manufacturers and we're at a dead end." He raised his eyebrows as if knowing that his words were somewhat inappropriate.

"From what you've said, the phones are still active, neither has been cancelled?"

"Yes, our procedure, particularly considering the circumstances."

"Keep them active. Inform both families and also notify Baines's business partner, Strong. Just say it's to do with forensics."

"Understood. I'm double-checking all numbers to see if any are duplicated. I've also tracked Claire Baldwin's. She had only one. I've called the number a few times but it goes straight to answerphone."

"Leave it now. Cross check Baines's and Stephens's numbers with her account too. With all the coincidences, I have a hunch that you might find a connection."

***

Cyril stood at the back of the auction resting on a shelf that ran across a radiator. The room was not large. A hotchpotch of chairs was organised in lines, leaving two narrow walkways down either side. Along each wall, smaller items of brown furniture were positioned, each displaying its lot number. The auctioneer sat behind what once was a pulpit and to either side of that were two Doric columns painted to look like marble.

Letting his eyes drift around the room, Cyril recognised a few of the people: the odd dealer and a couple of keen amateur art collectors like himself. As their eyes met, there would be smiles and the occasional nod. One pointed to a particular painting on the wall before pulling a fearful face and crossing his fingers. Fortunately, it was a Lowry signed print and Cyril had little interest but he politely mouthed, *Good luck*.

Checking his catalogue, he noted that his lot would be coming up in the next twenty minutes. The only painting he was interested in was *The Coal Cart* by Norman Cornish. He took out a pen and jotted notes to the corner:

Jag forensic results?

Interview with staff at Clear Foods. Outcome?

Claire Baldwin photograph distributed to press and social media? Results?

Librarian: Names, etc. from the day Baines was discovered.

He was sure that none of these factors had been discussed at a briefing nor had they been added to file or the boards.

"Lot 93, The Norman Cornish…"

Cyril was suddenly alert.

Chapter Twenty-Two

Shakti burst into Owen's office wearing a huge smile. A number of heads turned and offered greetings. Walking directly to Owen, she dropped a small parcel into his hand.

"Small for a stick of rock that, Shak!" He looked down at the parcel. "Always loved getting rock when people returned from being away, especially Edinburgh rock; it's so soft, doesn't destroy your teeth like the normal pink stuff."

"Sorry, don't sell rock in France, or Italy for that matter. Saw that though and thought of you."

He opened the packet and looked at the key ring spelling the word, *NICE*.

"Nice?" Owen mumbled. "Thanks."

"Nice not nice... give me strength, man!"

Owen winked, moved around his desk and gave her a hug. "Good to have you back. Have you seen Smirthwaite? You're taking over his part in the investigation and you'll need to get your skates on, things are beginning to warm up."

DC Shakti Misra had been with the team for a good while and she was a reliable officer who worked well, particularly with Owen, having taken him under her wing after the death of a colleague. There was a strong trust and a firm friendship.

Shakti rubbed her hands. "Can't wait."

"Me neither. Thanks for this. I have an appointment in York."

***

The *Clear Foods* factory was not what Owen had been expecting. He had imagined it to be relatively small, tucked away on an industrial estate on the outskirts of York and so to find it nestled on the outer edge of a relatively compact and quaint village came as a pleasant surprise. It was larger than he had envisaged too.

Three articulated lorries queued to the left of a designated delivery gate. Before the first wagon, Owen could see what appeared to be a trapdoor set into the ground. He would later realise that it was a weighbridge, there was also one on the opposite side of the security office for those wagons exiting. He watched as the driver inched the vehicle forward. Once in position, paperwork was passed between the security office and the driver. The lorry then moved away to be lost within the factory confines.

Owen walked to the main entrance. He had made an appointment and as he approached the security office, an attendant immediately greeted him.

"Detective Sergeant Owen?"

Owen held up his ID.

"You're expected. Mr Mott is waiting for you. Have you parked over there?"

Owen nodded and smiled.

"Good, thank you. I'll escort you to his office."

Before moving away, Owen was handed a fluorescent jacket, safety goggles and a hard hat. "Health and Safety."

"Do I not need steel capped boots too?" Owen said tongue in cheek but the joke soared over the man's head.

"No, only if you're in the warehouse working or loading and unloading the wagons but I doubt they'll have you doing that."

Owen smiled.

The office was small but pleasantly organised with one window looking down onto a view of the processing part of the factory. Owen observed what looked like potatoes tumbling down a mesh conveyor belt. Two people at either side watched as they bounced and rolled past. The stainless steel structure looked complex and very efficient.

"Detective Sergeant Owen?"

The voice made Owen jump.

"Sorry, you were engrossed. Chris Mott, I'm one of the factory managers. Pleased to meet you, sorry for the delay. Enjoying the view I see? The machines look complicated don't they? It's quite simple this side of the operation. The conveyors carry different vegetables. Some of those will go to make soups whilst others will be canned. We did try to make a mashed potato many years ago but it didn't catch on."

"I've come to talk to you about Arthur Thorndyke. I believe he was in charge of the area where you had a number of accidents, including one to himself?"

"Thorndyke, yes. He was initially hospitalised, quite serious and he's been off work now for some time. He's been suspended pending the inquiry. As you're aware, there were shortcomings on both sides during that period, one that we're not proud of, I might add. We had, or shall I say we thought we had, trained our staff to an appropriate level when dealing with machines, chemicals and gases. There are rules to keep people in the workplace safe and the factory functioning within the statutory legal requirements. We do, I can assure you, take those responsibilities extremely seriously and even in the most well organised factories and places of work accidents happen. One can never plan for every eventuality, as I feel sure you're aware, especially considering your demanding profession. The majority of incidents here are human error… and by that very fact… accidents! Usually when people lose concentration or simply get it wrong."

"So what happened and what happened to him? I've read the report but I'd like to hear it from you, Mr Mott."

"How long have you got, sergeant?"

Owen looked at his watch. "As long as it takes." He took a Dictaphone from his pocket. "Do you mind? It saves you coming to the station on Fulford Road."

"I think the best thing would be to go to the area where you can see everything first hand. That's why you've been issued with those and that's why it'll take time." He pointed to the safety apparel Owen had placed on the chair.

Within twenty minutes, Owen was standing in front of three caged large white cylinders which reminded him of parts of a rocket. Pipes and valves appeared from the bottom and disappeared to the right. A heavy coating of white frost had formed around some of the lower pipes.

Mott blew on his hands before rubbing them together. "Liquid nitrogen, sergeant. We use it for our purification and freezing tunnels. Food frozen rapidly keeps its flavour. Managed well, it's cheap and exceptionally efficient. It's computerised, the flow and use, even down to when we reorder. To put you in the picture, there are many ways of freezing depending on the product: air freezing, blast freezing, fluid freezing and de-hydro freezing, to name but a few."

Owen looked at Mott. Owen really was not interested in the history of frozen peas, more the story about Thorndyke's errors "So what was the problem on that particular day?" he asked, failing to keep the frustration from his voice.

"Sorry, yes, quite. The pipes travel through to the tunnels along here and then into here." Mott opened a door. "You can see from this monitor that all's well. An alarm would sound if there were a build up, a concentration of nitrogen gas. As you can see we have a normal reading so it's safe to enter. Each operative would carry a personal N2 detector." Mott lifted his jacket to one side and pointed to the bright yellow device attached to his belt. "One of the problems, sergeant, is with red tape. When working with liquid nitrogen we have to monitor the oxygen levels and have a change of atmosphere over a set period; this can be inconvenient as it takes energy to build up a working temperature. Ensuring that the air is changed at regular, statutory intervals, as directed by H&S, is a problem for our engineers in maintaining their energy targets."

Owen was beginning to lose the will to live. "Thorndyke?"

"On that day, Thorndyke was, for some reason yet to be explained, filling a Dewar of liquid nitrogen. A Dewar is a pressurised flask. When liquid nitrogen is stored it boils at a ridiculously low temperature, minus one hundred and ninety-six degrees Celsius. Gas is given off as evaporation and if the liquid were not stored in a vented, pressurised vessel it would simply explode. So, he said that he found a faulty valve and had burned his hands on the metal as a stream of liquid nitrogen, forced out from the valve under pressure, struck and affected his lower abdomen. When I say burned, I mean that those areas affected by the escaping liquid had suffered severe frost damage. It's minus 195, it's comparable to putting your hands into a naked flame considering the temperature differential, and consequently he'd been unable to turn it off. The leaking liquid nitrogen then 'burned' off, evaporated into nitrogen gas and as the area was confined the nitrogen gas filled the space. When it does that the oxygen is pushed out, purged and the nitrogen gas settled. Remember, sergeant, that although nitrogen gas is slightly lighter than oxygen, the cold vapour coming from liquid nitrogen settles. Thorndyke was receiving treatment, he'd moved away from the area but suffered breathing difficulties; no doubt his fight-or-flight instinct kicked in. Sadly, others working in the lower confines of that area were unaware of the danger. I believe you've read the reports?"

"I don't see why it was Thorndyke's fault, surely it was the valve?"

"We have engineers for that. We also don't know why he was filling a Dewar, that's certainly not his job. Had he followed the correct operating procedure, he'd have sounded the alarm and the other employees would have been evacuated from the area and then the valve would have been made safe. The nitrogen gas was going nowhere. Once the staff was clear and the ventilation improved, it would just dissipate, no harm would have been done. That's why we have, and I'm sure the police have, rules and procedures. They're there to keep the staff and the public safe. As it was, he put himself and other members of staff in harm's way."

"If they all had alarms surely they'd have been warned of the build up of nitrogen?"

"And this is what I said. When something goes wrong, the infamous Murphy's Law states that it tends to go wrong in a big way...."

The acronym, FUBAR came into Owen's head straight away. Fucked up beyond all recognition!

"Two had left their gas alarms in their lockers and the other person was well away from the other two. Just so happened the two without alarms were together. This is why the legal side to this incident is not clear cut, there were faults on both sides."

"So how dangerous is liquid nitrogen?" Owen asked, hoping to understand fully the nature of the gas.

"When controlled, like now, it's as safe as houses. Handled properly you have no worries. However, it can be deadly and a force to be reckoned with. Put some in a steel container without a vent and the pressure will become so strong it will destroy it, blow the container apart. These cylinders in front of you are vented for that very purpose. Like all things, give a car to a maniac driver and you have a killing machine. We've seen that too often recently, but handled well and driven safely it's a very different story. Millions of miles are driven every year without a problem, so too with liquid nitrogen, in the hands of a fool it can be lethal."

Those words set alarm bells ringing inside Owen's head.

***

Owen wasted no time. Once in the car, he rang Cyril. "Thorndyke failed to follow procedure, probably thinking he was doing the right thing but... liquid nitrogen, sir. Despite serious cold burns to Thorndyke's hands and lower abdomen as well as suffering breathing problems, Mott didn't consider the man to be a victim. According to him, it was his action that inadvertently put others in danger. He was, as you know, suspended even though he was ill. Mott said that they could never fully understand what he was doing there and they still haven't been able to get a full report from him. Even so, they say that they tried to ensure that he received the appropriate support but he failed to respond to their offers. I thought that the manager wanted to force all the blame onto one man, see an end to it all. A potential scapegoat maybe, sir. Not sure."

"So why get rid of the H&S company that was there to keep operatives and the factory safe if it's one man's error?"

"They allowed things to slip. According to Mott, after the accident and subsequent inspection they were seen to have given inadequate training, that and not following the latest H&S guidelines. Something to do with the number of air changes, the more changes, the greater the cost! They'd worked fewer changes in the past without a problem until Thorndyke's accident and subsequent closure of part of the works."

"Get hold of Strong. I want him to come in and talk to us about the Health and Safety issues around liquid nitrogen. I also want a representative from the gas supplier. As soon as, Owen, as soon as. And Owen, be courteous. It's info we need right at this minute."

Chapter Twenty-Three

Owen rang the bell. He waited in the entrance lobby, conscious of the cyclopic eye of a domed ceiling-mounted camera pointing in his direction. It seemed an age until he heard the door mechanism click. He was a few minutes late for his appointment as his meeting with Colin Strong had taken longer than anticipated but he had managed to organise two people from a gas supply company to talk at a briefing as Cyril had requested.

The waiting room was quiet and he heard the voices of the chiropodist and his patient in a room further up the corridor; they were obviously both running late. Owen stared at the framed posters and diagrams positioned along the walls. Some advertised comfortable and sensible looking shoes whilst one showed a cutaway drawing of a foot. Around the centre of the walls was a border illustrating the outlined silhouettes of different creatures' feet. He tried to match the animals to the feet. The duck, he thought, was the easiest.

Within five minutes, he was sitting facing Craig Gillan, his bare feet stretched out in front of him.

"How's your foot been?"

"It was a little sore to begin with but seems okay now, thanks."

Gillan removed the adhesive pad and inspected the verrucas. "They seem to be healing well, another week and you'll not know that they were there. Your nails, however, could do with a trim. Do you want me to do them while you're here?"

"Thanks."

He collected a tray of instruments from the store. "Solved the mystery murders, Mr Owen, or should we still be trembling in our beds?"

"Still ongoing." To quickly change the subject, he mentioned something that he had touched upon during his previous visit. "Last time I thought you'd burn the plantar warts off with ice, liquid nitrogen. Is it difficult to store and use?"

Gillan clipped the first of Owen's toes, the position of the chiropodist's hand ensuring that the nail travelled towards the floor before answering. "No, it's simple to use, as easy as a laser but a laser doesn't need storage vessels, doesn't need venting. You used to have to store the small Dewar or the flask but now there are more sophisticated ways. Just take the Cryopen, for example. It holds small cartridges containing cold inert gas in liquid form that are safe and easily stored. It's really accurate too, but like all new technology, too expensive for a small practice like this. I have used liquid nitrogen and other freezing gases when I worked in the hospital but here? No longer viable."

There was a pause. "You might recall an issue with a food factory over York way. They had a problem with liquid nitrogen and they were fined heavily for a blatant disregard of Health and Safety guidelines. It was in the press, local and national but no mention of LN. I heard that from one of my clients."

Owen immediately sat up.

"Please try to keep still, Mr Owen. You could have lost a toe!" Gillan smiled. "Only joking."

"Was your client directly involved?"

"I couldn't say… you know how it is with client confidentiality, sorry."

"Do you have the Dewar still, if that's what the containers were called?"

"No, this place is too small to store equipment I no longer need so I sold it. Strangely, there's a ready market."

Owen twitched as the nail clipper cut through a thick nail. He did not ask another question but concentrated on what Gillan was doing to his toes. "That nail seems to have some fungal infection, you'll need to watch that."

***

Cyril had finished working with the communications team. The images of Baldwin and Thorndyke would soon be posted on the North Yorkshire Police social media site. He knew that it was a long shot but one that he had to take. Shakti dashed into his office.

"Check your computer, sir. Mrs Stephens has received a photograph. It's from her husband's missing phone. On receiving it her son called 999. An officer is with her now and the image has been patched through. The recorded call is also filed."

Cyril allowed Shakti to bring up the image as he reached for his reading glasses. They both stared at the computer screen. Cyril moved a little further away trying to discern what he was looking at. From what he could make out, it was a close up of a face.

"We believe it to be Arthur Thorndyke, sir. He's in a freezer according to the report and has been for some time."

"And it was sent using Stephens's phone?" Cyril moved more closely to the screen.

"They're trying to find the location from which the call was made and although that's possible, it could mean nothing. It's a mobile after all." She shrugged. "But at least we'll know if it's in the right area. Here's the message." Shakti moved the cursor to the file icon and clicked the computer mouse.

Which Emergency service do you n—

Jonathan Stephens blurted out his name and address.

Is this your mobile number you're calling from, Jonathan?

Yes, yes. Please listen, please!

Transferring you to the police, Jonathan, stay on this line.

Jonathan, this is the police.

My father died a couple of weeks ago and we've just received a photograph of what looks like... There was a long pause. *A frozen corpse... When Mum's phone rang it showed Dad's picture, the one taken of him in France, the one she loved so she knew it was from Dad... problem is the police have been looking for the phone. It's been missing since he died. We need to see someone, we need help, to see the police. My mum's in bits, crying and shaking, she needs help.*

Paramedics and police are already on their way. Stay on the line, Jonathan. Where's your mother now?

She's here with me. He used to see a face... my dad that is... for weeks before he died... a person... I think it frightened him but he'd never show it. He...

The sound of a siren could be heard in the background.

Someone's here now. Thanks, thanks, bye.

Cyril turned and looked at Shakti. "Get that written up and then we're going to pay Jonathan a visit."

***

It did not take a detective to deduce that the young man was clearly shaken and far less confident than he had appeared.

"Mum's lying down." He fidgeted with his hands putting his fingers together and then spreading them over the phone that was on the kitchen table. "They gave her a sedative. Our GP came out, made a special trip. He's calling later too. She never goes to the doctor." It was clear that Jonathan had been chewing his lip.

"Is that the phone on which you received the call?" Cyril nodded towards the mobile on the table.

He shook his head. "The other police officer put it in a bag and removed it whilst the lady officer remained here. This one's mine. I'm keeping it near just in case."

Cyril turned and acknowledged the officer sitting in the corner near the Aga. "Gone to Technical, sir, as requested."

"Tell us about the face, the person you thought your dad had seen."

There was a long pause before Jonathan spoke. "Started a while back, I can't give you an exact date but maybe March. I think March because I clearly remember him coming in with some flowers he'd left in the car as a surprise for my mum's birthday the following day. It was late. When he came in, he was quite shaken which is not like my father at all. He said he'd seen someone at the end of the driveway, just staring, a mask-like face focussed on him, but then he thought he'd been mistaken, perhaps a trick of the light. My father was leaning into the car and as he was about to get out he said that he saw him through the windscreen. When he moved away from the car, the figure was gone. He told me that he went down the drive but there was no one, nothing."

"You said it was late. How late? Was it dark?"

"About eleven. There are lights down the drive and on the gateposts. That's probably why he was slightly confused."

"Had your father been drinking?" Shakti asked.

"Wine with dinner and some Champagne, mother's favourite. Not enough to make him hallucinate though." Jonathan paused again. "I'd wanted to tell you this when you first came round to inspect the car but Mum said that Dad had nightmares and occasionally saw demons and devils. Sometimes he'd wake up screaming and she thought that the face and the figure were all part of that. As you know, he liked cocaine too. I only found this out after he died, when the search dog found a small quantity in the garage."

"Do you have any idea where the drugs came from?"

He shook his head. "As I've just said. It's news to me. What with his health problems… I was shocked. I don't believe he took any that night. He appeared neither drunk nor under the influence of drugs. He had a cold, that's all, I remember that."

Shakti took a quick look at Cyril. It did not go unnoticed. The significance was not lost on him.

"Did your mum take it too?" Cyril asked.

Jonathan shrugged. "I don't! I can assure you of that."

"Did anyone else see this face, the late night figure?" Cyril asked keeping his eyes on Jonathan's expression as he considered the question.

"Do you know what? I felt as though someone was there the other day. I'd taken the Jaguar from the garage and I felt as though someone was watching me. It was bright daylight too."

"Did you look carefully?"

"Yes, nothing. To be honest I felt a little scared and got in the car and drove away."

Cyril looked at Shakti. He nodded, just enough for his colleague to notice. She folded her notebook and took out a card.

"Should you feel as though you're being watched again, call me no matter what the time." She smiled and pushed the card in front of him. "We're here to help."

Chapter Twenty-Four

Stuart Park looked through the logbooks for Stephens's aircraft. It surprised him that there was an engine log, a propeller log and one for the aircraft airframe itself. Noting that it was based on flight hours, he swiftly checked through each before boxing them and signing a receipt. The one good thing was that the logs were controlled by the flying club so he could be assured of their accuracy. The aircraft was occasionally used by club members to learn to fly an aircraft with a variable pitch propeller and retractable undercarriage.

The acknowledgement that the receptionist recognised both William Baines and Claire Baldwin when he showed the photographs had surprised Stuart. It was one of those moments when you do not quite believe what you are hearing. He had hoped that there might be a connection between Thorndyke and Stephens but to get a positive visual ID for two out of the three was not dissimilar to winning the lottery.

"Funny really, I remember them quite clearly, it's the circumstances you remember and then everything seems to click into place."

"Circumstances?" Stuart Park leaned forward, ready to note down what she was about to say.

"The weather had been dreadful, the weekend especially. David had returned from a trip to France and the cross wind here at Leeds Bradford, we still call it Yeadon, can be dreadful. It was the day he was due in. We're on a hill you see and exposed to all the vagaries the wind can throw at us. Anyway, he was expected in according to his flight plan at 1500 but he arrived early. The cloud base was low and a storm was threatening, contrary to the forecast.

It was touch and go whether or not he'd need to divert but he's a good pilot, safe. Anyway, ten minutes after landing, the heavens opened and he came in here wet through after getting the plane into the hangar. On that occasion he received a visit from customs, just his luck! Gave me a bottle of Champagne, made my day."

Stuart was a little confused, neither knowing where the story was leading nor what relevance it had regarding the photographs.

"That's what I mean by circumstance, the storm and the Champagne, you remember things. When he eventually came in here, he laughed and said he'd never fly again as it was the worst and most frightening flight he'd ever made. IMC all the way." To Stuart's inquisitive look, she explained. "Flying in cloud, officer. He was buzzing, probably all the adrenalin. I see that a lot after a student has just completed a first solo circuit or cross-country flight. It's like it saps everyone's energy.

"Two days later, I heard his helicopter land. It was then that I noticed the couple, thought that they were husband and wife. I didn't speak to them that day but the next time I saw him I pulled his leg about his promise never to fly again and we laughed about it. He said that the couple worked for him and that it was a reward flight. I should have their forms. Everyone coming into the hangars has to fill in a form… Well, the pilot does it for them they just read and sign it, as if we don't have enough red tape! Informs them of safety, just as you've done. You all have to sign your life away when you come in here. He left the forms in the hangar, there's a specific tray." She giggled as she moved towards a filing cabinet. "So sad to hear about David, though. Who'd have thought it? A heart attack and at his age too. I shouldn't be surprised as it happened to one of our instructors a few years back. One day he's flying students all day and the next he keels over at a football match. He'd just had his medical too!"

Park looked at the two forms. The addresses on both were that of Stephens but the names were different. Both forms appeared to be signed by the same hand. "Can read neither. David should have been a doctor with handwriting like that!"

"No, I can't make out the names on these forms and it looks like the same person has signed them both," Stuart remarked.

She took them back before looking at him. "These were handed in and simply filed. No one was injured or hurt while here and so they've never been looked at again until today."

"I'll need copies of those. And you definitely have never seen this man? Take your time."

She looked again at Thorndyke's photograph. The door opened behind her and a man in his forties appeared. He nodded to Stuart Park and blew on his hands before rubbing them.

"Frank, have you seen this man before?" She handed him the photograph. "Sorry, Frank, this is DC Stuart Park from the North Yorkshire Police. They're looking into the death of David Stephens. Frank is my husband. He owns the flying club or in these days of emancipation, I should say we own the flying club."

"Sad affair that," Frank said. "How's Jonathan taken it? Don't suppose he'll be up for flying for some time. Too many memories."

"It's never easy to lose one's father at that age and at such a critical time in the young man's life."

"So who's this?" Frank asked focussing on the image. "I've certainly seen him before. Yes, how could I possibly forget?"

Stuart's heart leapt. "Arthur Thorndyke?" he asked, knowing that he was leading him. Park noticed his expression suddenly change. "No, he's not who I thought it was. Thorndyke you said?"

Stuart nodded. "Who did you think it was?"

"Albert Baldwin, may have been Arthur. I'm not sure. How could I forget the man? It'll be on file."

Both his wife and Park looked at each other and then back at Frank.

"Absolute waste of bloody space. You must remember him, Pat. He was with us less than two months, temporary. Said he'd always wanted to learn to fly and would work for nothing in exchange for some flying lessons. David Stephens supported him financially too. Originally he flew with other students. He had two single lessons if I remember correctly, flew with David a few times.

More than likely took pity on the guy. He ran that Tomahawk into the back of a client's Chipmunk, removed part of the tail and damaged the prop when he was helping to close the place down one evening."

"David Stephens?"

"Yes. David was very generous, often took students with him if Jonathan wasn't flying. That's the kind of person David was. Bloody sad, his passing."

Pat turned to the computer and typed in the name Baldwin. "It's a while ago. A. Baldwin, thirty-eight. We have his address as, The Main Street, Appleton Roebuck, just outside Tadcaster."

"Bloody posh address for the guy. Always arrived in a battered, old van. Dripped oil, I remember that. You both look as though I've said something wrong." He tossed the photograph onto the desk. "He said he'd received a small inheritance that had allowed him to give up working for twelve months to realise his dream."

"Was he married? Kids?" Stuart Park asked with a degree of optimism.

"I think so. A daughter, Vicky, if I remember correctly. I know because I thought it sounded old-fashioned. She'd be in her late-teens I'm guessing from what he said. I never saw her so the age thing is a stab in the dark."

Stuart's skin tingled on hearing the name Vicky. He extended it to Victoria.

"She lived with her mother. Baldwin even made a mess of his marriage. As I've said, waste of time and space and believe me, you can ill afford incompetents in my line of work. Now if there's nothing else… any chance of coffee for the team, Pat?" He pointed to the office clock suggesting the coffee was late.

"Just one more thing. You said he was thirty-eight. Can you describe him?"

Stuart could see that he had just poked the bear.

"Medium build, about my height. Hair colour as your picture suggests, dark. Rubbed his hands a good deal. Kept himself to himself. To be honest he was a bit of a miserable bastard but then people sometimes say that of me." A forced smile appeared on his lips. "Now, if you're done?"

***

It was when Stuart Park returned to Harrogate that he called control for as much information as possible on an Arthur or Albert Baldwin living in or near Appleton Roebuck. It was then that Stuart suddenly remembered about the name and the coincidences with the addresses of those missing or dead. He dialled Cyril's number.

"Bennett."

"We have a match for two people at the flying club. Baldwin and…" He let the first name hover for a while.

"Thorndyke the second?" Cyril asked and from his tone, he was clearly not in the mood for guessing games.

"Baines, sir."

"Baines?"

"However, there's more. The owner recognised Thorndyke not as Arthur Thorndyke but as an Albert or Arthur Baldwin. Worked there in a past life. He had one child, a girl and the girl's name…."

"Don't tell me, Victoria."

"Sir."

"How the bloody hell does that stack up? If this gets any foggier we'll be flying on instruments ourselves. We're already in the bloody dark."

Park was amazed how swiftly Cyril connected the two but then that was why he was a DCI and not a DC; Park felt quite humbled.

"Do we have an address?" Cyril asked.

Park could detect a degree of enthusiasm in his boss's voice and quickly responded. "Being checked but my guess is it's false, sir. Pat, the receptionist and wife of the club's owner, recognised Baines and Claire Baldwin but could not recall ever meeting Thorndyke. It was Pat's husband Frank who clicked on to it resembling this Baldwin chap. Originally remembered his name as Albert but then wasn't sure. Find it strange that she didn't even take a second look. She was adamant that she'd not seen him and yet his name was filed as an A Baldwin."

"Get everything uplifted onto HOLMES. With luck, if there are links they'll be tracked. Get info on Arthur Baldwin then check it with Claire's history. Something's not squaring up."

Chapter Twenty-Five

Owen started the meeting, informing everyone that Colin Strong and two representatives from a producer and supplier of liquid nitrogen would be joining them at eleven. "They want to keep it informal. Elijah and Noah will brief us on the stuff." Owen smiled and nodded at Cyril. "I kid you not, two for the price of one!"

Cyril smiled to himself and thought immediately of April. He turned and grinned at her. "With names like that sounds right up your street, your chosen subject."

She pulled a sarcastic smile in return. "We'll see."

Owen continued. "Also, Forensics have reported back on the inspection of Stephens's Jaguar. Nothing. I got the distinct feeling it came with the title, *I told you so!*"

A number of officers chuckled.

It was April who brought the meeting to order. "So we know that Baines and Claire Baldwin were with Stephens in March. Interestingly, that's well before the accident took place at the factory and we'd assumed that Baines and Baldwin had never met. How wrong we were."

Cyril scribbled the word *March* onto the pad in front of him and circled it.

"They were there for a reward flight the receptionist told Stuart Park. Stephens took friends and employees occasionally as a mark of gratitude. The trouble is, neither was employed by Stephens and according to Mrs Stephens, she could never recall seeing either of them. Remember, however, that she's still in a state of shock."

"Was it just a local flight?"

"According to the records, yes. Out and back to Yeadon looking at Stephens's log. There were no names mentioned for that day's flight in his flying log but then there's no legal requirement to do so. The forms kept by the club were as good as useless. We're also relying on memory regarding Thorndyke or Arthur Baldwin or Albert. Yes, he worked for the flying club but he could be anyone who looked similar to Thorndyke. According to Claire's birth certificate her actual father was a Graham and not an Arthur or an Albert and there were no other children, just Claire, the daughter."

Stuart Park added that the owner of the flying club was adamant, immediately querying the name. "I guess when an employee partly destroys two of your client's aircraft you kind of remember them. Mind, he even questioned the Christian name so… but that was filed."

"Remembering the daughter, Victoria, can't just be a coincidence, surely?" someone piped in.

"Let's focus on what we do know." Owen stood and moved to one of the whiteboards. "We definitely know that Baldwin liked to keep cocaine in the fridge, Stephens liked to dabble and Thorndyke? According to Chris Mott from *Clear Foods,* he was partial to a drink but then again, he may also have had other bad habits. It has to be said that alcohol was never referenced on his disciplinary record. His poor professional attitude, bad time keeping and failure to follow procedures were cited and may well indicate that he liked a drink but it's purely conjecture. The traits he exhibited could certainly be similar to the Baldwin employed at the flying club. He might even have been under the influence of either alcohol or drugs when he damaged the two aircraft. The odd one out, the one without any vices, appears to be Baines."

Cyril was surprised by Owen's vocabulary, the words *cited* and *conjecture* within one sentence were certainly not Owen's normal style and as for the word *trait,* he would have thought Owen to presume that was something for carrying tea and biscuits on.

"But looking at the photograph of the frozen corpse, the answers to those questions may well remain a secret unless we can find out where and with whom he'd been staying the weeks prior to his death. His last known address has brought nothing other than it's clearly the home of a man who, let's say, had a few problems, not least alcohol and drugs."

Cyril looked at Stuart Park and immediately noticed that something was puzzling him. "Penny for them, Stuart."

"Just a thought. Could the aircraft have landed at a farm strip or remote location on that flight? I recall Jonathan Stephens describing their continental visits and saying that once in the country and after clearing customs, you can go wherever you please. They were here and staying within the country so could they, as the lad said, go anywhere and land anywhere? Granted if they landed at a registered airfield then that would have to be logged but…"

"From my experience, they could," said Cyril. "You're right and that's something we'll never be able to discover, particularly if it were for illegal purposes. You're thinking drugs… moving drugs. If so why take two spectators?"

There was a knock at the door and it opened quickly. A female officer popped her head round and looked directly at Cyril.

"Sorry, a moment, sir. It's important."

Cyril went to the door.

"This has just come through and I thought you'd need it immediately. Mrs Baines received it, texted to her mobile." The officer passed the image to Cyril. "After referencing with the photographs we hold it looks like Claire Baldwin, sir."

Cyril could see Claire's features through the layer of ice particles that covered her face and from his recollection of the photograph attached on the incident room board it was Claire. He brought the reading glasses from the top of his head and looked more closely. Her eyes were open, just the hint of blue from the iris seemingly trapped, frozen like a blurred opal. He also looked at the iced garland of what could only be described as ivy across her neck.

"It was sent from William Baines's missing phone."

"What's that in her mouth?"

"We believe it's a potato, just as in Thorndyke's photograph."

Cyril was taken aback and looked more closely. "A potato. I wonder why someone's done that."

Neither spoke as Cyril inspected the photograph, his arm outstretched compensating for the fact that he had lifted his glasses onto his head.

"One potato, two potatoes, three potatoes, four… used to play it at school for picking who was to be next. Next person to be *It*, sir."

Cyril raised his eyes and looked directly at the young detective.

"It," he sounded each letter. "*It*, the person to be chosen for a game. Do something for me. Find and copy as many of the variants of that rhyme as you can and let me have them as soon as. Have we tracked down any known relatives, boyfriends, acquaintances?"

"We know the mother lives in Essex, Woodford Green according to an interview held with local police. Last saw her daughter earlier this year, couldn't be more specific. Since university they rarely saw each other. The father went off the scene fairly early in her life. We know that he was a Graham and not an Arthur or Albert. Mother and daughter had what can only be described as a turbulent relationship. We've tracked down a boyfriend though. The details should be with you. Have you received them?"

Cyril felt a sinking feeling in the pit of his stomach as he metaphorically reached out a hand as if to keep another plate spinning. "I'll check after this meeting. Thanks. Potatoes, as soon as, thanks." He smiled and watched her leave to give him time to assimilate the latest piece of the jigsaw.

"We have another piece of the puzzle, people." He removed his electronic cigarette. He needed nicotine and he needed it right at that very moment. All eyes followed him. He fumbled for the glasses perched on his head before holding up the photograph. "Claire Baldwin, another person frozen in time, kept on ice so to speak, and another inventive use of a missing phone. Everything seems to be linked with bloody cold. We've had liquid nitrogen, ice, and frozen bodies."

"Cocaine is known as *snow* and crystal meth is referred to as *ice* owing to its appearance," April offered. "Two, possibly three, have known connections with one of those drugs. Both drugs, as I'm sure we're all aware, are produced differently, one coming from leaves whereas crystal meth comes from a chemical synthesis. However, they can be both smoked in the same way. Give a similar high too, a high that brings with it an increase in alertness. It's referred to as *amping* as in over-amped electrical wire. Wagon drivers have been known to use it on particularly long and difficult hauls."

"Pilots facing difficult flights?" Stuart Park asked.

"Same thing, I imagine."

Cyril frowned. He had certainly never heard of it being used during the time when he had held a licence.

April continued. "Cocaine gives a high for about fifteen minutes whereas ice, crystal meth, can keep you buzzing for eight to twelve hours. However, each will have its own downside."

Owen checked his watch and stood. "Sorry, our visitors will be in the meeting room in ten minutes and considering what we've just seen, I think four people will be enough to attend: Smirthwaite, Park, Shakti and myself. We'll report back."

"Owen!" Cyril called as he went through the door. "Remember what we said about Strong. You'll get a feeling."

The four left as Cyril checked off assignments to those remaining. He then went to see if Claire's boyfriend's file was on the system.

Chapter Twenty-Six

The three phones were placed in front of him on the work surface. All were by the same manufacturer but could be differentiated by either a personalised case, a designation number or letter. The SE looked the smallest of the three. Mobile phones seemed to have come full circle. Like a small brick originally, the manufacturers' quest was to reduce the size and within a couple of years they had succeeded but they were back, slim yes, but so big.

"Whoever would have thought that the world needed so many mobile phones?" he said as his gloved hands moved over each phone. "One potato, two potatoes, three potatoes, four…"

After a few recitals, he had removed two handsets before placing them in a cardboard box. Their time was done for the moment, but he would need Claire's phone shortly. He stood and moved through to the conservatory and admired the view, instinctively rubbing his hands. He glanced at the stone outhouse.

***

The Detective Constable had placed the photographs on the counter at the *Bauhaus Champagne and Cocktail Bar*. He watched as each member of staff viewed the images and noted their responses. Two members of staff recalled seeing both Baines and Baldwin, but they could not remember whether they had seen them together or separately. The third person, Thorndyke, nobody recognised.

***

The notes on Claire's boyfriend could only be regarded as sketchy at best. Her mother recalled seeing him once and had made it clear that Claire had a habit of changing her men on a regular basis. The one thing that made Cyril look twice was the man's age. On the whiteboard Cyril drew an extended green line, a circuitous route to some space. He added the details, his name, Eddie Lawson, and his date of birth. If the date was correct then he would have been nearly twenty years her senior. Cyril wrote AGE in block capitals to ensure that others would see the relevance.

Replacing the top to the pen, he studied the boards. He knew that there was something within all of these notes and images that was staring the team clearly in the face. He knew that the critical clue was more than likely hidden within the obvious. He recalled the words: *The face, have you seen the face? He was scared of a person. This face was looking back at him.*

Cyril reflected upon the notes and the reports on Stephens and Baldwin before moving his eyes along to the next board to search out the two photographs of Thorndyke and Claire Baldwin. Their blind eyes looked back defiantly as if mocking his inability to find a connection. Were the photographs deliberately planned?

"As requested, sir, the information on the rhyme."

Lost in his thoughts the words, Cyril was startled. He turned to face the officer to whom he had spoken with earlier. She held out some sheets of A4 paper.

"From what I can get from the Internet, they're all very similar. Some count up to ten but the more common one goes up to seven as in *seven potatoes… more.* They were known as counting or 'dipping' games. It refers to them as a way of starting a game, to find who was to be *It.* Kids would stand in a line with their fists clenched and one person would be the counter tapping his or her fist on top of the others. When it came round to their own fists, they would tap them either on their chin, like this, or tap alternate fists." She demonstrated both methods.

"When you got to the word *more,* then the fist you landed on was 'out', eliminated and the child put it behind their back. They began again and when both fists were 'out' then that person stood away, until they were all eliminated apart from one. The last boy or girl standing, you could say."

It was the word *eliminated* that had a resounding effect on Cyril. He turned and looked at the frozen feature of the two faces. "Eliminated… until only one remains and then they are…. *It*… whatever *It* can be in this strange game." He turned back, took the notes she had made and thanked her. Picking up a pen, he jotted the word *Eliminated* along the top of each board.

"That was some bloody show, sir," Owen said with a great deal of enthusiasm.

Cyril turned. "Really, and what was that?"

"Strong and the double act. Just to get things clear from that meeting, I don't believe Strong is involved in any criminal way. You asked me to come back with a gut feeling."

Cyril nodded. "And the double act?"

"Very clever. They brought in a Dewar and some liquid nitrogen. Blimey, if science lessons had been like that at school I'd have been hooked. It's magical to watch, and according to the guys it's as safe as the handler. If you know the rules it's simple, but if you fail to adhere to them it can have a habit of seriously biting you."

Cyril leaned against the wall, his face revealing intense interest.

"Poured some into a bowl, then stuck a flower into it before removing it. He crushed it in his hands."

"Did he wear protective clothing?"

"Only safety glasses but he said that really they were unnecessary. He poured the stuff into a bowl of water. Huge clouds of white rolling smoke tumbled and flowed everywhere. He even let some fall onto his hand and run off without damage. The danger is if you stick your digit into the stuff apparently. And then there was a trick with a balloon…"

Cyril raised his hand. "I thought it purged the air of oxygen and that would be dangerous."

"I talked about that very thing. It depends on the size of the space and the quantity of liquid nitrogen. He gave me this chart. A Dewar of this size full to capacity with liquid nitrogen and left open in an enclosed vehicle would push out all of the oxygen as every vehicle is vented and anyone stepping into that car would immediately be affected by it. Initially they'd be rendered unconscious and then they would die."

"The vents on the Jaguar and the Volvo were closed."

"According to them, a car isn't a sealed box. When the nitrogen gas is released the pressure builds, but in a car there are enough gaps to push away the oxygen and prevent too great a pressure build up. If the vents were closed it was deliberate to allow a quicker…" He paused and looked at some notes he had written on the back of his hand "… Enrichment of nitrogen. Importantly, to create a safe space you simply let air flood back in."

"Open the doors and leave them ajar so that there's no trace. The flattened carpet that Forensics discovered was probably where someone positioned the Dewar or flask."

"You're now asking the same question I am, sir. Who has or had access to liquid nitrogen?"

Cyril raised his eyebrows. "Thorndyke? But he's dead, frozen."

"What about Paul Ashton? He kept it in the cocktail bar."

"Stephens had just saved him from bankruptcy. Never went near the aircraft or was seen at the flying club. Make some enquiries. Check on their distributor. It's worthy of some time."

Chapter Twenty-Seven

He lined up seven potatoes on the dark grey work surface. All were about the same size and shape, obviously chosen for their consistency. Music drifted from the lounge, an orchestral number, containing a plaintive plea from a soprano. He had chosen this piece as it perfectly suited the morning's clarity and the task that lay ahead. He emptied a polythene bag of coloured plastic pieces; ears, lips, eyes, onto the surface. Picking up various plastic facial features, he pushed them into each potato. The point attached to each perforated the potato's shallow skin allowing the vegetable to bleed transparent, starchy fluid. He giggled occasionally, interrupting the melody as each potato took on the appearance of a disgruntled face. He constructed every character with care; the ears, nose, and, usually by choice, a sad mouth. He had even selected the type of plastic hat to either match the colour of certain parts or the character's demeanour. The fifth one, however, he adorned with a large, green moustache for no apparent reason.

"You never expected that! How very, very smart for a potato, a perfect appendage, even if I do say so myself!"

The final potato, created to look like a policeman, was wearing a hat comprising a shield-shaped badge labelled, 'Spud 1'. The *officer* sported a smiling, upturned mouth, the only face in the line-up that was depicted with a positive expression; the others all appeared sad. Like a child, he took the final potato and bounced it down the line as if on parade and inspecting the others.

"Very smart. Chin up, cowboy. Nice moustache. Oh! Look at you, first in the line!" He returned it to the end.

Once satisfied with his work, he adjusted the setting on Claire's phone camera to *video* before placing it on a small flexible tripod in preparation, ready to focus on the seven Mr Potato Heads sitting in a neat line. He stood and started the music again, a specific piece he had planned to match the moment's mood. He rubbed his hands and blew on them before picking up the phone. Slowly panning along the row of heads, he paused momentarily at each one to allow all the features to be seen and fully appreciated. Only then did he move on. Once done, the phone's camera was positioned at a suitable distance to capture them all in the row. He stood and changed the music, an opera, for him, a total contrast to the previous piece as it commenced giving a more intense and sinister atmosphere. He was ready for the denouement. If all went to plan well then the effect would be perfect. He pressed the record button.

A gloved hand slowly came into shot, removing one potato, then the second whilst quietly and slowly whispering the rhyme in an exaggerated French accent in time to his hand's movement:

One potato… two potatoes… three potatoes, four.

Five potatoes… six potatoes… seven potatoes.

Mort.

On whispering the word *mort*, sounding like the word *more*, the French word for dead, he let his hand hover over the final, remaining potato head before deliberately removing his hand. The camera stayed focussed for a few seconds on the last head, allowing the viewer time to see clearly the police potato's features. It was only then removed and the camera was kept running, the music gaining in strength and intensity as if rushing and tumbling; a plaintive cry that sounded emotionally close and yet seemingly at a distance. Hidden hands quickly spun the upturned, grinning mouth round through one hundred and eighty degrees. The whole of the potato's facial demeanour was changed, the downturned mouth immediately bringing an air of sadness to match the melancholy of the music. It was returned to the work surface so that the camera could focus fully on it once more. Hopefully for him, importantly, the subtle but significant change would be noticed. Within thirty seconds he switched off the camera.

***

Julie sat opposite Cyril. The Italian restaurant was small and a favourite. Tomaso Wilkinson, the chef, had tried to tempt Cyril away from his usual dish but had failed. He had also observed that he was not his usual self. Resting a hand on Cyril's shoulder he spoke quietly and sensitively. "Next time, Mr Bennett, next time." He smiled at Julie and returned to the kitchen.

"Next time. Thanks, Tom."

Although the conversation was not as flowing as usual there was something about the restaurant's familiarity, its comforting aromas and ambience that brought them back time after time. Julie gave Cyril space and observed her man who seemed distant and often deep in thought. She watched him toy with and rearrange the bowl of risotto, his favourite dish, but seldom did she see him eat.

"Are you eating that or are you just going to maul it to death?" Julie reached across and tapped his hand. There was no anger, threat nor admonishment. "Still undecided about the Bentley or is it work?"

He put the fork down, removed his napkin and stood. "Do you mind if we just walk?" He held out his hand and a shallow smile cracked his lips. "Sorry…but…"

Julie was taken aback by his sudden move. "No… no, not at all."

Cyril helped her with the shawl she had brought, paid and sent an apology to Tom. "Please tell him he will choose my meal next time."

The light summer evening lifted Cyril's mood as they strolled hand in hand along the edge of The Stray. Only the light breeze whispered in the sun-dappled leaves contrasting with the low rumble of the traffic.

"Four people dead, two possibly through natural causes but the fact that we know someone has access to the dead men's phones tells us everything we want to know. We both had serious concerns regarding the two fatalities from the outset and now with the frozen bodies, it seems we're looking for one person, someone who maybe has an axe to grind, someone who is out to seek revenge or, and this is the worst case scenario for me as a bobby, someone who is just doing it for the fun of it, the buzz of killing, the challenge."

Cyril turned to look at Julie. "Because they can. These people are the most difficult to track down as they've spent time and care in the planning. History tells us that they're usually intelligent, often scheming and underhand, possibly secretive, and without any doubt, extremely calculating in their actions. They've been fathers, uncles, neighbours. They're chameleons, shadows and invisible all at the same time and to cap that, for me and my team, they're a pain in the arse. We've seen that so often in the past… Neilson, Lee and then we have the so-called Yorkshire Ripper. How he managed to escape capture for so long…"

"With the advances in forensics that we have today, Cyril, he'd have been caught far sooner than he was."

"That may well be the case. I personally don't believe that. Human nature brings human error and you only need to miss one vital clue and that gives them the opportunity to take another life. It's a feat to them, like climbing a mountain. Often they don't care about themselves, they just want to see how far they can get, how many victims, how much suffering they can inflict. As I say, it's a game."

"What about the link; the cold and the ice? Surely the possible use of liquid nitrogen, the bodies in the freezer… That's the route the investigation is following?" Julie sounded convinced.

"Yes," he paused and looked around and then skyward. "Let's not rule out the aircraft, the cocaine and our knowledge that these people knew each other before the first death. Strangely that death was of the man who seemed to bring them together in the first place. Who did what to whom? And if that's the case, how long ago?"

"Thorndyke could have been dead well before Stephens. We know almost to the day when Claire Baldwin went missing and therefore have an approximate of her time of her death. Thorndyke's the only one we're unsure of. He's the unknown in the equation. We've still have no idea as to when and how he died."

They sat on a bench. The horizon was turning into warm lines of rich colours that seemed to be smudged into what became a perfect late evening sky. The sun hovered still just above the trees silhouetting the church spire in the far distance. A dog barked somewhere behind them and Julie turned to look as the owner threw a ball.

"It's April!" Julie pronounced, grateful to break the conversation that had seemed to linger near to its conclusion moments before.

Cyril turned to see her throwing a ball for Ralph, a Great Dane. The dog's gangly legs propelled him along in a clumsy, uncoordinated but efficient manner.

"She's done wonders with that dog since she got it," he said, a smile coming to his lips for the first time since leaving the restaurant. "It was such a sad case. I feel a little like Ralph; clumsy and less coordinated the older I get. Sometimes it's as if I can't see the wood for the trees." He lifted Julie's hand and kissed it. "Our killer wants to be found, why else would he send the photographs, why play the game using the dead men's phones? Why tell us that he's…" Cyril paused and frowned before stating what he believed to be the obvious. "A serial killer?"

The sun dipped quickly behind the trees and the sky turned a deep red. Cyril did not fail to see the prophetic irony and he laughed, leaned over and kissed Julie. "Red sky at night."

Ralph bounded towards them, a deep bark breaking their thoughts. Julie waved towards April who immediately came jogging over.

"Evening. Hope Ralph hasn't disturbed your quiet time."

Cyril pulled at Ralph's ears and rubbed his head. The dog yawned.

***

Cyril stood looking out of the bay window of Julie's apartment. The streetlights still cast an orange glow as they competed with the early dawn's growing light. He smiled thinking that slowly, this warm sodium light was being replaced by the more energy efficient LED white. He did not fail to see a metaphor for his own life and career. Progress, he knew, was an inevitable factor in the passing of time and in the changes within one's career. It seemed only natural that his mind should turn to Wendy, his stepmother. He should call her soon. It had been a while and he had promised himself that he would maintain contact. He sipped his coffee between inhaling the menthol vapour from his electronic cigarette and his thoughts turned to the Bentley. He must also make a decision about that and his heart sank a little.

Chapter Twenty-Eight

The relocation of the North Yorkshire Police Headquarters from Newby Wiske to Alverton Court had brought a number of local complaints, not because the police were leaving but because of the building's pending future. It had to be said that progress and technology made demands on a modern police force, and the old hall no longer met its needs.

The replacement was deemed perfect. Until recently, the new building had looked across to the old Northallerton Prison but the demolition teams had moved in and swept away all but the listed buildings. First built in 1788, its time, like Newby Wiske, was at an end for the maintenance of law and order.

Cyril turned off Crosby Road and into the Police Headquarters.

Within fifteen minutes he was waiting to see the Chief Constable; a mixed blessing at any time but today it was one element of his responsibility Cyril could have done without. He believed he had more important things to do. Looking around he realised quickly that the charm of the old hall had been replaced by modern-day efficiency or so they had convinced everyone. *A clock is only as good as the person who winds it up*, he thought. Noticing the brass plaque positioned to the side of the double doors, he stood and walked across knowing whom it commemorated:

In Memory of DS Liz Graydon who died…

Cyril brought his hand to his lips, kissed it and placed it on the plaque without reading further; it was carved in his memory, he did not need to. He had read it so often on The Police Roll of Honour Trust site. "Miss you young lady. Miss you."

To focus his mind and try to leave the past behind, he recalled that much of the contents of Newby Wiske had gone for auction in Scotland and Cyril had been delighted to secure a Robert 'Mouseman' Thompson bowl, a souvenir. He had remembered seeing it on one of the many tables by the staircase on his numerous visits and had just wanted to keep something as a memento, something that brought the past into the present.

It was only upon entering the Chief Constable's office that Cyril realised that things do not always change for the better. He stared at the desk facing him, *The Eiger*, as he had always called it was still there, maybe not as high but certainly it was present; a horizontal filing system of loose papers and documents secured by pebbles and rocks of differing sizes and colours. A second feeling of security embraced him, knowing that, like himself, you could not teach old dogs new tricks.

After accepting coffee but rejecting the guided tour, Cyril was soon on his way back to Harrogate. It was only then that the idea came to him. The obvious that had been staring him in the face struck him like a slap and he cursed quietly for not having noticed the connection sooner.

***

Within twenty minutes Cyril pulled up outside the Flying School. A quick call to control after leaving Northallerton had secured an appointment with the Chief Flying Instructor, a Bob Ryan. A large aeronautical chart of the north of England was spread out in front of Cyril and Ryan on the planning table.

"You could have used mine, you didn't have to buy this one."

"I'll need to take it with me," said Cyril. "Have you been here long?"

"It's one of the biggest clubs in the north east and I've been flying in this area for years. Without blowing my own trumpet, I think I can honestly say that I know every official and unofficial landing site. I often mark out specific fields in mind when my students are working on their engine failure scenarios. A number of wealthy landowners and farmers have their own strips too, although we see a lot more using helicopters now. It's the convenience. Many are still involved here to enjoy their fixed-wing pleasures; bit of a drug as you may well remember."

The word made Cyril turn quickly and it did not go unnoticed. "Indeed. I see you offer customs and immigration facilities here."

"Not wholly. I'd use Leeds Bradford if I were flying to the continent regularly but we offer a service by appointment only. Suits our members and those visiting from abroad. So to focus on your enquiry, Detective Chief Inspector…" Ryan marked the possible landing sites he knew using a red chinagraph pencil to circle the farms and the buildings. There were eight. "They're mostly used throughout the summer. Some keep older type aircraft and hangar them on site but it varies. Mind you, I have seen aircraft on the ground in a number of unusual locations in my time. I often wonder what they're up to." He turned and smiled whilst raising his eyebrows.

"Microlights?" Cyril quizzed.

"No, a mixed bag. Once saw a twin engine Cessna parked on the moor. Called that in, what with people smuggling you can never be too sure."

"Would anyone know? Can you land anywhere, the odd field, old airstrip?"

"If you know the lie of the land and have the owner's permission, why not? Just picking a field and landing could be wrought with dangers and I'd certainly never recommend that unless the big fan at the front of the plane has decided to stop… when it does, it's amazing how suddenly every field looks inviting."

"If I were a qualified member of your club and I hired that Cherokee outside, would I be able to just go off and land where I liked?"

"If you're qualified, you should know what you're doing. We assume that you don't want to kill yourself and so we have to trust you to fly according to your training and qualifications. The answer is yes, within reason. May I ask why you wish to know?" He paused. "Maybe I get the idea, seeing it's the police doing the asking: aircraft, continent, smuggling, people, drugs? If it's people, then you have to land, but for drugs you don't. Why take risks you don't have to take? You just have to overfly and although it's illegal to drop anything from an aircraft, it is possible. It's been done before and will be done again."

It was like a sudden epiphany. "Wood for the trees, Bob, wood for the trees. The whole of North Yorkshire is a potential drop off area!"

Bob Ryan simply stared at Cyril as he rolled up the aeronautical chart. "If I can be of any further help, here's my mobile number."

Cyril held out his hand and Ryan shook it. "Appreciate that."

"Before you go I'll show you a couple of the older aircraft we have in the hangars if you've time and if you're interested."

Cyril smiled. "Wonderful."

Ryan had read Cyril's love of aircraft well. The two imposing corrugated hangars stood next to each other, their gaping doors open wide. The sound of an aircraft flying in the circuit droned as it climbed away, its screaming engine note reverberating against the steel hangar side. The interior appeared dark until Cyril's eyes grew accustomed. Three people were working on a plane near the entrance, the engine cowls removed. Ryan and Cyril walked into the depths of the building and Cyril saw the two aircraft standing side by side.

"Chipmunk and Tiger Moth, both built by de Havilland," Ryan remarked. He could immediately see the look of admiration in Cyril's eyes as he inspected both aircraft. He watched as he ran his hand down the edge of the cockpit. "Owned by the same man, Captain for Easyjet and ex-RAF."

Cyril walked round each plane before suddenly spotting a photograph on one of the boards which ran down the full length of the hangar. He felt a shiver of excitement move down his back as he walked towards it. This sudden move away from the aircraft to the side of the hangar appeared to surprise Ryan. He watched as Cyril stopped in front of one of the large noticeboards filled with photographs taken and displayed by club members. He followed him. Cyril tapped the aerial photograph held by three drawing pins. "The bloody beer mat!" Cyril exclaimed and Ryan laughed.

"Nope, crop art. Taken last year, I believe. A small piece of crop art in the shape of an open mouthed emoji, it's very original. I've seen a few crop circles. Can you believe that I've even seen proposals of marriage cut into the fields in my time here. Not far from this flying club, a farmer makes a huge corn maze every year, a favourite for a pleasure flight destination."

"He sees a face…" Cyril said out loud.

"Sorry?" Ryan looked puzzled. "Who does?"

"Something someone said to me," Cyril answered. "Where was that located?"

"I don't know. I didn't take it, but I can try to find out."

Cyril studied it looking for buildings or positional clues but the image had obviously been cropped to just show the smiling face. Removing his phone, Cyril took a picture of the photograph. "I'd be grateful if you could. To locate the position would be so useful."

"The airfield manager can send out a message to all our present and past members to see if they took it or have any memory of its location."

Cyril thanked Ryan and handed him a card containing his mobile number and email address. "Anything, anything at all, I'd appreciate a call."

Cyril returned to his car and felt for the first time that he could see a light at the end of the tunnel.

***

The incident room was busy when he entered. April raised a hand, a signal for his attention, and he quickly moved across the room, avoiding the occasional file left on the floor next to the tables. His hand reassuringly touched the shoulders of those working.

"We had, as you requested, linked the mobile phones of Mrs Baines and Mrs Stephens so that we can intercept specific calls made from their husbands' missing mobiles. They're routed directly to us saving the family any further trauma. It was prophetic, sir, to include Claire Baldwin and Thorndyke's phones."

Cyril smiled to himself at April's use of vocabulary. She was becoming an invaluable member of his team. Never did he feel as though Liz would ever be replaced, but April was proving to be equally efficient, astute with a keen eye for detail.

"At 1.57pm we received this video. It was sent simultaneously to both the wives." April clicked the mouse and Cyril dragged across a chair, put on his glasses and watched.

"Mr and Mrs Potato Head, yes! There's more." She paused the video briefly. "The first piece of music you can hear is part of Symphony number 3, Op 36 by Henryk Mikolaj Gorecki, and the second is a section taken from an opera. Strangely, sir, it's a favourite of mine but I guess the way the case is going, not for much longer. It's *The Ice Maiden* by Rimsky Korsakov."

Cyril immediately turned to her, his expression revealing everything before he turned back to watch as the camera scanned the heads.

"What's interesting, sir, is that the first piece of music was inspired after the composer read a kind of prayer, an inscription on a wall in a former Gestapo prison cell. It was written by an eighteen-year-old Polish girl. The composer suggests in his notes that there were other writings too on that wall; whereas the other prisoners all called for revenge, this girl, this teenager, asks simply for comfort and support even though she knew her fate. To be honest, it brings a lump to my throat when I listen and think about the composer's inspiration in writing such a tragic piece. The captives were all just waiting, knowing their fate, understanding fully what was to happen to them, alive, dare I say, to the gruesome fact that soon they were all to be eliminated."

Cyril could see pools welling in April's eyes. He removed a handkerchief square and slipped it into her hand. She dabbed her eyes as she whispered her thanks.

"It's so clever, sir, so cruel and yet… this is well planned and well exec—" She didn't finish the word. "Sorry! We have Claire imprisoned in what we believe to be a freezer, a cell, the music is suggesting to us that she's not seeking revenge but is simply asking for comfort. The fact that the message portrayed has been sent from her phone suggests that it's her wish, like the writing on the wall and that it's directed at Baines and Stephens and maybe even Thorndyke. The very nature of the visual message, the removal of the characters one by one, the chant of the rhyme, the French accent allowing the play on words, the elimination process, all precise, strangely playful and yet so calculated. But to me, the visual and the audible interpretations of this message are at loggerheads, a contradiction in themselves. Do you see?"

There was a long pause as Cyril and April watched it play through again.

"I do, April, thanks to your musical understanding, I do," he admitted as he placed a hand on hers. "And who is to be the last, can you tell me that? Maybe the French is a nod towards Stephens and his trips."

Both looked at the paused image. The potato head of what could loosely be seen as a police officer stared back. The initial smile that had seemed so benign and yet so sinister had suddenly been changed. The mouth, downturned, mirrored very much that of April's as she sat holding onto the handkerchief. Cyril's stomach churned. He knew that they had to work quickly before the next victim was taken.

"One potato, two potatoes. Surely we're not waiting for three more?"

April turned and lifted her shoulders. "Who knows what the rules of this person's game are. I think there's more to this than we've seen. I need to watch it a few more times."

Cyril printed the image of the emoji and stared at it. "Are you the face that comes back to haunt, are you the disappointed one?" he said out loud before walking through and pinning it on the board in the incident room. Going to the aviation chart, he focussed on the circled areas completed by Bob Ryan before calling Shakti over. She had just entered the room with Nixon. Cyril explained what they were looking at.

"I want each and every one of these locations checking out. Owners, who flies in and who keeps what where and I don't just want you to take their word for it. Look… Look in the hangars and in the outhouses. You're searching for a freezer, chest freezers. If they won't cooperate we can get a warrant. Look in whatever cold store they might have. Anything from our enquiry about Ashton?"

"The records for his supply of liquid nitrogen are scrupulous. However, there's no log of when it's used. You have to take account of evaporation so you'll never achieve a perfect record." They left.

Cyril stood in front of the boards and focussed on two photographs, one of a cocktail glass and the other of the beer mat. It was clear the connection the mat had with the crop art but why? He was still puzzled by the cocktail glass.

Chapter Twenty-Nine

The room allocated for the early briefing was full. They had all watched the video of the potato heads and April had bravely interpreted her thoughts on the music and the actions revealed. The room was opened to debate.

Cyril showed the photograph of the corn emoji and explained the circumstances in which it had been discovered before emphasising the link with the beer mat that had been removed from Baines's car. He knew that it was a strong clue and clearly matched the evidence that suggested two of the victims had seen a face and the other had been recently unsettled. He was determined to develop the idea that the case revolved around the smuggling of drugs but he still did not have any vital evidence to support his belief.

"Stuart and Shakti are investigating eight possible landing sites but currently there's no evidence to suggest that this face was created in any of those places. They're also looking for any deep freeze storage at the sites, as there is likely to be a link. At the moment, no one can recall where or when the photograph was taken. I'm confident we'll find that information but not when. As I said at the beginning of this briefing, time is against us if we believe our killer plans to make the game run to seven." He paused, allowing those in the room to assimilate the information. A number of group conversations immediately started until Cyril continued speaking. "We're looking for a motive, a reason for this action, and I want all possibilities put into the frame. Just call them out, there are no right or wrong answers here, just your personal interpretation of the evidence you have to date. As I said earlier, keep an open mind."

"Thorndyke. Could it possibly be industrial espionage? Could he have been wanting to get back at them and therefore thrown a metaphorical spanner in the works?"

"Who? Stephens, Baines, Thorndyke, Claire are all dead."

"Someone linked with Claire's place of work?"

"Drug cartel, local. Maybe York or Leeds. Stephens has trodden on toes."

"Stephens's business partner, Paul Ashton. He'd nothing to lose but plenty to gain."

Owen quickly interrupted. "He'd everything to lose. The business was dying before Stephens got involved. Besides, how would he know Baines and Baldwin, let alone Thorndyke?"

"They were both known to have been in the bar," someone interjected.

Cyril stood and waved a hand. "Stop! This is not as yet a discussion, it's simply a way of tagging possible suspects within a frame. The whys and the wherefores can come in a minute. If you call out a name then you have reasons, sound, intelligent, professional reasons that will be based on what you know. Now, any more?"

Cyril knew that there would be a pause from the previous free-for-all. It took a while but an officer at the back of the room raised his hand. Cyril noticed it immediately but was unable to attach a name. "Yes?"

"Been on my radar for some time, sir. Jonathan Stephens I mean."

Cyril added the name to the board.

"I hope this doesn't sound stupid," Owen said. "Someone we've yet to find, someone who isn't connected with anything we've looked into, someone who's got just what he wanted and is closing everything down. The game has either run its course or is just about to commence. The person we seek is without a face."

Cyril looked at Owen knowing full well what he was thinking. The last two suggestions had been sound. He turned and drew an outline of a head on the board and added a question mark within it before turning back, like a teacher demanding more from his pupils. "Right, take each name in turn and jot down why they shouldn't be there."

Within forty minutes they had two lists showing potential weak and strong candidates based on the clear evidence they had. The third column simply held a question mark but was as important as either of the other columns. Cyril's phone rang.

"Bennett." He listened whilst scanning the board. "When?" He picked up the pen and drew a ring round Jonathan Stephens's name.

"Jonathan Stephens has been missing for fifteen hours. He was last seen in Pool-in-Wharfedale. CCTV had him at the garage there with the Jaguar. He had informed no one as to where he was going but it's on the road to Leeds Bradford Airport. He wasn't expected at the hangar. We're monitoring ANPR and traffic in West Yorkshire has been alerted. Let's hope we've not lost another potato."

Cyril looked across at the officer who had first mentioned Jonathan Stephens's name. Even from across the room, Cyril could see the puzzled frown and somehow knew just what the officer was thinking.

***

Cyril sipped a cup of tea in his office as Owen, sitting opposite, nursed his Harrogate Festivals mug. Fine lines had appeared within the glaze, stained brown with the appearance of ancient tree bark.

"Why do I keep returning to the conclusion that the murders and the discovered cash point to drugs, Owen? Help me."

Owen pulled a face. "Stephens's autopsy, cocaine, cocaine in the fridge at Baldwin's, Baldwin linked to Baines. A good deal of money sloshing around with Stephens, plane and helicopter, great house… on three relatively small business interests."

"The drugs could just be superficial, a mere link. However, what if someone managed the workplace incidents? People like Baines, Baldwin and Thorndyke were paid to ensure that it would fail, be lacking in the eyes of the H&S executive after the accident. Imagine for a moment that it was supposed to be controlled but it went seriously wrong. That's why Thorndyke, who broke all of the factory rules, simply disappeared and was put on ice."

Owen placed his mug on Cyril's desk. "Was he stealing liquid nitrogen? If so, why? Chris Mott suggested that he was filling a Dewar at the time of the incident and that there was no reason for him to be doing so. Why photograph the body? Why tell us? Why kill Stephens and Baines and then send those images too? Why kill Claire Baldwin and show off? Surely whoever is responsible would have just got rid of Thorndyke and that'd be it. Job done. Thorndyke, in my opinion, was involved from the start. As I said in the briefing, sir, the person we seek is not yet in this script."

Owen lifted his mug and Cyril noticed the brown watery ring. He pulled out a tissue from the box and mopped it up. "So many questions, Owen, but no real answers. Why the liquid nitrogen, why the bodies in the freezer, why the music links and why the potatoes? Let's hope we get something positive about the emoji and more importantly, let's hope that we find Jonathan Stephens."

Before he's had his chips! Owen wanted to say but looking at Cyril's face knew better.

"What have we found out from the address given at Stephens's flying club, Appleton Roebuck?"

"Checked all occupants around the area for the address given. We found a family who were actually called Baldwin with two kids, one of whom was Vicky, but they're both in their mid-seventies and Vicky lives in Cyprus. Seems to me the guy they employed gave false details of his address and therefore we can assume that his name is too, probably just used their identities."

"So why go to all the trouble?"

"Stephens, that's why."

Cyril picked up the phone after looking up the flying school number at Leeds Bradford.

"Day Flights Flying Club. How can I help?"

"DCI Bennett. May I speak to Frank?"

There was a pause. He could hear the scream of an aircraft engine in the background and then a door banging.

"Frank." The voice sounded breathless and impatient.

"One of my officers spoke with you regarding a Thorndyke who might be a Baldwin who worked for a short time with you. You mentioned that he drove a van. You wouldn't happen to know the registration and make of the vehicle, would you?"

The pause was palpable and Cyril was aware that the man at the other end of the line was not the most patient. "Detective Chief Inspector, if I had that information don't you think I'd have mentioned it to your detective at the time? The answer is no. It was a mix of blue paint and iron oxide, if that helps. He'd daubed a rust proofer on various bits of bodywork giving it the appearance that it had some kind of pox."

"Do you hold a collection of photographs taken by students of the club which might have the car in the background?"

"Look, I'm a busy man with a living to make. The guy was a pain in the arse when he was here and now he's coming back to haunt me. I have neither the time nor the inclination to look through the club photographs—"

"This man might be responsible for the death of David Stephens and three other people," Cyril interrupted him in mid flow. "We know that he has an agenda to kill more. We don't know who is on the list but we do know that he's not finished. If it's our man, who knows why he selects his victims, Frank. At present there appears to be no pattern and the next victim could well turn out to be someone he worked with or for."

"Are you suggesting…" He paused. "I'll get them looked at immediately. Do we have your number?"

"There are more ways of killing a pig than to stuff it full of cherries," Cyril said to himself after he put down the phone.

Within twenty minutes he had received a return call. They had discovered two photographs showing not only the car but also the man himself. Cyril was assured that they would scan and mail the images immediately and he gave them his email details.

On receiving the two images on screen Cyril was disappointed not only by the quality, but also by the position of the man and the vehicle.

Within minutes he had sent them to the technical IT team to see if they could enhance them. He needed a make and a registration number but he was not optimistic.

Chapter Thirty

It was two hours after receiving notification that Jonathan Stephens had been reported missing that the Jaguar was discovered. It had been left parked on the roadside near the centre of Ilkley. The car was locked and there was no sign of Jonathan. Owing to its proximity to other parked vehicles, it had not been spotted for a number of hours. Apart from the missing driver, all seemed to be in order. Cyril immediately requested the CCTV images for the area to be checked.

Within twenty minutes, an image of Stephens entering the train station had been confirmed. Checking the time against the image there was one train timetabled for Bradford, Forster Square.

"Now why would the lad leave his car and go to Bradford on a train? He's gone backwards to come forwards. Why, in fact, go by rail?"

Cyril looked up the stopping places of that specific train and then picked up the phone.

"Dan, did we keep a track on Jonathan Stephens's phone?"

Dan Grimshaw shook his head flustered by his boss's question. "No, we were instructed to keep open those which were missing."

"Jonathan Stephens appears to have gone missing. Can we get onto that?"

"Has he taken his phone?"

Cyril suddenly felt foolish, he had not checked. He kicked himself for making such a basic error. "I'll get back to you."

The call to the Stephens's house confirmed that Jonathan had left his mobile and that was one of the reasons there had been such urgency to notify the police. He usually was never parted from it.

Cyril immediately felt the anger bubble, anger with himself as he organised an immediate request for a missing person's bulletin to be issued as a matter of urgency. Control had managed to notify all the stations on the line to check CCTV images for the time after Jonathan had been seen at Ilkley Station. It took barely forty minutes for a response to come through. Jonathan Stephens had left the train at Burley-in-Wharfedale.

***

Cyril Bennett and April Richmond parked outside the Stephens's house. The front door opened before the pair had left the car and Mrs Stephens rushed towards them. April quickly got out and met her.

"Have you found him?" Jonathan's mother's words came through gasps of obvious anguish.

April held Mrs Stephens's shoulders as Cyril came to her side and addressed her. His tone was controlled and reassuring. "We have a positive ID and know that he got off a train at Burley-in-Wharfedale just over two hours ago after leaving his car in Ilkley. Let's go inside so that we can try to understand what's going on."

Once inside, Mrs Stephens calmed down; Cyril's words were slowly penetrating.

"What's he doing there? Why not take his phone? Why not just drive there?"

"Did anyone contact Jonathan before he left the house?"

Mrs Stephens raised her shoulders. "He's always looking at his phone. I don't know, maybe someone contacted him through Facebook, Messenger or such. I really wouldn't know."

"We know that his phone is here, yes?"

She stood, walked into the kitchen and returned with Jonathan's phone. "Never leaves it, that's why we rang. His sister was shocked to see it sitting on the kitchen table." Mrs Stephens handed it to Cyril.

"Do we know his entry code?"

"He has a pass phrase. He is very conscious about mobile security and hackers, and it will be difficult. It'll have a four in it, his so-called lucky number." The smile was clearly forced.

"Bloody phones," Cyril mumbled as he looked at the locked mobile. He tapped 4444 but the phone vibrated in his hand, showing it to be locked.

April held out her hand. "May I, sir?"

"The last time you saw Jonathan was?"

"Yesterday. It was about eleven. He was in the hangar fiddling with something, a container. The next thing he'd gone, his car too. No note, message, nothing. After ten hours we were getting worried."

"Can you show me the container?"

Cyril's request seemed to surprise her. She stood and took him to the hangar. Clicking the door remote, the helicopter appeared. "It's there, on the shelf."

Cyril slipped on a pair of nitrile gloves before picking up the container. The word *cryo 5* was written on the side. He gently shook it and was surprised by its weight; it seemed excessively heavy for its size even though it appeared to be empty. Next to it was a larger one and some smaller stainless steel containers. He brought the original container outside, inspecting the top as he tried to work out how to open it. It took a moment before he gently unclipped what appeared to be a safety catch. He cautiously removed the lid; his assumption was correct, it was empty.

"What do you know about these, Mrs Stephens?" Cyril asked as he crouched next to the container that stood about fifty centimetres in height.

She came towards him to look. "That's the one I saw him handling, thought it was to do with additional fuel for either the helicopter or the car but they might have been used in the bar. I don't know. They take them from the car usually. I've seen them put them here." She pointed to two pods that were secured to the helicopter's landing skids. "They take them when they fly, especially when they're going to France. I've seen them load them into this part."

She moved inside and touched the pod. "He had these fitted just after he bought it, gave more room inside for bags and those when he took them. David had told Jonathan that they…" She pointed to the containers. "…Should never be carried in the cockpit." Her face was blank. It was clearly telling Cyril that she was ignorant as to their true use.

Cyril noticed April and Jonathan's sister approaching. Cyril stood.

"Joanne's told me that if we try to get into the phone it will delete everything. He told her that he'd set that facility for security. After ten attempts the phone is rendered useless as far as evidence and information for this investigation is concerned. She also believed that his father had set that on his too but knowing that someone had access to it maybe not."

"Does he have a second phone, Joanne?"

"I couldn't say and if he did I doubt he'd share that information with me."

"Have you ever flown carrying these?" Cyril pointed to the container in front of him and the one in the hangar.

"You've seen my logbook. I haven't flown for ages. Dad pushed us…"

Joanne's mother was quick to step in. "That's not fair, young lady."

"He did. He wanted us to both be the youngest pilots and I did it to keep the peace. At first it was fun, something boys and my friends looked up to me about but to be honest, it frightened me at times, especially flying on my own. I was alright with another pilot with me or even Mum but on my own, no."

"And the answer to my question, Joanne. Have you ever had to fly with these, take them anywhere or collect them?"

"They might have been in the pods when I flew but I never saw them being loaded or unloaded."

"Surely you did your pre-flight check and that would include weight and balance. You'd have looked in the pods?"

She started to cry. "I've done nothing. I don't know why he's gone. He did the pre-flight or Dad did after they brought it from here. I've told you I didn't and I don't like flying." She turned and stormed back away from the garages into the house.

"You must forgive her, since her dad's death she's been so uptight. What she was telling you is true. She wasn't a natural Amy Johnson. She flew for her dad and that's it. I, on the other hand, would never go in anything that doesn't have a first class lounge and continuous and generous offerings of Champagne throughout the flight."

April had to smile. There was a woman who knew her own mind.

Chapter Thirty-One

Cyril had organised a forensic search of the Stephens's hangar and the adjoining garages. They had quickly acted on information that the *Bauhaus Champagne and Cocktail Bar* received a regular but limited supply of liquid nitrogen for use when creating their special cocktails. The exotic drinks had not proved to be as popular as they had hoped, after worldwide news reports of members of the public sustaining serious injuries from inexperienced or overenthusiastic bar staff mixing varying quantities of the liquid directly into cocktails rather than using it to freeze the products going into the drink.

News of the incidents had spread rapidly and not only had sales declined nationally, but a formal tightening of operating procedures and practices had followed. Many bars and clubs had withdrawn the service. Bauhaus had also considered stopping but no direct decision had been taken. With David Stephens's death, more important issues had arisen. They had checked the records before and this second investigation corresponded with the first. It was clear that Paul Ashton's name would move to the outside edges of the investigation.

Even with extensive media coverage and appeals to the public for help, there had been no further sightings of Jonathan Stephens. The one consolation Cyril had was that they had received no further calls using the missing mobiles and therefore assumed and hoped that there were no more frozen corpses.

The follow-up on the potential landing sites that Bob Ryan had circled on Cyril's aviation chart had also proved fruitless, apart from eating into more vital resources. However, it was important that his hunch should be followed. It was one fewer lead to pursue.

***

On vacating the railway station, Jonathan lifted the shoulder strap of his bag over his head, leaving both hands free before checking the details on the paper he held in his hand. He felt lost without his phone, in fact not having a mobile at all seemed totally alien and strange. Feeling isolated and unsure, he tried to recall the last time that had happened. It never had.

Once down Station Road, he checked his notes detailing the buildings and waypoints before turning right. Walking quickly, he soon passed the Queen's Head pub on his right and to his amazement, he noticed two Celtic crosses positioned to his left. They were set just off the pavement to the front of the stone community-type hall; their presence seemingly incongruous. He had little desire to stop and look. His destination, if he had written down the directions correctly, should require a turn to the left a few metres ahead. This route would take him down Iron Row, a narrow lane comprising the former factory workers' cottages and a row of modern garages. The path would soon lead him between two gateposts, the original mill gates and a modern tunnel under the busy dual carriageway that bypassed the town.

After fifteen minutes he found himself standing in front of a stone house. Gates to the right were closed but they blocked only a cobbled road. There was neither wall nor fence to the right of the gates; they protected nothing but at one time they had secured the entrance to the part-derelict Greenholme Mill. He continued, unsure as to his real destination or as to who or what was to greet him.

On the roadway by the side of the house, his eyes were drawn to a metal oblong set into the cobbles. Concrete filled the central space, the old and the new set in marked contrast. Had he known the history of the place he would have realised that this was once the gatehouse to the mill and the oblong, the weighbridge. He had little interest other than in trying to control the fluttering nerves of uncertainty crashing about in his stomach.

As he approached the ruins of the stone-built mill, he noticed a number of large red signs announcing and warning of demolition and the advice to *Keep Out*. He paused feeling uneasy. He listened for bird song but there was none, there was nothing other than the drone of cars speeding along the bypass hidden behind the barrier of trees.

The road running past the mill was patched occasionally with concrete, careless repairs of convenience with total disregard to the historical value or cobbles' symmetry. The cobbled road surface seemed to stretch as far as a distant bend behind the furthest section of the mill site.

Part of the building to his left had already been torn down. Only the lower portion of the wall remained, encapsulating a hollow in the ground but still offering a clear picture of what was once the footprint of the structure. It was then that he saw his first real marker; the mill clock. Its ruined metal remains projected at almost right angles to the wall of the deserted building. Checking his notes they described the clock; he had reached his destination. He read the last instruction on the page.

Once at the clock you must wait and look. I shall be there and when I am ready you will see me.

He stopped beneath it. He must wait and see. On one side, the face and hands remained intact but frozen at a time in the past, thirty-seven minutes past six. On the other side was a void where there had once been an identical clock face.

It's right twice a day that clock, he said to himself trying to calm his nerves. He screwed up the notes and tossed them on the ground.

Suddenly he sensed it, the feeling that he had experienced in the driveway at home, that sensation of being observed and scrutinised. He let his eyes drift along the row of windows set at regular intervals along the building's façade. Surprisingly few had suffered at the hands of vandals. It was then that he noticed it. Initially he was unsure and he passed over the window, but slowly he returned his gaze and there it was, a face set back in the shadows, a face he thought he knew and had seen before. The figure, semi-silhouetted against the northern lights set high and angled into the roof, stood motionless.

A tingle of warm fear ran through Jonathan's body and his instincts screamed to move away, turn and tell, but that was not the deal. He fingered the bag's strap that ran across his chest and realised that avoiding this meeting was against everything he had achieved to get there. He had to see it through.

Chapter Thirty-Two

Owen sat looking at his computer screen whilst chewing his thumbnail. There was very little to nibble at but he persevered. It helped him think of the times when his gran had told him that he would end up looking like Venus de Milo. That brought a smile to his face. It was only years afterwards that he had realised who she was and the significance of the comment. He looked at the remnants of the nail before removing the bits from his mouth and depositing them in the bin. He wandered towards April's desk.

"Do you think Stephens is up to his armpits in all of this even though he was the first to kick the bucket?" Owen perched on the side of her desk and picked up two CDs that April had left there. He looked at each and turned them over as he listened to her reply.

"Second, Thorndyke was the first to die. In my opinion, Owen, what was once a smooth and possibly long-standing operation has gone wrong for some reason. The trips to the continent, the returning with so-called products and now the Dewars and the additional helicopter pods. You couldn't fly with liquid nitrogen in the cockpit, it's an enclosed space and should there have been a leak, what with altitude and pressure and all that, the pilot's judgement and ability to function safely would be seriously impaired. You witnessed the demonstration. I've contacted the flying school where he kept the plane and sent images of the Dewars giving dimensions and approximate weights to see if they recognise them. I asked the question about separate stowage on his aircraft too. Then again, there's the food factory and the fact that Stephens, Baines and Baldwin were acquainted. I'm talking about Claire, that is, and not Arthur or Albert Baldwin. He's a mystery who doesn't seem to have existed other than for a couple of weeks whilst working at Yeadon."

Owen looked at the top CD cover. "Sympathies... need bloody sympathy with that picture on the front!"

"Symphony, Owen. *Symphony of Sorrowful Songs.*" April smiled and hit his thigh whilst shaking her head.

He looked again and then smiled back. "I've felt like that chap on occasion when trying to work out this puzzle... pull my hair out and scream." He tapped the part of the cover image before dropping the CD in front of her and copied the pose of the character pictured. "Pulled all his hair out already... look!" He paused and his expression became more serious. "I've seen that face before."

It was only then when his remark registered did they stop and look at each other. He felt a hot flush run through him.

"Edvard Munch. It's called *The Scream*. You've seen the white masks you can buy at Halloween." She turned to her computer and tapped the words into the search engine; a number of images appeared. "Yours for just 99p. Flash will know more about Munch. Funny how Stephens thought he saw a masked person looking at him, remember when he was getting flowers from his car?" She flicked through the notes in the file she had on her desk, first checking the index down the side, impressing Owen. "There, Jonathan Stephens said..." She read from the notes:

"*... He'd seen someone at the end of the driveway, just staring, a mask-like face focussed on him, he said but then thought he was mistaken, perhaps a trick of the light.*"

"So this Munch bloke painted and made music?"

"No, that's..." She didn't finish, but took the CD from Owen and her file. "Come on. Is Bennett in?"

Cyril had just entered the incident room when Owen and April appeared.

"Owen's made a discovery, sir, an important one, one that might answer some questions." She passed him the CD.

"$120 million that sold for a good few years ago, 2012 or maybe a little later, and it was one of his two pastel works and not the oil."

Owen plonked himself on a desk.

"How much? One hundred and twenty million?" He sounded each word as if he were chewing it. "For that? I could do better with one arm tied behind my back!"

Cyril simply raised an eyebrow. "Really? He's a Norwegian artist, Victorian… lived in the reign of Queen Victo…" It was unusual for Cyril to state the obvious but he was talking to Owen. He did not finish the sentence. "She has a number of streets, roads and avenues named after her throughout the world and throughout this bloody case. You have my full attention, tenuous as the link might be," he announced, alternating his gaze between each officer.

April handed Cyril the CD cover. "That's the music we heard on the video with Mr Potato Head, the first piece. Owen said he'd seen the face; that face, *The Scream* and of course, you see it every year on Halloween masks. They're all over the Internet. The victims said that they believed that someone was looking at them, that they'd seen a face!"

April moved to the whiteboards and focussed on the two photographs of the frozen faces. "Look at the mouth. It's open and remains slightly dark because of the potato. The faces are now white and crystalline, not too dissimilar to that of the masks. Look at the position of the hands too." She held the CD cover next to the images and Cyril had to admit that there was clearly a resemblance.

"Surely the coincidence with Victoria Avenue can't be so tenuous."

"Sir."

The voice of the detective who had supplied Cyril with the details of the potato rhyme had been working at one of the desks and approached. "I studied history and specifically Queen Victoria for A level, I was fascinated by her. She was the longest ruling monarch until our present queen. Came to the throne on 20 June 1837 and stayed there until she died on 22 January 1901." Cyril could sense the enthusiasm in her voice.

"You need an anorak," Owen muttered.

She frowned looking for reassurance from Cyril.

"Ignore the sergeant, please continue."

She moved closer to Cyril. "It was a well known fact that she kept a number of mourning relics, something the Victorians did. She wore black after her beloved Albert died. I was fascinated by a relatively bizarre fact, sir. She also had a post-mortem photograph of him taken as if he were on a bed asleep, she had it accurately hand coloured and framed in an evergreen wreath. Her relationship with that photograph was quite intriguing and some would say morbid as wherever she were to spend the night, the photograph was hung above the vacant side of the bed."

Cyril stared at her trying to take in the information.

Owen broke the silence. "On the photographs here and here, there are what look to be some frozen leaves. Evergreen maybe. Looks a little like grey-green ivy. We seem to have our mysterious Albert or Arthur."

Cyril turned to the young detective. "It was you who brought the photograph?"

"Yes, sir. You asked me to research the elimination poem. I'd considered the connection then but thought you'd think me foolish like the sergeant did."

Owen quickly apologised. "A silly joke."

Cyril nodded. "I should think so! I'm grateful for your diligence, thank you. We missed an opportunity on that occasion but fortunately I believe we might have a link, thanks to your quick mind and enthusiasm."

She blushed slightly.

He tapped the photographs. "So, my trusty hounds. Who is speaking to us and why? Are we being led forward or are we simply being distracted? What is staring us in the face?" He looked across at the photograph of the emoji. "We're surrounded by faces, some real and some fictitious but all are expressive, all are open-mouthed, conveying either a sense of shock or fear. There's an explanation. Are we dealing with revenge, or just simple madness? The jigsaw pieces are on these boards. All we have to do is find the correct sequence to put them together."

Owen sighed. "We need the bits that go around that emoji, the ones that show a building, some trees. We need something to give us a clue. Have you heard nothing from the pilot chap Ryan?"

Cyril shook his head.

***

Jonathan Stephens managed to take his eyes from the motionless figure staring from within the mill building. The dirty windows and the light shining from behind only allowed him a limited view. He glanced at the frozen clock face and then back at the window. The figure had gone. He felt a stab of panic as his eyes searched every dark window. It was then that he noticed the door set at the top of some wrought iron stairs swing slowly open. It was his invitation to step inside.

Chapter Thirty-Three

It took a while for Bob Ryan to get to the phone. "Sorry, Detective Chief Inspector, just finishing some groundwork with a student. Hope that you're well and have found your mysterious landing field."

"Sadly not, we checked all the fields marked on the chart but nothing. Did you have any response from your enquiry regarding the corn face, the one photographed on the hangar pin-board?"

Ryan sounded surprised by the question. "Yes, you should've been informed. One of our old students remembered taking that shot when he was on, and I quote, *a photographic detail.* Some amateur pilots clearly suffer from delusions of grandeur once they qualify!" He laughed out loud before giving Cyril the answer. "The secretary said she'd left you a message but alas… Anyway, do you have your chart close to hand? It would be a lot easier to give you the co-ordinates? I'll just be a few minutes, I have them in my case."

***

Jonathan pulled open the door and looked inside. The long upper floor of this portion of the mill was naturally lit by the angled northern lights that ran in rows along its length. It was empty apart from an echoing silence that seemed to bombard his ears. He stood momentarily, checking every part of the space, ensuring that one foot kept the door ajar. At the bottom of the room was a pair of large doors, the only other exit excluding the old fire doors he stood by. He let the door close quietly before starting to walk towards the others. His eyes scanned the metal bars that formed the skeletal frame supporting the roof. As he passed each window, he looked out onto the cobbled road, the same road he had walked down minutes earlier; it was now bathed in sunshine but still deserted. Nothing moved.

Reaching the doors, he took a deep breath before quickly pushing them and to his surprise they too swung open silently and with ease. The room he entered was much larger, but darker having lost the ceiling windows. There was another floor above and this space was not empty like the last. He cautiously took two steps. In front of him were seven naked figures, mannequins, shop window dummies, positioned slightly apart to form a neat arc. Their arms were all bent in the same way so that their hands were arranged at the side of their heads. A chair was positioned in front of the semi-circle of figures on which was placed an envelope. He paused, assimilating the scene. He wondered if they were remnants of the mill, abandoned and unwanted stock; the possibility helped calm him. He felt sweat run down his inner arm and the bag he carried suddenly seemed to weigh heavily.

As he moved further into the room, a startled bird flew and crashed against one of the windows, causing him to panic and instinctively look towards the sound and movement. The bird soon recovered to flutter clumsily onto a steel girder to his left. Watching it settle, he allowed himself the same opportunity to gain control of his mental and emotional equilibrium before walking towards the motionless group. Giving the figures a wide berth, he moved around the mannequin furthest away from the windows before he turned round to look. It was only then did he hear the gasp, his own gasp, that broke into a short but sharp cry of anguish that seemed to fill the space, causing the bird to flutter again and crash once more against the same glass as if trying to find freedom. It fell, confused and injured onto the soiled wooden floor. It fluttered again briefly for one last time and then lay still. He watched its final moments but felt nothing. He was numb.

It had been the emotionless laughing face of his father staring back at him that had caused the sudden shock and explosive cry. He let his eyes rest on each mannequin's face before moving to the next. He recognised the face of the woman from the photographs that the police had brought round to the house and the man too, Baines if he remembered correctly. Each was merely a life-size monochrome photograph secured to the mannequin's head.

Jonathan's confused and frightened mind tried to rationalise, add names, put into perspective what he was contemplating but it could not. Even though they were photographic masks, life size and accurate, black and white, they seemed real. The other dummies wore masks but were simply blank, featureless. However, the final one terrified him. When his eyes fell on the last of the figures he emitted a second gasp as he tried to comprehend the scenario. Astonishingly, it was a full-size photograph of his own face staring back at him. He remembered when the photograph had been taken and by whom… his father.

He moved to the chair and collected the unsealed envelope. His name was clearly written on the front. He removed the contents to reveal a handwritten note.

***

Cyril stood in front of the aviation chart and carefully plotted the co-ordinates as they were given.

"There are two possibilities, life is never simple, Mr Bennett, but he assures me one of these locations is correct. Being an arse and a flying snob we are also blessed that he appears to be anal about his flight records. Any normal flyer would have just pointed the camera, pressed and forgotten about the location but not our boy. He even wears all the gear; tie, epaulettes and carries the obligatory pilot's case." He laughed again.

Cyril had stopped listening and was circling the two co-ordinates. "Do we have a name and contact details for this person?"

Making a note, Cyril thanked Ryan before looking carefully again at the marks he had made on the chart. He estimated a two-mile radius around the two marks and circled them but it was the second mark that drew his focus as the area in which it was situated was close to the village of Bedlam. He paused searching for some kind of logic but to him the word Bedlam was linked with Bethlem, the famous psychiatric hospital, the first and oldest in Europe. It might also have given origin to the word for chaos and madness and from where Cyril was standing at the moment it certainly fitted.

***

He read the note twice:

There's no rush, take a seat and reflect on those faces before you. I'll be along very soon. If you've brought everything, I can assure you that you have nothing to fear.

Jonathan's mind was a jumble of options. Should he do as the note said, wait, or should he just dump the bag and go? There was nobody close to stop him. He turned the card over:

Do not run, as that would be the last thing you will ever do. You must now trust me. You will leave here safely if you just do as I ask.

He reluctantly sat and looked into the bag. Everything was there, everything that had been specified.

***

Owen, Shakti and April entered the incident room as Cyril stood by a flip chart. He quickly explained that the location of the emoji crop circle could be in one of two places.

"Owen and April to this location. I want it searched. You'll have backup waiting, a drug and police dog handler. I've not requested an armed presence at this stage but if at any time you feel as though…" He did not finish as somehow he felt as though he was trying to teach old dogs new tricks. "Shakti, you're with me. The property owner's details are in the file with a map and images of the location. If they have nothing to hide, you'll receive full cooperation."

Owen and April read through the notes. "We go in thirty minutes. Keep me informed throughout. You're looking for some kind of deep freeze, a chest freezer or a cold store but as always, keep an open mind." Cyril slipped his e-cigarette into his mouth and looked at Shakti as she read through the details. He watched her frown and then look up.

"Bedlam?" she asked as she observed a light cloud of vapour erupting from Cyril's mouth.

Chapter Thirty-Four

After the second roundabout at Ripley, Cyril turned towards Burnt Yates. The A6165 was relatively quiet. The police minibus containing four officers and two dog vans followed. The handlers and their dogs were both attached to the operational base in Harrogate and would, after the search at Bedlam, go on to support Owen and April.

***

Jonathan heard the door, the one he had used to enter the mill, suddenly slam shut, the sound echoing through the near-empty space. He immediately stood, his hands fumbling with the strap of the bag as the note and the envelope fell to the floor.

"Good of you to come, Jonathan Stephens." The voice came from the other room and was still some distance away. It suddenly seemed as though the shock of hearing someone speak turned his insides to liquid. A shudder of fear spread down his back.

"Turn around and don't look towards the doors, not yet, not until I give you permission. That would be so unwise. Now we understand that one simple rule, let me thank you for following my instructions. You might not believe me but I'm sorry to bring you here, to what you might think is a godforsaken remnant of a Victorian carbuncle, to me this once-proud gem is a masterpiece that may soon be lost forever. Some of the buildings have gone following the demolition of the mill chimney." He paused as if to bring solemnity to his words. "I noted when you arrived that you saw the clock, Jonathan. How many lives did that clock control over the years? How many families did this mill support? You probably have no idea and neither do you care. Why should you? You are more interested in your possessions, your trophies of wealth, just as your father was. This building was the lifeblood of the community. It supported and enabled them to make a living, but it did more for the owners; this mill gave them immense wealth and power. Not for them the toil and hard graft. Your father was the same and I…?"

Jonathan's heart rate had not fully recovered, his senses still heightened; he could hear every sound, even the breaths taken between the words of the person who controlled his every move. His eyes, as instructed, remained focussed on the distant paint-flaking wall.

"Why?" Jonathan pleaded, the words dribbling stickily from his dry lips. "I don't understand this. Why?"

The stranger approached one of the figures. Jonathan sensed the movement before he saw him in his peripheral vision. Dressed in a white boiler suit and white training shoes, the mask he was wearing was the same photograph as on the last mannequin; it depicted himself.

"You may turn."

A bizarre sensation filled Jonathan's body, a prickly, hot tingle. Seeing his own face looking back, it was like staring into a moving mirror but yet the eyes, obviously behind the holes in the mask, seemed to speak a different language. There were no accompanying facial expressions to support the look, just the occasional movement of the head.

"It's really quite simple, my young friend. It's a game, you remember, you probably played at school… One potato, two potatoes… You know the rhyme. Three potatoes, four… you can join in if you like." The stranger pointed to each static figure as he counted.

"My father did see you. It was true. Where did you get that photograph of me and the one of my dad? Who gave it to you?" Jonathan's voice was high-pitched but he kept a degree of control.

"You did. You posted it on social media like many other photographs… like this one of your father here. Surely you remember as you boasted about your helicopter, your plane,

your holidays and fancy cars. You put everything out there; you made it so easy for me. Look, I've cloned you. It's been so simple. Look!" He pointed to his own masked and covered face, then to the mannequin furthest away. "You are here and you are there…" Before pointing at Jonathan. "And you are here. You've not met this man and this young lady before but you have seen them, you have seen their post-mortem photographs and you could say, like the clock face outside, they're now frozen in time."
"I've brought what you asked me to bring." Jonathan removed the strap from around his head and tossed the bag on the floor. A small cloud of dust rose from the boards but settled quickly.

The masked head remained focussed on Jonathan; the eyes moved freely behind the perfect circles cut exactly where the mask's eyes were positioned.

"Frozen… in… time. You know all about the cold, the extreme cold, as your father utilised it to bring him wealth. Just the two of us, he said, but then we have Baines and that silly bitch of a girl Baldwin. She was always an untrustworthy schemer right from our first meeting. All she was meant to do was to spill the beans and Baines was to act upon it. Five grand each for bugger all, and what do they do? She was having an affair with both of them. Your father always did have a soft spot for young ladies, money attracts, you see. She then threatened him.

"Blackmail is such a wicked sin but then I discovered it was Baines, he put her up to it, more money and next a share of the products you brought back. With blackmail and then greed, the situation needed to change. So, Jonathan, from only your father and me, we now had two leeching parasites and that, to my mind, couldn't be tolerated. I took a page from their book and performed a simple risk assessment for my health and my safety's sake and decided it was time."

Jonathan stared at the masked figure. "An affair?"

"Took them flying, told people that they worked for him. He began to lie, to cover up. How could I trust him then? You tell me."

"You..? You killed them?"

Chapter Thirty-Five

The building was to the right of the road and the vehicles swung onto the small private lane that led to the front of the house. Cyril wanted the dog trained to detect drugs at the ready. The tracking dog would remain in the van with its handler should it be needed to give chase. The Harrogate Dog Section had been enhanced since recent amalgamation of the forces of Cleveland, Durham and North Yorkshire.

Cyril pushed open the gate and walked towards the stone building. It reminded him of the type of house a child might draw, with symmetrical windows and a central door. All it needed was a sun containing a smiling face but then he remembered that it might have had one of those in the field opposite.

The garden was orderly and Shakti lowered her hand to brush against the lavender, releasing its delicate perfume.

"I love lavender and rosemary, rosemary for remembrance." She smiled to herself.

Cyril ignored the comment, focussing on the job in hand.

***

Owen was sitting with the farm owner's wife. Her husband was at a market in Gisburn.

"Picked a bad day, love. He doesn't normally go that far, we don't even go that far for us holidays." She giggled. "That's not strictly true. We once went to Filey for a week. Which is closest?"

"There's probably not much in it but I'd say Gisburn is the closer." She smiled but received only a look that said *snotty bitch.*

"*Anyroad up*. I can tell you one thing, Sergeant Owen, my Stan wouldn't be going to the expense of growing a good crop and then destroying it by making a stupid face in it. How big did you say it were?"

Owen explained again.

She shook her head. "Bloody stupid that. Some people are just plain daft. Tea?"

Owen smiled.

"You 'n all?" She looked at April. "Sugar and milk? Them in the van too?"

"Can we look around your outbuilding, just to tell my boss we have?" Owen realised that she would have no objections by the way she kept putting her hand either on his knee or arm as he spoke to her.

"As you please. Take your shoes off when you come back in, there's shit and all sorts round them barns."

They were leaving when she called after them. "Mind that daft bloody dog of ours, it doesn't take prisoners. It's chained mind."

As they left the room, Owen beamed at April. "Like putty in my hands!"

April pretended to make herself sick.

***

Cyril knocked again and then went to look through the front window. The net curtains proved successful in keeping out prying eyes. He went back to the lane where the officers were leaning against the wall. One, the female on the team, had taken the opportunity to have a swift cigarette but dropped it and extinguished it with her boot on seeing Cyril come through the gate. She was surprised to see him come over to her.

"Name?"

"Naylor, sir."

"I'd pick that up, Naylor if I were you. We might be at a potential crime scene. Think before you act. Be professional, that's all I ask."

"Sir, sorry." She blushed and when he turned away she breathed deeply, realising that she had let herself down.

Coming up the lane were two people on horseback. Cyril walked down to meet them. He held out his ID at arm's length. "Do you own the house?" He pointed with his other hand.

"Owned by the Wilbors, they live in the large house just outside Bedlam, up Pye Lane. They've rented this place out for a couple of years, usually holiday lets but occasionally long term stuff. I believe the last person who stayed any length of time was a head teacher and his family, taught in Harrogate and rented whilst looking to buy something. I had a beer with him a couple of times in the New Inn. Not seen him or the family for a few months now. Possibly school holidays but more likely he's found a house to his liking." He spoke like a newsreader of the forties, using long and drawn-out vowels.

"We have the owner recorded as Wilbor as you have confirmed, Donna and Christian Wilbor."

"Lovely couple. As I say, Pye Lane, the largest house on the right. Can't miss it, bloody pretentious gargoyle things by the gateposts. Still, it wouldn't do for us all to like the same thing. Chief Inspector did you say? Major Collier and this is my daughter Pip."

Cyril smiled, nodded to Pip and thanked them. "Just one more thing. Do you remember a large corn face made within any crops round here?"

Pip giggled and looked across at her father. "That would be Harvey the farmer, does these things to make a bob or two. He's created all sorts in the large field over by his barn. You can see it from here. Usually it's a message… Marry Me or a birthday wish. We even had a heart last year. They usually fly over with the person to whom it's dedicated. Mind, most now film the things with these new drones."

"And the face?"

"You'll have to ask Harvey, although I doubt he'll say much where cash is concerned."

Cyril thanked them again as he followed the horses' slow walk. Back at the car, he instructed Shakti and one of the officers to go and speak with the owners and to get them there as soon as possible. "Call me with details of the tenant and a contact but I need to get in this house."

It would be forty minutes before the police car, followed by a Bentley Continental, would turn down the lane. He spoke with two officers and instructed them to pay Harvey a call. He outlined details of the information that he needed and the possible consequences of withholding vital information relevant to a murder case.

Chapter Thirty-Six

Jonathan stared at the motionless, expressionless figure and was afraid of the consequences of any degree of conversation.

"It's all there, all that we have; the drugs and the money. It's what was in the hangar safe, his secret stash."

"Thank you. You do not know who I am. I'm pleased your father protected you from that fact. Had he not done so then the consequences of this meeting would be very different."

The figure pushed the nearest mannequin, the one wearing the face of Jonathan's father. It wavered precariously and then began to fall. "One potato…" he whispered. The model hovered briefly before crashing to the floor, its arms separating from the body; another cloud of dust particles rose up to meet the second and then third toppling mannequin. "Two potatoes, three potatoes… You see I have spare potatoes."

As the boiler-suited man approached the next dummy, Jonathan moved as quickly as he could, curving a path as far away from him as possible. He crashed through the double door and then focussed on the next exit. He could see it was closed. The push bar ran across the centre and he flung himself against it. It opened with his full force behind it, colliding with the metal handrail and bouncing back, threatening to knock him off his feet. He stumbled but maintained his momentum, taking the metal steps two and three at a time before he was on the cobbles. He neither noticed the sun's warmth nor the face from the upstairs window watching his escape.

A hand reached for the mask and removed it for a moment allowing the cool air to bathe his face before replacing it. He smiled as he watched the badly shaken youth veer frantically towards the bypass.

***

Owen wiped the soles of his shoes across the boot-scrape outside the front door but still removed them on entering. The tea sat in two large blue and white striped mugs next to a tray with four more mugs. "I'll take these to the boys outside."

"Biscuits on the table. Find owt?"

Owen shook his head.

When she came back in Owen was quick to ask. "You don't have a chest freezer I see." Flecks of biscuit dropped from his lips as if to accompany the start of the question.

"No, small one on top of the fridge. We try to eat fresh stuff here not that frozen processed muck and my husband'll eat what I give him."

"Thanks very much and thanks for the tea. Can I take a biscuit with me?" Owen's grin spread across his face when she told him he could take two and that they had been baked freshly that morning.

As they got in the car, he put them on the dashboard. He waved as she stood at the door. "Like putty!"

"She's old enough to be your mother!"

The police minibus pulled away. "Call Cyril. Tell him this end's clear. If he doesn't need us we'll see him back at the station." Owen stuffed another biscuit into his mouth, selected first gear and headed for Harrogate.

***

Jonathan Stephens did not take the bypass tunnel and retrace his steps to the railway station, instead he kept to the road and jogged towards the dual carriageway. Watching for a suitable gap between the fast-moving vehicles, he crossed to the side where the traffic was heading in the direction of Ilkley and held out his thumb.

Within minutes a battered transit van pulled to the side, its hazard lights ablaze. Jonathan ran up and pulled at the passenger door.

"Where you going?" the driver enquired, keeping one eye on his wing mirrors.

Jonathan was still breathing hard. "Ilkley."

"Get in, shouldn't stop here owing to the traffic," the driver said. The van was moving before Jonathan had closed the door fully. The journey would take them twelve minutes.

***

Cyril opened the driver's door and a sprightly lady well into her seventies climbed out.

"There're not many of you left, gentlemen, that is, not police officers." She looked at Cyril again. "Mind there aren't as many of them as there used to be."

Cyril smiled. "DCI Bennett. Sorry to drag you all this way but my colleague has informed me that the last tenant is due to leave in the next few days. When is that exactly?"

"Mr Monk. This Sunday, took it for two weeks and then extended. Normally we do holiday lets with the occasional long term. The clients need to be the right sort of people, if you know what I mean. No riff-raff. You want to look round?"

Cyril smiled before leaning towards Shakti. "Get on to Owen and April. Our man here goes by the name of Monk but my instinct tells me that's bullshit. Ask him to translate Munch from the Norwegian to English and he'll see why."

Cyril turned back to Mrs Wilbor. "Did you receive any client details when he made the booking?"

"For a holiday rental? He saw the local advert and rang, like many do. He said, if I remember correctly, that he saw the advertisement in the *Dalesman* when he stayed on the first occasion. We get a lot of our bookings from either the Tourist Office in Harrogate and Ripon or from the occasional adverts we place in magazines and local papers. We try to keep away from the Internet, attracts the wrong sort."

"This is not the first time he's rented?"

"Goodness, no. I should say about three maybe four. I'd have to check. That's why I was surprised by all of this palaver."

"So you'll have his contact details, Mrs Wilbor?"

"At home. He paid cash in advance including the deposit against damages and the like, as always. Left the place better than he found it usually, immaculate."

Cyril followed her up the path as he waved an arm to direct the remaining two officers to go to the back of the property. The police dog and handler were to follow him. They stopped at the door and Cyril explained to the owner justification for the sniffer dog. "Do you have an alarm?"

She shook her head. "You'll not find drugs, not if I know my guests."

"Alarm?" Cyril pointed to the box on the front of the house.

"It's false. The original alarm caused too many problems for the guests and we were forever coming to silence it." She passed Cyril the key, her face full of disgust at the thought that someone would use drugs in her house.

"If you'll wait in your car, please."

Cyril donned overshoes and gloves.

The dog entered after being unleashed, the Spaniel's tail animated as it excitedly began working.

***

Jonathan Stephens jumped from the van whilst waiting at the traffic lights on Leeds Road. He waved as the driver pulled away. He was less than a minute's walk away from where he had parked the Jaguar. Turning up Victory Road, he saw the car. He breathed a sigh of relief. Slipping his hand in his pocket, he felt the comfort of the car keys. The doors immediately unlocked as he approached, his hand went to the driver's side handle and he pulled it before jumping in quickly.

***

Back at the mill, the masks were removed from the mannequins and the various limbs that had become detached as the figures had crashed to the floor were moved to the side of the room. They would remain along with their owners, leaving only the bag that Jonathan had dropped in the centre. The man rubbed his hands together and blew on them before retrieving the bag. Feeling its weight, he knew that there should be four kilograms of high quality cocaine and some crystal meth with a street value of a quarter of a million alongside the cash. At this stage, he could only hope that the youth had been honest as there was no going back, for Jonathan there would be no second chance.

The vibration from his phone made the man pause. He knew what it meant. There was someone in the house and they had activated the motion sensors on the wireless cameras, triggering the alarm on his phone. Removing his mobile, he quickly watched the scene as the dog moved around the corridor leading from the front door. He observed as each door was opened and rooms were checked. He sat back and split the screen showing the live images from the three cameras. His finger hovered over the green alarm button that would allow him to sound a siren within the room as they approached. He pressed it and he laughed as the phone app asked if he were sure. He let his finger hover over the command. As the police dog came into the lounge, the man pressed and as the remote cameras were designed to transmit images and audio, he heard and saw the immediate effect.

The officer and the dog responded in different ways, the dog simply ran from the room and down the corridor, almost knocking Cyril over before dashing through the front door. It settled by the wall where the pulsating sound was much diminished, its tail still and between its legs. The officer, after the initial shock, covered his ears and ran towards the sound. He quickly removed the camera and thrust it into the pocket of his cargo pants, blinding it and muffling the alarm's shrill scream.

"If there's one camera there are more," Cyril announced. "You get the dog and bring in the others. I want every one of them located." His voice was filled with frustration.

***

Removing the white overall, he rolled it up, ensuring that the photographic masks were safely wrapped within it before leaving by the fire escape. He scanned the area but there was nobody about. The demolition notices seemed to have achieved the desired effect. He walked down past the clock round the end of the building to his car. Lifting the boot, he added the bag and the boiler suit between the suitcases. He was prepared for every eventuality; he was just a couple of days early but his objective had been reached.

Climbing into the driver's seat, he removed the paper mask. Would the police ever understand the reason for the potatoes? He doubted they would fully grasp the relevance of the cocktail glass and the beer mat. If they found the mill before it was torn down and discovered the mannequins, then maybe. However, should they discover the masks… then who knew? As he drove out he glanced at the mill clock.

"Eighteen thirty-seven," he said out loud, "simply frozen in time." He then let his eyes fall on the pile of stones tucked within the remains of the demolished section of the mill.

Chapter Thirty-Seven

The dog re-entered after the cameras had been removed and it was soon evident that drugs had been used or stored in the house. Cyril was aware of recent reports suggesting cocaine was so common that one in ten people have traces of the drug on their fingers. He had read about eighty per cent of bank notes carried traces. Nine toilets in the Palace of Westminster had previously tested positive. Finding drug residue within a holiday property would be circumstantial should Mr Monk be traced.

Cyril stood in the conservatory and looked out across the garden. He observed one of the officers check the hedge and then move to the stone outhouse. He watched as he tried the door. It was locked. The Spaniel came round the back of the fence and worked the garden area. Cyril marvelled at its enthusiasm.

Mrs Wilbor was still sitting in her car. Her eyes were closed and the sound of classical music could just be heard. Cyril gently tapped on the window. It startled her. He smiled and opened the door.

"Do you have a key for the building at the bottom of the garden, please?"

"It's on that ring, fits the padlock. It's not accessible to the tenants, just a place we keep some old things. Should be thrown out but you know what it's like. You keep things believing they'll come in handy one day!"

"We've tried that key, and according to my officer it's both the wrong size and the incorrect make."

"I can assure you that it was fine a month or so ago and we haven't been in there since." Her whole demeanour changed, more defensive than ever. What with the alarm and the key, she felt as though she was losing control. Climbing from the car, she walked round to the stone buildings and stared at the lock. "That's certainly not right. That's been changed." She swiftly took her mobile from her bag and dialled. "Have you changed the lock on the outbuilding at the holiday let?"

Cyril watched her expression.

"Well someone has. The police can't get in. The lock's been changed!" She turned to Cyril. "My husband is on his way with some tools. You will get in. We've nothing to hide, Chief Inspector."

One of the officers who had been talking to the farmer approached Cyril. They both moved towards the tree at the far side.

"Two hundred quid, sir, to make the face. Told us and I quote, *it were a piece of piss to do.* The guy renting this place, Monk his name is, he said it was to impress a lady friend who'd be flying over. Told us that it attracted a lot of aerial traffic and some came quite low. I asked if he had seen anything being dropped but he said that he wasn't watching it at all times during the daylight hours and I quote again, *How the bloody hell does I know? Christ, it were a bit of fun and these things always attract attention. You should have seen the traffic the huge red heart I made a while back brought over.* He told me that his work now even attracted people with drones who come to take pictures. He charges them a fiver to go onto the field if he sees them."

A Range Rover pulled up alongside the Bentley. "DCI Bennett? Wilbor." He leaned offering his hand. "Sorry for this mess. More bloody trouble than it's worth. Should sell it but then it's been in her family for some time."

He went to the boot and brought out some bolt cutters and a crow bar. "One of these should do the trick!"

***

Owen received the call as he was just making a mug of tea. "Which hospital?" He poured the tea away and quickly moved to find April. "Jonathan Stephens, he's in a bad way. He's being taken to

Airedale Hospital Accident and Emergency as we speak. Touch and go according to the paramedics who attended. Give Flash a call and let him know we're going over to interview the officer who got him out of the car. Tell him I'll ring with further details once we know more. Meet me downstairs."

With blue lights and sirens, Owen managed to even make April feel more than a little sick.

On arrival at the hospital, he left April to recover on a bench outside and he entered A&E. He saw the PCSO immediately.

"DS Owen?" She smiled. "Hazel, Hazel Barnes. He was in a bad way."

Owen sat her down. "So what happened? You were to keep an eye on the car."

" I took over at 2.30pm and was told to just keep coming back to see if the car had moved. I wasn't to watch it all of the time. If it had gone it would be tracked. About forty minutes later, I turned down the road and saw a bloke I now believe to be Jonathan Stephens open the door and get in. I ran down to the car hoping to stop him but he was slumped over the wheel. Throwing the door open, I was met with a vapour-type stuff that drifted over the footwell. To be honest I thought it was smoke and that it was on fire. I just grabbed him and pulled him half onto the pavement. A passing member of the public helped. Stephens had stopped breathing and so I gave him CPR whilst the guy dialled 999. Funny thing was that whilst we were down there, in the gutter with his legs still in the car, I started to feel unwell, dizzy and a little sick. The bloke decided to drag him well away from the car and he did what I instructed. He continued with the resuscitation until the paramedics turned up. They gave me oxygen too."

"How are you feeling now?"

"Okay, thank you. They've checked me over and they tell me I'm fine, that I'd done the correct thing. They also said if I'd tried to help him in the car they might well have had two serious casualties. It was just whilst I was down by the side of the vehicle. Something else too, it was really cold. We found a black insulated flask in the passenger side. One of the attending medics suggested that it was liquid nitrogen. They closed the lid. It's still with the vehicle. I believe Forensics are taking it away once it's been assessed. They also found four small potatoes!"

He could tell from her voice that she found that hard to comprehend.

"Potatoes?" Owen said nothing more about them. "Did you or your colleague see anyone near the car at any time?"

"People walked past occasionally but I certainly didn't see anyone open a door or stand by it. Had I done so, I'd have been straight there."

"Well done. Do you have a lift back?"

She nodded. He gave her his card. "Call me. We'll await your report but let me know you're okay. Congratulations, Hazel Barnes, you saved someone's life today, you should feel proud." He tapped the hand that rested on her thigh before moving to reception. He showed his ID and within minutes was with one of the doctors who had treated Stephens.

***

As the door opened, Cyril immediately saw the chest freezer. "Please wait in the conservatory. Is that your freezer?"

Wilbor looked and Cyril noted his puzzled expression. "Yes. Where have that bloody bar and the three locks come from? Wasn't like that when it went in."

"Did it still work?" Cyril saw the cable running up to a plug socket on the stone wall.

"It did, just expensive to run, must be twelve years old, maybe more."

Cyril watched him go to the conservatory but saw him stop and pick something up from the grass before entering. One of the officers put the bolt cutters to the first padlock and watched as it fell to the floor. Once the three locks were cut and removed they slid the bolt. Shakti cautiously lifted the lid. As the cold air hit the warm, it condensed forming a grey vapour cloud that hovered above the void.

Staring back through opaque eyes was Claire Baldwin, her hands by her face as if she were about to scream. Cyril turned his head to look at the figure trapped beneath hers. He looked more closely; the face seemed strange. Through the encasing crust of white crystals, it was the face of Thorndyke that stared back but as Cyril put his gloved hand to the side of the face he realised that he was actually looking at a photograph and that the trapped body beneath the frozen corpse of Claire Baldwin was not human. "It's a bloody mannequin!" he said lifting his eyes. "The bastard. We're looking for Thorndyke. He's led us along all the while. Bloody clever that! Like Albert's post-mortem photograph it was put there to keep her company!" Cyril allowed the lid of the freezer to close, his frustration and anger getting the better of him. He moved to stand outside, before resting his head in his hands.

"Inspector, sorry. This was in the grass." Mr Wilbor handed Cyril an earring. He knew exactly where that had come from.

Chapter Thirty-Eight

Cyril sat at home listening to Gorecki's Symphony number 3, the Symphony of Sorrowful Songs that had been played to accompany the opening sequence of the Mr Potato Head video. He had to admit that it did nothing for his mood but he was enchanted by the quality of the soloist's voice. He wrote down his thoughts on the case as they came to him, trying to work retrospectively. Occasionally he kept stopping to wonder how Thorndyke, a man initially on the periphery of the investigation, a man whom they believed to be the first murdered, could be the killer. He needed to identify a motive. Yes, he could see the associations between Baines and Baldwin but then those connections did not seem to be a strong enough reason to kill. Revenge was always a possibility, but for what? The link had to be with Stephens and the likely illegal importation of drugs, but then why the potatoes, the cocktail glass? Unless they found Thorndyke, Cyril doubted that the truth would ever be known, after all, who was he looking for, Thorndyke, Monk or Baldwin?

***

Owen was in bed when his mobile danced across the bedside table, its shrill and annoying ring awakening him. His uncontrolled hand flapped about, trying to catch it but he did nothing but send it crashing to the floor. He could see the name of the caller on the screen. He sighed.

"Good morning, sir," his tone sarcastic.

There was a pause as Cyril checked the time; it was well past midnight.

"Sorry, Owen. Were you in bed?"

"For the last two hours. I'm trying to redress my work life balance, sleep being a vital part of that balancing act, seeing as I did fourteen hours today." He wanted to ask if his boss had wet the bed but thought better of it.

"When Thorndyke suffered the injury at work, do you recall whether we checked all his personal details? He must have had a hospital record."

"To be honest I don't, but I could always get out of bed, shower, dress, drive to the station and check then give you a call back."

"Are you sure? That would be so helpful, Owen. Always said you were as keen as mustard."

"I was being facetious, sir. It's the middle of the night. Ring control, they'll get someone to look. I take it you're not with Dr Pritchett?"

Cyril's tone immediately changed. "I'm sorry, Owen, I never thought. I'll see you in the morning. My apologies."

Owen looked at the empty space next to him and smiled.

***

"Sorry for last night, Owen, wasn't thinking straight, forgot the time."

"Hospital records. Do we have them?"

"Description is that of Thorndyke and we've checked the address he gave. Shithole if I remember, but it hadn't been lived in for some time. We've nothing on Albert Baldwin, that was a fictitious address he gave the flying club. The farmer and the Wilbors have confirmed Monk to be our man. They remember a car too, blue Honda CRV, 4x4. Parked at the house. No idea of registration number. We're running checks from the local ANPR records. If he's changed his name then he'll have a number of registration plates. Any news on Jonathan Stephens?"

"We've arranged round the clock armed security. As soon as he can be interviewed we'll have someone there. The flask, the Dewar found in the car seems a likely match for the one placed in Baines's vehicle. Liquid nitrogen is the silent killer according to the lab people, takes just three breaths if you're in a confined space where it's released. It pushes all the oxygen and you're out for the count. Within a minute or two it's goodnight, Vienna. He's a bloody lucky lad."

Shakti knocked on the office door and pointed to Owen's computer. "We've intercepted another video from Claire Baldwin's phone. This one was sent to Jonathan Stephens's mobile. We've had it here since he went missing, to help monitor any activity. The video is, we believe, directed at both you and Owen, sir."

"Owen!" A degree of urgency rang within his voice.

He moved quickly to the desk and brought up the relevant file. The familiar strains of Gorecki's Symphony number 3 could be heard against a black screen before a slide show commenced. The individual images of the masked photographs of Thorndyke, David Stephens, Claire Baldwin and Jonathan Stephens appeared before reverting to darkness. A video started. The decorated potato heads were again shown in a line, this time, however, the first was sitting in an identical cocktail glass to that found in Stephens's car. The second was sitting on a beer mat, the same as that found at Baines's murder scene. Owen immediately pointed to them.

"Look, sir. They must represent Stephens and Baines."

Cyril leaned forward, his reading glasses on the end of his nose.

The camera slowly panned to each face, to every potato before pulling back. Suddenly a hammer crashed onto the first one in the row. Owen jumped back. It had appeared from nowhere and the act of aggression had taken him by surprise. Pieces of potato, cocktail glass and plastic fragments flew in all directions before the hammer crashed down onto the second one and then the third.

"Bloody hell, wasn't expecting that!"

The hammer was then rested in front of the last potato in the row; the one they believed represented a police officer. The screen went black again and the music slowly died. All three watching said nothing for a few moments.

"Location of the call?" Cyril knew the answer before he asked the question.

"Harrogate, sir, and strangely enough, less than a mile from here. That, however, means nothing as it could have been a delayed post."

"Counting the damaged potatoes, he thinks that Jonathan Stephens is dead. The officer who saved Stephens, is she being watched?"

"No. She wanted to stay in work, said she was fine."

"I want full protection, I want someone with her. We take no chances. Owen we're going to pay the flying club a visit. I'd like a word with…" He glanced at the notes he had made the previous evening. "Frank. I think he knows more than he admits to. Shakti, make some enquiries about the club, finances etc. and keep me up to speed on Stephens's condition. When he's awake I want to know."

"What about April coming along too? She'd be able to befriend the receptionist, Frank's other half."

Cyril smiled and nodded.

***

Owen turned off Victoria Avenue, Yeadon and into the airfield pulling up in sight of the flying club. Two aircraft sat some distance away. Cyril stood leaning against the car as the sound of a distant jet from over by the passenger terminal mixed with the wind bringing a slight smell of jet A1 fuel. It brought back memories of his time at Speke and Liverpool Flying School. Owen and April stood looking at their boss.

"Those things make me sick and I'd rather not bother," Owen announced looking across at the Piper Cherokee. "Bean can with wings and bloody dangerous to boot!"

April giggled. "For a big man you can be real soft."

Cyril smiled at the memory of flying back from Nice with Owen, recalling how he had turned the most gruesome shade of green.

As they entered the flying club, a student and an instructor were sitting together looking over one of the charts. The student was plotting the wind using a handheld device; neither looked up as they entered. They walked to the reception desk. Owen smiled and held out his ID.

"Good morning. Sorry to bother you but we'd like a word with Frank."

"I'm sorry but he's off for a few days. Can I help?"

"Off where?" Owen asked; the politeness had leached from his voice leaving her in no doubt that their visit was serious.

"He's taken an aeroplane to sell; a private sale. Should be back tomorrow either with it or…"

To Cyril, her smile seemed false and wrapped in a degree of insincerity as well as uncertainty. "We'd like to look around David Stephens's aircraft."

"Now that's difficult as that's the aircraft he's taken. We part owned it, as you know, and his family were happy to sell it. Maybe too many memories."

"I take it he filled out a flight plan?" Cyril knew immediately from her expression that something was amiss.

"Was he flying alone?" Cyril watched her eyes.

She shook her head. "Baldwin." She pushed the flight plan across the desk.

Owen and April looked at each other and both instinctively thought of Claire but quickly remembered Albert Baldwin.

"It's Thorndyke!" Cyril snapped before taking out his phone.

He rang police control and asked them to link with Europol. He checked the flight plan, next his watch and read out the aircraft registration. "Should have landed at Le Touquet approximately four hours ago. I'm informed that he might then have headed to a small airfield near Abbeville, a club which was interested in the aircraft. On the other hand he might be returning here unannounced. I want a check on all public crossings so liaise with Border Force. Let them also know there's a chance that he could return by private aircraft. He has the necessary connections."

Cyril thought about it and knew that tracking a light aircraft would be near impossible considering it could land almost anywhere. "It's urgent. Let Owen know when everything's done."

The three officers simply stared at the woman behind the reception desk. They could clearly see the anxiety that had spread across her face.

Chapter Thirty-Nine

Jonathan Stephens stirred. Opening his eyes, his right hand went immediately to the transparent oxygen pipes that ran into each nostril.

"You can leave those be!" The male nurse quickly went to his bedside. "Good of you to join us in the land of the living. For a while we didn't know whether you would or not."

The bleeps and audible sounds showing that life continued echoed within the room. They were constant and ignored. It was only when they stopped or changed tone did anyone take notice and act.

It was clear from Jonathan's facial expression that he did not fully comprehend what was being said. His eyes followed the nurse as he approached. Jonathan blinked a few times as if trying to focus and then he lifted his hands as if in self-defence.

"You're fine. Safe. My name's Keith. You're doing fine." He held Jonathan's wrist and monitored his pulse. "As I said you're doing fine."

Jonathan moved his head, his eyes scanning the room as if trying to make sense of his surroundings. He held up his hand to see the cannula taped securely to the back of it. He tried to speak but made only a small grunting sound. Keith watched and waited knowing it would only take a moment before he found his voice.

"Where?"

"That's a start. Airedale Hospital. You're in the High Dependency Unit. Poorly sick when you came in, but once you were stabilised you were subsequently transferred here to be cared for by my specialist team. Another day or two if you keep on making these improvements and we'll be moving you to a normal ward."

"What? Why?" Words dribbled from his lips, the weakness still clearly audible.

Keith said nothing but noted down his exact words on the chart table positioned just by the door as he had been instructed to do.

"The man and the masks, the mill, the manne… dummies? What happened to them?"

Keith added further notes and then leaned outside to call the seated armed officer. "He's talking. I'm notifying the consultant and if he thinks he's strong enough he might be okay to interview later today."

The message was sent for Cyril's attention.

***

The instructor and student had left. "Who's booked in today?" Cyril asked.

"We've that one and then one at five. It's quiet at the moment." Pat Blackwood's voice quivered and she fidgeted with her hands.

"Owen, please wait by the door. No one in."

Owen moved to the entrance but remained inside the reception area.

"Anything you say…" Cyril cautioned Pat Blackwood. "I'm not at this stage arresting you for being complicit in the possible murder of three people…" He did not have to say any more. He could see from the way she suddenly crumbled that she was going to talk openly. She was broken.

"It's really not how it looks. It wasn't meant to be like this. He promised me that we wouldn't get into trouble."

April observed as the woman broke down but neither moved nor spoke. They simply waited knowing that the vacuum of silence would help elicit more of the truth.

"It was a case of putting a blind eye to the telescope, of knowing but not heeding. What or whom is a little contraband booze and other bits and bats for personal use going to harm?"

"The flasks?"

"I don't know. Hidden from sight, part of the aircraft to unknowing eyes." She looked up hoping that they would understand. "It helped keep the business afloat. We live in difficult times."

"So tell us about Albert Baldwin."

"David Stephens introduced him to us as a good friend in need of some work. He said that he couldn't work in the licensing trade and we assumed that he had a dependency. He also wanted to gain a pilot's licence. He had the necessary CAA medical. Stephens said he'd pay if he were allowed to help out, washing aircraft, cleaning, anything, he said, to keep his mind active."

"So was he responsible for the Stephens's aircraft?"

"Only with certain things. David was very particular. Everything had to be just so, but he allowed Albert to help unload, and as I said wash and clean. When the aircraft returned from abroad and it faced a possible customs check, I often saw Albert take certain things and put them in his van."

"And the damage to the aircraft your husband mentioned?"

"David, Albert and my husband had a huge row, something about dropping things from the aircraft. It's illegal, as you know. Frank had heard that on a few occasions during these 'reward' flights an object had been dropped from the aircraft. It was usually in the same location. He had told David that, should it occur again, his aircraft was no longer welcome and that he would have to buy out our share."

"Did it stop?"

"I don't know. That's when after another argument between Albert and Frank, he climbed into one of the planes and crashed into the other. He simply walked away, climbed into his van and left. We never saw him again."

"Were the police involved regarding the malicious damage?"

Her look told him everything.

"I take it that's a no?"

"How could we?"

"You denied seeing him when one of my officers came here. Remember you're under oath. The DC here is making notes." He turned and looked at April.

"I recognised him but I really didn't want to be involved. I believed then that he could have been responsible for David's death. I saw his anger, his manic expression when he left the day of the crash and I really believed that he could be capable of doing anything."

"So your husband just flies him over to France for fun, this dangerous man, as you describe him?"

"I didn't know. He'd filed the plan online and I printed it after he'd gone. I wasn't concerned as it shows just one occupant." She pointed to the relevant section. "He sent me a text saying that he was with Albert Baldwin and he was all right. He also said to say nothing to anyone, that this would be the end of it. Those were his words. *The end of it.*"

Cyril's phone rang. Owen turned to look and then went outside.

"Bennett." He moved away from the desk and listened carefully. "Get Shakti there plus one other. See if she can get a full statement from him. As soon as she has anything I want to know."

Cyril returned to the interview. "There's no van in the car park."

She shook her head. "I looked when I got Frank's message. I checked with security and they have no record of his arriving on site. The only thing I can think of is that Frank smuggled him in."

April spoke next. "You don't seem too anxious, Mrs Blackwood. If it were my colleague, let alone husband, I'd have contacted the police straight away even knowing that the proceedings here in the past might have been against the law."

She broke down again and nodded. "Whichever way I'd have moved I would have been in the wrong."

Owen opened the door. "A minute, sir."

Cyril went outside.

"The French police. The aircraft landed but not at Le Touquet. The flight plan was altered mid-flight and he landed at a small airfield near Abbeville where we believe the aircraft was due to change hands. Strangely, the transponder appeared to have been switched off mid-way over the Channel too whatever that means. The story of a sale has not been corroborated. No deal was done."

"The loss of the transponder code means it would be difficult to track the aircraft and if he flew in low… The head count was correct, one passenger?" Cyril asked.

"Customs was cleared at the field by special arrangement. Took on fuel. There was no mention of an aircraft purchase but what we do know is that within the last twenty minutes the French police have received a report of a light aircraft touching down briefly at a disused airfield just west of Amiens forty minutes before our man landed at Abbeville. I'm assured that the timing corresponds for it to be our man. This could have been the dropping off point for Thorndyke."

"Like SOE all those years before, Owen. Get him to keep you informed." Cyril returned to reception. "He's on his way back, his job's been done. It seems your husband changed his mind half way over the Channel, decided to travel straight to Abbeville. Apparently the aircraft wasn't sold, in fact, there was never a sale lined up was there?"

She shook her head. "Albert Baldwin is a dangerous man, believe me."

"Let's hope your husband has the common sense to head straight back home."

"Owen, I want an armed police officer here within twenty minutes, one from the airport. April, notify air traffic control to put out a watch for light aircraft coming from the east." He turned. "Mrs Blackwood, when he arrives we'll be arresting you…"

Chapter Forty

Shakti perched opposite Jonathan Stephens who was sitting up. The oxygen was still routed into each nostril but despite the tubes linking the back of his hand and the surrounding machines, he looked well.

"So you received a message to go to the mill in Burley. For what reason?"

"He mentioned the face and that we would never be rid of him until he received what my father had stored in the safe in the garage."

"You knew just what that was; you always knew."

"No, when I was cleaning the Jag the day my father was killed, I found an envelope under the driver's mat. It was addressed to me with the instruction that it should be opened only if anything were to happen to him. I told you about seeing the face and that Mum had said he'd been so scared."

"And did you open it?"

He nodded. "I didn't wait. It was the combination to the safe he had installed in the floor of the garage. It was then that I realised why he might be in trouble. There were drugs and bundles of cash. There was also a list of names. Three, I believe, along with my father, are now dead, Thorndyke, Baldwin and a Baines. I saw the photographs. I never knew that he was mixed up with all of this shit. Christ he'd lecture me as a kid about drugs and said he'd kill me if he caught me with them. I see the irony now. He alleged that his trips to France allowed him to bring back a few luxuries and he used to quote the Rudyard Kipling poem, you know the one about smuggling."

Shakti smiled knowing the poem well. "Yes, I do. You should remember that fathers do say things when they have strong feelings. We've probably all said something like that. How did you know where to go, Jonathan?"

"He sent very clear and precise instructions about where to leave the car and how to proceed to the mill. I have to tell you I was scared shitless even though he said that it was to just be a drop, to leave the stuff and go. The note said that I'd see the derelict mill and once there, that I'd have to wait by an old mill clock face. I'd know when the time was right to enter. It was only then I knew that someone was inside. The door that had appeared tightly shut at the top of some iron stairs opened."

Shakti just let him speak. He simply stared at the foot of the bed and continued.

"The mannequins all wore masks, those photograph-type ones you see of the Queen and pop stars that crowds wear. Well, the first mask was my dad's face, then there were the ice faces and mine right at the end. It was then that a guy came in dressed in a white boiler suit. He also wore a mask; it was my face looking back at me. It makes me feel like jelly just thinking about it now."

He stopped speaking and turned to look at Shakti. She could see the fear still in his young eyes. Glancing at the monitor to his side, she noticed that his pulse rate had climbed considerably.

"You're safe, your mum and your sister are safe. You did the right thing," Shakti reassured him.

He smiled briefly. "Anyway, I put down the bag in front of these figures and suddenly he started to say that children's rhyme, one potato… He pushed over the mannequins one after another and they fell like dominoes. Christ, it was so controlled and so well planned but for what? I couldn't fully understand why all the drama and theatricals. He removed his gloves and showed me his damaged hands, parts of his fingers were missing. *Lost to the cold,* he said. He collected the liquid nitrogen my father used to smuggle the drugs. Once they had been placed in the flasks they would be frozen. There would be no smell, nothing to attract attention and when they fell to earth they were solid. *Snow and ice falling from the sky like Manna from Heaven,* were his words as he laughed. To be honest, he'd lost me, confused me. My father, he said, cheated him after the accident, didn't need him, said that he had brought in the stuff for use in the cocktail bar. The latest craze in cocktails had come at an appropriate time. He said that he'd given him a glass. That's the glass I found."

"Did he mention the others, Baines and Baldwin?" Shakti encouraged.

"They were both used, both worked in Health and Safety, both knew Dad, both small time users, clients. Also said that she was having an affair with Baines. He said that he'd put drugs in Baldwin's fridge and sent a package to Baines. He didn't elaborate but said that once they were dead these would be discovered and that they would be seen by the police to be up to their necks."

"The psychology of murder, multiple murder, is complex. They want people to know just what they've planned, they want to see their victims' fear, they get off on it. Probably watching you watching him representing you gave him a huge kick, believing that he'd put everything in place to ensure that you'd not be alive to report it. He was very nearly successful on that score," Shakti explained.

"He didn't try to stop me. He could have locked the doors, kept and murdered me but he didn't. He didn't come after me when I ran."

"Because he knew you'd go back to your car, and like with your father and Baines, he'd left an open Dewar in your vehicle. The atmosphere was toxic and he knew that within three breaths you'd be dead."

"I only remember opening the car door and then waking up here."

Shakti simply smiled.

***

The plane had landed and was immediately instructed to stay behind the *follow-me* vehicle that brought the aircraft to a standstill out in the open, away from the main airport and surrounding buildings. There was one customs car parked close by. Cyril watched a marshal climb from the truck and signal to the pilot to close down the engine.

Frank Blackwood followed the instruction and then climbed down the wing. On seeing the armed officer's weapon aimed at him he instinctively raised his hands. Owen removed the handcuffs and taking each wrist in turn he locked his hands behind his back as Cyril quoted his rights.

Chapter Forty-One

Once the Blackwoods were safely collected, April travelled with them. Cyril and Owen drove straight to Burley-in-Wharfedale, a sixteen-minute journey. The interview with Jonathan Stephens had been patched through and Owen read the notes out loud as Cyril drove. Turning off the dual carriageway, they moved slowly and cautiously towards the mill, now easily visible, and he parked under the clock as instructed. Another car was waiting.

"That's the door." Owen pointed to the top of the staircase.

A man in his sixties climbed from the parked car. "DCI Bennett?"

Cyril turned. "And you are?"

"Jones, I own this white elephant. Sadly it has to go, as we can't seem to get planning permission to turn it into apartments. Crying out for homes but..."

"That door. We need to look around."

Jones went to a door towards the lower end of the building. "Two minutes."

Both detectives waited. Cyril looked at the clock face, its frozen hands stuck at six thirty-seven. Suddenly the door swung open and crashed against the iron railing. Cyril and Owen mounted the steps and entered. "Mannequins?"

Jones pointed to the next room. "There are more downstairs, also shop fittings if you want to see."

Cyril counted the prostrate disfigured dummies. There were seven.

"They were downstairs a couple of weeks ago, maybe just kids pissing about. I pay a fortune for security too although nothing seems damaged." Jones looked at all the roof lights as if checking for breakages.

"Who else has a key, Mr Jones?"

"Demolition lads and the architect at one time but that's it. Do you want to see the rest of the place?"

"So only three sets of keys?"

"Yes… yes three sets but I had to get one replaced for the demolition team as they lost one, must have dropped off the ring. The guy thought he'd left it in the door but was obviously mistaken. It happens."

Owen just looked at Cyril.

"No one must enter this room until my Forensics team has checked it. Notify any key holder. There'll be a police presence here until it's done. Get a cadaver dog too to give the place the once over. If there is anything, the dog will find it."

Cyril enjoyed watching the frown appear across Jones's forehead. "You think that there could be a body stored here? Surely the dog will only find the mannequins?"

"It uses its nose not its eyes and it'll find a corpse even if it's buried lower than six feet. You don't know of any by chance do you, Mr Jones?"

Jones shook his head. "Most definitely not and I hope you don't find any either. It's been a bloody noose around my neck this place."

***

The Blackwoods had been extremely co-operative and had given more information than both Cyril and the French police could have hoped for. It surprised them all to learn that as Frank had crossed the Channel, the transponder had been turned on and he had given details over the radio of the clandestine landing and an accurate description of the person dropped off. The French police had been informed and taken immediate action, resulting in a quick arrest. They had seized a sizeable quantity of drugs and money.

"Once the Gordian knot of red tape has been sliced through, by Alexander and not Victoria, Owen, we'll have our man safely back in the fold. He has a few puncture wounds courtesy of a French police dog but that's all. We can then tie the knot back together or to use your metaphor complete the jigsaw."

"I think I need a brew. I haven't a clue what you're on about. Want one?"

"Clean cup and saucer, Owen, and a celebratory biscuit would be in order." His phone rang. He lifted his eyes to the ceiling. "Bennett."

"Owen! Leave it. Our dog at the mill has found a bone or two." He smiled tapping his stomach. "Gut instinct, Owen, always follow what it tells you."

***

Within the hour, Cyril stood near a pile of rubble close to the damaged clock face that had clung to the mill wall since the early eighteen hundreds.

"That face again, Owen." He pointed to the frozen hands that clearly had not moved for years. "Where have you heard that before? Strange, isn't it, how we now discover a corpse, right in front of that face, a face with frozen hands. And what do you notice about those static hands, Owen?"

Owen looked up with his usual puzzled expression. "It's buggered?"

Cyril shook his head. "You're not wrong. Six thirty-seven or to tell the time another way, eighteen thirty-seven. Now if you'd been listening to the detective you thought should be wearing an anorak, as you so cruelly suggested, you'd have known that was when Queen Victoria, the lady who has featured strongly throughout this case, ascended the throne."

Owen raised his eyebrows. "Like many coincidences throughout this case." Owen spotted Jones, the owner of the site, sitting in his car. "Speaking of coincidences, that car there's a Bentley, sir, like yours."

Cyril ignored the comment.

A Forensic tent stood out amongst the broken stones and lintels. It looked like an island protected and surrounded by a flimsy ring of blue and white tape. Julie Pritchett appeared. She stretched and walked over to Cyril, her smile increasing the closer she came.

"Owen. From the state of him, he's been here a while, six months, maybe a little longer. Can't be more than that as the building that stood here came down about that time. Before you ask he was put under the stones, the building did not fall onto him. Besides, they don't just knock these places down any more, the stone's too valuable for a crash, bang, wallop job. From the state of his teeth I'd say he was a tramp, a vagrant. Nothing to identify him but we'll do our best."

"Albert!" Cyril exclaimed. "Twenty quid says that you'll find that to be Albert."

"We'll have to wait and see, Cyril Bennett."

Chapter Forty-Two

Two days later

The briefing was full and the noise from the group was louder than Cyril could ever recall. This case had certainly taken some strange twists and turns and the recent findings had generated a great deal of excitement. At long last, they could, they believed, see the wood for the trees. The Chief Constable was sitting next to Cyril, a rare moment indeed.

Owen tapped the side of his mug with a pen and the room slowly went quiet.

Cyril let the silence add a frisson of excited anticipation before he spoke. "Firstly, I want to thank each and every one of you for the way you've handled this difficult case. We have, I believe, been taken down some very unusual and obscure pathways by one scheming criminal who murdered for what appears to be very little financial reward. It appears, however, that his motivation, his appetite were not necessarily only financial. Neither was this a case of pure revenge, it was simply because he could, it was a game, a cold and sinister game. Yes, there was money and yes, there were drugs involved and he did enjoy these but no more than your average street dealer. This man had a different addiction. He enjoyed playing a game; scheming and planning.

"Initially we wrongly believed that the first corpse in this twisted game was that of Thorndyke, Arthur Thorndyke, who went missing after being found responsible for failing to follow operating procedures. He demonstrated his sheer incompetence, an incompetence that might, and some say should, have resulted in a case of gross, if not criminal negligence. But why should he have been killed, who would want him dead?"

Owen shuffled his feet waiting to see if anyone would steal the boss's thunder but they did not.

"The only person who wanted him dead was Thorndyke himself, and that clever ploy brought with it a cloak of invisibility. He needed us to believe that he was a pawn in a game, and we did so. We thought he had cocked up. It had been easy collecting and taking the liquid nitrogen, the odd Dewar here and there. Nobody would know providing he followed the safe practice which he had done each time until... There should have been no real risk. Once the accident had happened, the proverbial hit the fan when Health and Safety and working practices were questioned. It was like watching ripples in a pond that he hadn't anticipated. That he didn't plan, but once things went wrong and he could see Stephens look elsewhere it was game on."

A voice came from the back of the room. "What about the chap at the airport, Albert Baldwin?"

Cyril pointed to April and smiled. "Thorndyke using a false name. We now know that he was on holiday from his job when he worked there and once the task was finished he decided to leave in a spectacular way. Stephens needed Thorndyke to design the compartment to store the flasks in transit. It couldn't be in the cockpit for obvious reasons and so it was stored within the fuselage.

"On this particular aircraft the stowage is through a small external door but it leads directly into the cockpit behind the rear seats. This was totally unsuitable for transporting the Dewar containing the drugs and the LIN or LN and so they engineered modifications. The space had to be sealed from the cockpit, but also secret and well ventilated to prevent the build-up of pressure. It was designed so that the door could be opened electronically to allow the object to be ejected without compromising the airframe or aircraft in flight.

"It was difficult to detect and the fact that the cocaine was within the LN before it got anywhere near the aircraft meant that the customs dogs would not find any trace. It was so simple. If you look at Thorndyke's work history, his career was in cryo, freezing, fridge design."

"So who started it all off, Stephens or Thorndyke?"

"As Stephens can no longer speak for himself, I would imagine that the guilt will fall there. Our man in captivity is saying nothing, just occasionally rubbing and blowing on his hands whilst rocking backwards and forwards. We assume that he befriended Claire Baldwin when she was employed in her advisory capacity. We also know from Jonathan Stephens that she was having an affair with Baines; they both liked the odd line of snow or ice but Baines needed cash. The likelihood was that once established, she would work with him.

"According to the file, Baines and Stephens were seen at the flying club. It was stated that they were his employees. Turn to G16 in the file. April will go through this."

"A reward flight it was termed, a reward for what we may never know; moving drugs, keeping quiet, misinformation… Let's say they both had need of something and Stephens had a supply of both cocaine and cash."

"The corpse at the mill is that of a Mr Albert Edward Brown of no known address, missing for over a year," Cyril interjected, smiling and looking at Owen who scratched his head.

"You said that at the scene, sir."

Cyril rested a hand on his colleague's shoulder before bringing a new twenty-pound note from under his folder. "DNA tests will determine whether Thorndyke and Brown had ever met. What we do know is that he probably died in the same manner as the others. Now, I have a twenty-pound note for the first person to give me the link between our corpse and the case." Cyril looked in anticipation at each person in the room.

"The name, Albert Edward is the hospital in Wigan!" one bright spark shouted, causing a ripple of laughter to run around the room.

The officer who first brought Cyril the details of the elimination game stood. "Queen Victoria, sir." She continued to speak as all eyes turned to her. "Victoria Avenue mentioned in three places, a Victorian Mill, the elimination game, more than likely Victorian. Albert, the sending of post-mortem images with evergreen like Victoria's picture of her husband. Albert, the name used by Thorndyke. Albert again with the corpse found at the mill. Edward was Victoria's son and finally, Brown. This is the interesting part. It is rumoured that Brown became Victoria's lover after Albert died. Many people saw it as a betrayal of her love very much like Stephens betrayed Thorndyke after his accident."

Cyril walked across the room, handed her the note, and continued.

"Those things were planned, they were not coincidences. He used one coincidence and that was the road outside the airfield and Claire's address to kill Baines on Victoria Avenue. He could have killed him at home had he wished. Thorndyke had worked within the industry for years and believed that he had the perfect solution to eliminate those who crossed him should the need have arisen. He has revealed in his statement that he was betrayed. *They wanted liquid nitrogen so I gave them what they requested and by the third breath they stopped asking.*"

"Why leave the cocktail glass?" Nixon asked.

"Jonathan Stephens said that he told him that it was because he was now getting the stuff from the cocktail bar, The Bauhaus. That may be but the cocktail glass was designed in such a way that it could be held by the stem so that the liquid in the bowl would remain cold. Maybe it was symbolic of a Dewar… unless he talks we'll never know."

April looked across at Cyril. "You used to fly, sir. I find it difficult to believe that in this day and age people can still fly freely, not only in this country but also abroad, and land when and where they choose. They neither need a radio nor is it required to communicate their intentions. No wonder we see more and more drug and people trafficking."

Cyril just looked at her. "It's about human freedom. There are rules in place in all walks of life, April. You'll find those who will bend and corrupt them for their own ends. Considering the number of private pilot flights a year, very few are illegal or clandestine. Liberty is something we take seriously in this country and this should be exalted. On this occasion they might appear to have got away with a great deal over a considerable time but, like us all, eventually they made errors, and it was then that they were caught or, in this case, died. We cannot watch everyone all of the time."

Chapter Forty-Three

Cyril looked at the grey-washed sky that hung like wet sheets above the Pennine Hills. The M62, a ribbon of gloss black, snaked its way over the reservoir and beneath the concrete span of a bridge. The windscreen wiper, a metronome, kept time.

Within minutes, they passed the isolated farm trapped between the two carriageways, the Little House on the Prairie as it was affectionately known to traffic reporters. As the red rose appeared to his left, the sky seemed lighter, a shallow crack revealing blue beneath.

"Not enough for a pair of sailor's trousers but it's a start."

Julie heard nothing. Her eyes were closed and the sound of her breathing seemed to match the click of the wipers.

Cyril pictured Thorndyke sitting within the confines of the interview room, his face displaying neither anger nor remorse, but static and mask-like throughout the whole of the one-sided interview. From the psychiatrist's assessment, it was clear that Thorndyke was not of sound mind. According to his ramblings, it seemed to have been one moment in time when he felt rejected and no longer relevant. The relationship between Stephens and Baldwin had been the catalyst for his sudden and dangerous transformation. The injuries he had sustained and the sudden exposure of his negligence were the point at which the future was set.

The thought of that one instant changing the lives of so many haunted Cyril. Suddenly he was again on his bicycle, touring the country lanes of his youth, excited to be riding home until he saw the car and heard the animalistic grunts, their faces, Wendy and his father locked in a bestial embrace. That was his moment, a second in time, where his anger and feelings of rejection had brought about a hatred of a man whom moments earlier he had loved. It was then that he felt a pang of sadness for Thorndyke, for had he been older, he wondered what he might have done when the red mist fell.

A blast from a car horn brought Cyril back to the present. He swerved the car back onto his side of the road.

"Are you okay?" Julie had opened her eyes.

He quickly looked at Julie and counted his blessings. Someone somewhere was looking after him. He smiled and nodded. "Go back to sleep."

He pulled up just before the gates of the family home, knowing that he would make the decision about the Bentley's fate. He had no need of it and yet everyone to whom he had spoken seemed to believe that he was the luckiest man alive. There was no option but to scrap it, to follow his father's last and only request.

The gravel beneath the wheels crunched a warm welcome as Wendy opened the door. A broad smile brought a youthful glow back to her eyes. Cyril allowed Julie to greet her first and then he gave her a hug, something he thought that he would never be able to do again. It felt right.

"I've made crumpets, Cyril. I know you loved them as a boy."

He smiled and went inside. The sound of a classical piece of music streamed from the lounge, it was surprisingly familiar. Wendy saw him pause.

"It was one of your father's favourite pieces of music, surely you remember it, Cyril? It's by Gorecki, it's the Symphony of Sorrowful Songs."

It made Cyril stop; it was the same music that had taunted him in the videos. He smiled inwardly before turning to Wendy. "This world is full of coincidences and do you know what?" He held both her hands. "Sometimes we try to read too much into them."

After the crumpets and tea, Cyril walked towards the garage and Julie looked at Wendy, knowing just where he was going. Wendy winked and smiled.

Dragging the cover away from the car, he stared at the cocooned behemoth that had plagued many of his waking moments since his last visit. He had resigned himself to the fact that it had to go, to be destroyed. He was a copper, for goodness' sake, he could not be seen in this. Opening the door, he slid onto the leather bench seat and held the wheel; taped to it was an envelope. His name was clearly and neatly written in black ink. Opening it, he read the letter.

Cyril,

Julie tells me you have a bit of a dilemma. Your father has asked you to either keep the Bentley or destroy it. I know from my daughter that you have decided to scrap it. Now, that would be foolish as I have a better option. I'll keep the old girl and look after her, drive and polish her just as your father would want and all you have to do is occasionally take Julie out for the odd spin. How does that sound?

Best wishes,

Fred.

Cyril read it again and smiled. He had a solution. He wondered how this letter was here in the car when neither he nor Julie had been to the garage. He realised that Julie had been working with Wendy behind his back. She knew that in his heart of hearts, he needed to keep it.

He let his hands caress the wheel and allowed his eyes to look along the sweeping bonnet. It made him realise just how much Julie meant to him and that very soon he needed to ask her a very important question.

Acknowledgements

'Watch the wall my darling while the Gentlemen go by.'
'The Smuggler's Song' by Rudyard Kipling

'Ay, but to die, and go we know not where;
To lie in cold obstruction and to rot;'
'Measure for Measure' by William Shakespeare

***

Concluding book seven, 'The Third Breath', is of great significance to me as a writer. Had someone said to me a few years ago that I would not only have written a successful crime series as a published author but that I would also be responsible for seven books… I would have been amazed. For this to happen I have many people to thank.

If I knew just what makes a book successful I would have found the Holy Grail for authors. What I have realised is that it takes a great deal of hard work and soul-searching. I also know that the members of the many book and reader's groups and the social media supporters, the bloggers and the readers are indispensable; they are the wind beneath a writer's wings. I have been blessed by their wonderful support.

Without meeting and chatting with so many readers over the last two years, I would never have known the people who have supported the Bennett series and inspired me. Some of them have been with me from the very beginning and I am lucky that they have stayed and we have become friends.

My first thanks, as always, go to my wife, Debbie. She never lost faith and has been so supportive throughout this adventure. I love you. x

Bloodhound Books made a decision to sign an unknown author in July 2016 and it has been a pleasure working with them and watching them grow, not only in terms of the number of their dedicated staff, the now-burgeoning kennel of wonderful writers but also in Bloodhound Books's standing within the world of publishing. Thank you and congratulations.

I am lucky to have a guardian angel. Caroline Vincent was the very first person to comment as an advanced reader on my work and I know that without that initial intervention things might well have been so different. Your friendship, dedication and support are more than any author could wish for. Thank you. x

To Debbie, Carrie Heap, Stef O'Leary, Christopher Nolan, Monica Mac and Kath Middleton for offering your thoughts and corrections on the initial draft of this novel. You are all so generous with your time, my sincere thanks.

To Andrew Forsyth for your help and continued support.

Imagined Things Bookshop, Harrogate. Always there with support and a healthy stock of Bennett books to sell. It's wonderful working with you. Thanks, Georgia.

Georgie and staff at Cordings, Harrogate.

Dr C Gray - Thank you.

Martin and Janet Keen, owners of Liverpool Flying School. Thank you for showing me around the aircraft and answering my many questions. It was lovely to come back into the fold.

To a friend who has spent a lifetime working in cryogenics and for the hours spent in conversation. You know who you are. Cheers.

Thanks too must go to the following people for their support with this novel: Claire Bent – thank you for your technical advice regarding the Jaguar – Michelle Corbin, Dee Williams, Craig Gillan, Pete and Ann MacNamara, Morgen Bailey, Nik Plumley,

Nancy Doherty, Stephen Barr, Christopher Holland, Donna Wilbor and Alison Wheat and staff at the Harrogate Library.

I hope you like your character, Chris Mott. Your continued support is very much appreciated.

I must also thank Nicholas Camm, the voice behind the Bennett audiobooks.

I feel sure that I have missed someone – my apologies, if so.

Emily Shutt - a princess, a warrior and a little angel.

Finally, I have self-published a short story on Amazon entitled 'The Penultimate Man' to commemorate the one hundred years since the conclusion of WW1. All the author royalties will be donated to the Poppy Appeal. If you can support this worthy cause I would be most grateful.

Thank you.

Malcolm